Michelle Boule

Lightning in the Dark

Turning Creek

Book 1

Lightning in the Dark
Copyright © 2014 Michelle Boule
All rights reserved.

www.wanderingeyre.com
Cover design: Design Book Cover http://www.designbookcover.pt/en/

This is a work of fiction. Names, characters, businesses, places, events and incidents are either the products of the author's imagination or used in a fictitious manner. Any resemblance to actual persons, living or dead, or actual events is purely coincidental.

ISBN: 1942339011
ISBN-13: 978-1-942339-01-4

To Jennifer Murrell
for being a better sister than I deserve

ACKNOWLEDGMENTS

Writing a book is an endeavor which takes a village. It has been a long journey and I apologize if I forget to include someone here. I love you all dearly.

Humble thanks and gratitude go to: My fabulous editor, Brenda Errichiello, who pushes me to be better and gives my words finesse. My copy editor, Stephanie Petersen, who gives my writing polish. Alexandre for a cover even more beautiful than I imagined. My fellow authors who have encouraged and supported me along the way: Nancy Kimball, Kelly Maher, Stephanie Leary, Sandra Schwab, Nicole Deese, Danielle Monsch, and Jax Garren. My friend, Laura Wardlaw, who supported this book with her generosity and endless encouragement. Pam Thompson who sent me encouraging words on my lowest days. All the ladies at University Baptist Church who have sustained me with prayer and love. My beta readers, Katy Ernst and Jennifer Murrell, for their eagle eyes, attention to detail, and their willingness to read the raw form of my stories. My family and friends for their love, support, and unfailing belief in my ability to weave words. My adorable boys for challenging me to be a better person than I would have been without them. My husband, Ries, who is my partner in all things and the love of my life. The Lord because He calls me redeemed.

CHAPTER 1

Colorado Territory, 1858

Petra flew over the frightened cattle, and bubbles of laughter sparkled within her. The livestock below resembled awkward dancers as they trotted away from the harpy swooping above them. While cattle in the area had many four-legged predators, they were not used to being hunted from above by a creature as black as the night sky and as large as a cow herself. Petra decided to try the maneuver again, brushing the talons of her feet against the backs of the three closest cows. Frightened lowing emitted from the terrified animals as they hopped into the brush in an effort to escape the fiend on their flanks.

Feral joy, the joy every predator feels when its prey is well and truly scared, coursed through her. Petra yelled after their retreating forms, her harpy voice screeching and caustic, so different from her human one. A cow was more docile prey than Petra preferred, but she still enjoyed watching them run. The wind danced over her feathers and the moon coated the mountain valley in a silver glow. It was a perfect night for flying.

Petra pumped her wings and climbed higher into the night sky. She found the warm air currents and slowed her wing beats to glide through the air. She flexed the clawed hands on the tips of her wings. Chasing the cows had awakened the baser needs within her, including the desire to hunt, and there were still plenty of hours in the night to indulge her violent side. She kept flights during the day to a minimum so she would not be seen, but under the moon she could let herself go.

Petra opened herself up to the violence within, and it thrummed through her veins. In the time of the gods, Zeus had created the first four harpies to torment souls on their way to the underworld. The harpies had wielded their savagery to influence mortals and wreak havoc upon the very god who had created them. If the written myths were to be believed, those first harpies had been little more than foul monsters, but Petra knew from experience that the written myths did not contain the whole of the truth.

Generations after the Fall of Olympus, Petra carried the legacy of violence from the first harpy of her line, Celaeno. She did not often indulge in the dark corners of her soul; there was a deep fear in her heart that the darkness would be her only legacy. Violence and solitude were an inextricable element of every harpy's life, but Petra did not want them to be the only constant in hers.

With her senses wide, Petra scanned the ground. She flew lower, silent as a summer breeze, searching for movement. With her enhanced harpy eyesight she could not see as well as an owl in the darkness, but she could see better than a mortal. A quick movement caught her eye on the edge of her vision. It was a raccoon, looking for its own nighttime meal. Petra wanted something larger and more challenging, and she left the raccoon to its search.

Against the grey of the mountain rock, the white outline of a ram became visible. The curved horns of the bighorn were unmistakable even in the low light of the moon. Petra changed direction and dove, stretching her talons forward like a raptor. Seconds before she made contact, the ram sensed the danger and jumped forward on nimble, sure-footed hooves. Petra adjusted to its movement and landed on the back of the fleeing sheep. Its high-pitched scream of terror was sweet in her ears as she sank her talons into its flesh.

The ram jerked and bucked, trying to throw off the laughing harpy, but it could not dislodge the predator on its back. Petra wrapped her wings around the animal's neck and squeezed its windpipe until her claws ripped through its jugular. She could feel the sticky warmth of the ram's lifeblood as it spilled in a black shower on the stone of the mountain. The wildness in her leapt in delight.

In the moment before the animal released its last breath, Petra used all of her strength to dig her talons and claws as far into the animal's flesh as she was able. She brought her face into the back of ram's neck and sank her pointed teeth into the flesh of her kill. The taste of blood rushed over her tongue, and her soul danced. The ram succumbed to its fate. Its cries ceased. The night was quiet once more.

Petra released the body and licked the blood from her lips. Her feathers were coated with blood, but she would wait to clean them. She inspected the large frame of the animal and was glad her cabin was just on the next mountain, on Atlas's Peak. She could carry the ram while she flew, but she would be tired by the end of it. Pleased and looking forward to mutton stew for dinner, Petra gathered her kill in her talons and flew off toward home.

***

She woke in the morning, after her third night chasing the poor cows and a superb bowl of stew, and stared at the log beams supporting the roof of her tiny cabin. A finger of guilt tickled her conscience. She knew the owner of the dairy cows in passing only. The town of Turning Creek and the surrounding region was sparsely populated, so while you could go months without seeing another soul, everyone knew everyone else, at the very least by reputation. James Lloyd, the owner of the unfortunate cows, lived a few miles down the mountain from her cabin. If she were in the habit of being neighborly, she would go down and offer Mr. Lloyd some help in rounding up the cattle.

Petra looked around her clean, but comfortable, one room cabin. The small bookshelf overflowed with books and papers. A rocking chair with a cushioned seat was positioned before a window, through which the top of the range was visible. The mountains glowed with promise this morning, and Petra snuggled deeper into the covers. If she shut her eyes tight, she could go back to sleep and ignore the voice telling her that, after eight years, it was time she got to know her neighbor better. Since moving to Turning Creek she had not felt the need to expand her circle beyond her sisters, Iris, and one or two others. She was civil with people she encountered, but those she defined as friends were few.

Perhaps it was time to branch out.

It was no use staying in bed. Petra flung off the covers and swung her human legs toward the smooth, wooden floor. It would take her no time to fly down to the Lloyd farm in her harpy form, but few mortals knew their world was littered with the descendants of Greek gods, goddesses, and their creatures, long forgotten but not dead. When Zeus had been overcome and Mount Olympus lay in ruins, those who remained had faded into the mortal world to start over, raise their families, and live free from the shadow of Zeus's rule. Remnants, as these descendants were called, were everywhere, but first introductions were generally not the time to educate a mortal on the truth of the world.

Petra made the bed and dressed in a simple cotton blouse and a skirt of her own design, which was really two extra wide pant legs. It looked like a skirt when she was walking, but allowed her to ride astride. There was nothing more irritating than being forced to ride sidesaddle. She checked on the goat and her kid and spread feed to the chickens before saddling her mare and heading down the mountain. The morning air mixed with the smell of wild summer flowers, and Petra let the peace of the mountains fill her.

It took her a little over an hour to reach the Lloyd farm. There were three buildings on the farm, a log cabin much larger than hers with two sections, a large barn made of rough-hewn planks and logs, and a smaller building tucked behind the barn. The house and barn were weathered, but not old, and well-kept. Petra smelled smoke from a kitchen fire curling from the cabin. Petra took a gamble and went to the barn first.

She swung off her tan mare and rubbed her sweating palms on her worn cotton skirt. There was little cause to be nervous, but a ripple of the unwanted emotion went through her as she pulled open the side door of the barn. No sounds escaped the hinges to alert anyone to her presence. The rich aroma of hay and warm animals assaulted her. She breathed deeply and shook herself to relax.

"Hello. Anyone here?" Petra squashed the brief hope that they would all be out chasing cattle and that she would be free of the business of being neighborly for one day. The gods were not with her.

"In the back. Who's there?" The reply was laced with irritation.

Petra cleared her throat. "My name is Petra Celaeno. We've met before. I live up the mountain and I noticed your cattle are scattered this morning. I came to offer my help." She kept the part about the reason why the cows were dispersed across the mountain valley to herself.

A man in his early thirties emerged from a stall. He was leading a roan, who snorted at Petra. Disheveled brown hair curled over his ears and wary brown eyes met hers. Something pricked at Petra. She concentrated, and then she felt it. It was minute, but James held the hum of power that all Remnants possessed. As a harpy, Petra knew her power radiated thick and bright. A Remnant meeting her would know she was a predator and not to be trifled with. If she pushed her power, a mortal could be made to feel uneasy, like the feeling a rabbit had knowing a hawk was nearby. James gave no indication he sensed anything strange about Petra.

The tight set of his shoulders eased. "That's the best news I've had in days. We could use the help this morning, as the cattle have lately taken to nightly jaunts around the valley." His clipped English accent did not match his rough western attire, but Petra was not the first person to seek and find refuge in the vastness of the Rocky Mountains. "My name is James Lloyd. I remember meeting you. Pleased to meet you again, Miss Celaeno."

James gave a small formal bow, and Petra felt her cheeks warm. She had almost forgotten the formality of the upper class. She ran a hand over her shirt, brushing off dirt that was not there. The stiffness of most people's manners wore away with the application of time and mountain living.

"We're neighbors, and there's no need to be formal. Please, call me Petra."

"Then you may call me James, but if you help with the cattle, you may call me whatever you prefer." James held out his hand and Petra shook it firmly.

"Deal."

James ran a hand down the neck of the horse he was leading. "Do you have your own horse? We have some spares, if you need one."

"No, I have a horse. I could've walked, but it would have taken me considerably longer to get here." Petra followed James out of the barn and retrieved her mare where she had left her tied.

James peered down at her from atop his horse. "Miss Petra, have you ever herded cattle before?"

Petra did not like being so far below his piercing gaze. She mounted and answered, "Just Petra. And, no, I haven't."

James pursed his lips. "I suppose beggars can't be choosers, as they say. We'll teach you as we go. Follow me. Robert and Adam are already waiting in the south pasture gathering the easy ones who didn't get too far." Petra kicked her mare into motion and followed James to the pasture. It was the same pasture Petra had flown over the previous three nights, but in the summer sun it was alive and smelled of green grass.

James reined his horse to a stop beside a young man with twinkling eyes and a boyish smile. "Robert, this is Miss Petra from up Atlas's Peak. She's come to help us this morning, but she will need some guidance. Petra, Robert Mullins."

Robert swept the hat off his head. "Pleasure to see you again, Miss Petra. We could use the help today. If you're learning cow wrangling for the first time, you've come to the right place."

Another man rode up with the same smile as Robert, but with brown eyes instead of blue. "Don't let my brother tell you any lies. I'm the best cattle man in Colorado, and if you want to learn how to be a proper cowboy, I'm your man."

Petra had never been on the receiving end on so much easy charm. If she'd thought the brothers were flirting in earnest, she might have been uncomfortable, but it was obvious they were treating her no different than any other woman they would meet. It made her like them instantly. "Today, it appears, is my day to learn new things."

"You two start on the back west side, and Petra and I will take the back east. Work your way across until we meet up. We will check the fringes after we round up the ones who didn't go so far. And keep your eyes open for tracks. Something has been spooking them." Petra examined the reins she held as James spoke. They would find no tracks to indicate a bird of prey with a woman's head and clawed hands had stampeded the herd.

Herding cattle on horseback was much harder than flying overhead and scattering them without rhyme or reason, but James was a patient and methodical teacher. He talked in a calm and easy voice while he showed her how to move her horse in a sweeping motion behind the cattle. Once they got into a rhythm and the cattle were moving along, he observed, "They are unsettled still by whatever spooked them, but they are used to being moved twice a day so they should gather easy. Move back and forth behind them, nice and easy, pushing them slowly in the direction of the milking barn."

Petra led her horse in a sweeping motion and the cattle meandered in the right direction, snatching mouthfuls of grass as they went. It was a slow, methodical process. She could see Robert and Adam making the same movements with their horses. The cows and horses kicked up little clouds of dust as they moved across the pasture.

Petra pointed to one or two cows lingering on the edge, away from the rest of the cows who were starting to bunch into a loose group. "What about the stragglers? Shouldn't we go after them?"

"They will come along. Cows like to be together. There is safety in numbers. Once we get this group going, they will realize they're being left and follow the rest."

James continued moving past Petra as they swept the cattle toward the barn. On the next pass by, he asked, "Where are you from? Your accent is peculiar." Her deep olive skin also betrayed her distant origins, and Petra was thankful this was not, instead, the genesis of his question.

Petra thought about giving her usual answer, but instead she found something closer to the truth coming out of her mouth. "I grew up in Venice, but my mother is from Crete. After I left home, I traveled around and lived different places. Some of the languages stuck more than others."

James perked up at the mention of Crete. "Crete is the origin of the myth of the Minotaur in the labyrinth." The comment was out of place, and the strangeness of it curled up her spine. James must have seen something in her expression, because he looked abashed and added, "I have a fascination with Greek myths. I did a lot of reading as a child."

He liked Greek myths, and yet had not said anything to her when they met in the barn about being a Remnant. This morning was becoming more and more strange. It was true that Remnants kept to themselves, but this would have been the perfect opportunity for James to reveal himself to her. If he was reluctant to discuss his origins, she would respect his lead. She had enough secrets of her own to keep.

She shrugged and said, "Everyone needs a hobby. If you want, I can tell you some of the stories my mother told me about Crete when I was growing up." She would leave out the fact that the Minotaur was much more than a myth. The Remnants of Theseus likely still told tales on late nights of how the first of their name slayed the monster and returned home a king.

James smiled at her and Petra's heart skipped. "I would love that. Thank you."

"If you two are done yakking it up like two society matrons over there, we've got cattle to get to the barn." Adam winked at Petra.

Robert rode up to the small group. "Like your mouth is ever shut, brother. One time, we missed a train stop because Adam here was telling the most ridiculous tales to the engineer. He had him really going about this time we went over the border to Mexico, and the engineer blew right through this little town. Once the man realized his mistake, he had the conductor throw us off the train and was forced to back up to the town. That was a day filled with walking."

Petra laughed. The laughter between the two brothers was infectious.

"Adam, take Petra along the pasture border and make sure none of the cows crossed the river. If you don't find any, come back and help us finish up at the barn." James turned to Petra before the pairs split off. "You're doing wonderful for your first time out."

Petra glowed with the praise.

Petra rode beside Adam, who talked almost non-stop and needed little help carrying on a conversation—which was appreciated, as small talk was not her forte. He spoke easily about his brother and his past. "Robert and I grew up on various ranches in Texas. We wrangled cattle before we could shave, which for Robert was just last year." Adam stroked his short cut beard for emphasis. "Can't imagine doin' anything else. We left Texas to find some new scenery. We thought to give the mountains a try and Mr. Lloyd is the best boss we've ever had. It's a small operation here, and he gives us a lot of the responsibility since he does all the cheese making himself."

Petra was already familiar with James's cheese and knew that he sold it at the mercantile in Turning Creek or sent it out to other places in the region. She had a large wedge of the sharp cheddar in her dry pantry right this moment.

Before Adam could continue, Petra said, "You picked the right place for mountains. I have a biased opinion, but the view from Atlas's Peak is the best view in the world." Every day she woke and thanked the gods for the way the mountains made her soul sing with their changing moods and landscapes.

Adam slowed his horse and pointed. "We got a couple stragglers right there." Two cows had wedged themselves into a copse surrounded by bushes. Petra could see where they had crashed through the bushes and then lost their way out. "Something must have really scared them to get them to barrel through those brambles like that."

Petra turned her head so Adam would not see her smile. She made a show of looking at the ground for tracks. "I don't see any wolf or coyote tracks." There were none to find, she knew.

Adam swung down from his horse and untied a long length of rope from behind his saddle. "I'm going to tie this to the horn of your saddle. Once I get the cow closest to us tied, walk your horse backwards and pull the cow, steady but firm, out of the bushes. Hopefully, her friend will follow along once the way is clear."

Petra did as she was instructed and the cow, reluctant at first, pushed its way back through the hole it had made in the bushes. The second cow followed along with no problem. The two stragglers saw they had been left and trotted forward to join the herd. Petra and Adam joined James and Robert in the final push into the paddock beside the milking barn.

By the time the last cow went through the fence, Petra was coated in dirt and sweat. It was the longest amount of time she had spent in the company of near strangers in her sixty-nine years. She was tired, dirty, and hungry. It had been marvelous.

James latched the gate behind the cows. "I think we have all earned a break before starting the milking."

James offered Petra a mug of water from the well, and she collapsed in a happy heap on the ground beside Robert and Adam.

"I think the cows are half in love with you," Adam elbowed Robert in the ribs, causing him to spill half his water down his shirt.

"They love you better, brother. Next time they scatter, we'll simply send you out to moo lovingly at them 'til they all come a runnin' home." Robert slapped his brother hard on the back, causing him to choke on the water he had been drinking. Adam doubled over, shaking and coughing around his escaping laughter. He let out a small hiccup at the end, and Robert guffawed.

"If you two loons are done, we still have the morning's milking to do." James shook his head. Petra covered the giggle welling up in her throat with a cough.

Petra was not ready to leave. "Do you need an extra hand?"

"If you can milk a cow, I'd be grateful, unless you need to go back to your own place and family."

"There's no family and nothing I need to get back to. I live alone." At his questioning look she added the old lie. "I'm a widow. My husband died before we reached Turning Creek, and I never remarried." The lie tasted worse in her mouth than normal. It was easier for people to accept a woman living alone if she was a widow.

"I'm sorry for your loss."

The sentiment both touched and annoyed her. The lie gave her safety, but she did not have to like it. "It was a long time ago."

"We could use the help, then, if you are willing."

She squinted up at James. He was standing with the sun at his back, and she could not see his features clearly. Petra had been milking cows longer than James had been taking in air, but she was still not about to explain that the world he knew hid another in plain sight. It was not something you discussed at the first meeting. It was not something you discussed at all. She tried to suppress a half smile.

"I can milk a cow or two."

"Great. Let's get to the barn. You two loons as well."

Petra sat on her stool in the barn and let her mind wander as her hands moved up and down in the familiar pattern. The smell of cows, warm milk, and hay mingled together and filled her nose. She had always loved the way a barn smelled; especially in winter, when the air was cold outside and the barn was a haven against the whine of the mountain winds. The chill air would be coming soon. Summer was on its last breath this high up.

Her mother had loved the cities, had thrived in the swarm of people struggling for survival against each other. She well remembered the freedom she'd felt when she left that life behind. A barn smelled of pure intentions and comfort. Two things she had been unable to find either with her mother or in any of the cities she had tried to make her home before settling in the Rockies.

The struggle in the west of the young America was more honest than city life. Here the enemy was nature and the only race was to gather enough to survive whatever the gods sent you each winter. Every morning, she looked to the peaks of what they were calling the Territory of Colorado and checked their mood. Every morning she rejoiced that Venice was thousands of miles and decades away.

Eight hands made for light work, and even though the cows would have to be milked again before the end of the day, Petra felt a surge of accomplishment at completing the task. It had been pleasant to work in tandem with the others and listen to the brothers' chatter. Adam and James took the cows out to a pasture near the barn while Petra and Robert loaded the large containers of gathered milk onto a cart. They rolled the cart to the smaller barn situated behind the larger milking barn. The smell of aging cheese wafted over her as they passed through the door. A large trough was set off to the side, and there was a door in the floor that led into an underground cellar, where it would be cool enough for aging the wheels of cheese.

James met Petra and his hands as they emerged from the cheese house. "Stay for a late supper. It's the least I can do to thank you for all the help,"

Petra swallowed the quick acceptance that bubbled to the top. "I don't want to be a bother." If he knew the reason they had worked so hard this morning, he would be running her off the premises.

"No bother. Please. Stay."

Petra could hardly say no to the man smiling before her. He had a handsome smile, but his eyes said he was unsure about her. He was not one who opened up quickly, unlike his two farm hands. Petra appreciated the novelty of the brothers' friendliness, but she understood James's wariness more. He was questions and mystery, and the hunter in her wanted to know more.

The meal they shared was a simple one, a thick stew, dark brown bread, and some of the last leafy greens from the summer garden. They sat at an outside table with benches in front of the cabin. Petra took the spot next to James, across from the two brothers. Though she deliberately sat with some space between them, every nerve ending on her right side reminded her of James's proximity. The novelty of having dinner with others was the highlight of the day for Petra. The foreign rumble of the men's voices surrounded her and tickled her ears.

Petra turned to address James. "Where in England are you from?"

James directed his attention to her, and Petra felt the weight of his gaze. "I grew up in Sheffield."

"I know the mountains draw all sorts, but English gentleman tend to stay closer to the cities." At the question in his face, Petra added, "You have better manners than most cattlemen." Petra looked at Robert and Adam. "No offense."

Adam flashed a smile. "None taken, Miss Petra."

"I was a gentleman farmer in England, not quite a gentleman. I grew up on a small family dairy estate. I needed to cut ties from my family, and I wanted to have something all my own." The shield of wariness in his eyes dropped, and, for a moment, Petra saw the melancholy and fierceness in James's gaze.

Petra knew those emotions well. She knew them so well they kept her awake during the longest nights of winter. She refused to look away from the exposed truth in his eyes, though it was mirrored in her own. His words stripped her bare with such ease. Petra felt the harpy inside her uncurl and take notice of the man before her. Warmth pooled in her middle and still she did not look away. A faint stain of red traveled up his neck, and James redirected his attention back to his food. Petra shifted her weight and moved a fraction closer to him on the bench.

It had been eleven years of wandering from city to city, continent to continent, after her mother had forced her from their house. Harpies were created by Zeus to torture souls on their way to Tartarus, but the violent nature he imbued in them also gave them power. To curtail their rise, Zeus cursed them to only produce one female progeny, who was required to leave her mother's house on her fiftieth birthday. Mothers who failed to push their daughters from the nest sickened and died. Thus the gods had assured the harpies would spend most of their three hundred years alone. Like James, Petra had come to Turning Creek looking for a place to have something of her own and to build a life that was not all about isolation and violence.

Adam and Robert watched the exchange without comment, though Petra saw their hidden smiles as they shoved more food in their mouth. She tried to redirect their attention. "Robert, how did you get hooked up with James?"

He swallowed his food and answered, "We heard there was a need for men who knew cattle up here. We ran into this poor bugger on the train north."

"Language, brother. We herd cattle, but I don't want her thinking we're without manners," Adam admonished.

Robert inclined his head. "As if you had any. Sorry, ma'am. We ran into James on the train north. He needed help and we needed a job."

"Oh, tell the truth. Robert was afraid Mr. Lloyd, with his high accent and manners, would be dead on his first day out here. Robert said we had to go with him to save himself from his crazy ideas about a dairy farm out in the middle of the Colorado Territory." Adam gestured as he talked.

"I'm so grateful to know you both have complete faith in my abilities to care for myself, though I do admit the first year would have been exceedingly difficult without you." James raised his eyebrows as he took another bite of meat.

"You've turned into a fine rancher, Mr. Lloyd. About twenty more years, and you'll be as good as me." Robert raised his glass of water in a salute.

James snorted in response and turned back to Petra. "What brought you to the Rockies?"

Petra rolled the answers around in her mind and chose the simplest. "It was time for me to leave home, and I've always loved the mountains. Turning Creek was barely a speck in the valley, and I wanted solitude without being totally alone. Civilization does have its advantages at times. I do appreciate not having to make my own cheese, for example, especially when it is as good as yours." James colored at the compliment and Petra gave him a small smile.

When the meal was over, Petra found herself offering to help with the second milking. By the time she swung up into the saddle to return home, the sun was sinking toward the tips of the mountains and she ached in muscles she had forgotten existed. It would be full dark by the time she reached her own tiny, quiet cabin up Atlas's Peak, but the time here had been worth a ride in the dark. She did not think, after today, she could continue her nocturnal raids on James's herd, although they had been fun.

James walked over to her after she was in the saddle. The sun was in his eyes, and he squinted up at her. His hand closed over her ankle, and Petra jolted. With the sun behind her, she knew he would not be able to see the shock of heat that transferred from his hand to her face.

"I can't thank you enough for today. I hope you'll come again, for a proper visit and not simply to work."

She found her voice. "That would be nice. It's been a pleasure." To her surprise, the entire day had been one of the best she could remember.

"Indeed, it has, Petra Celaeno." James bowed instead of tipping his hat in the American fashion. She kicked her horse into a gallop and did not look back.

CHAPTER 2

Petra took a deep breath and knocked on the door of the cabin on Jolly's Folly, a mountain to the west of her own and a couple thousand feet shorter. As soon as the door opened, Petra knew she should have gone to see her other sister. Marina was the youngest of the three harpies at sixty-two, and the Remnant of the harpy Ocypete. Out of the three harpies, Marina had an easy way with people, bordering on the brash. It was why Petra had chosen her over Dora, although she now regretted her decision.

Marina's sun-kissed skin shone with pleasure when she saw who stood on her doorstep. "And here I thought I was going to have to go looking for trouble."

Petra rolled her eyes. "Good morning to you, as well."

Marina laughed. "Don't be a grump already. The day just started, and I haven't had anyone to pester for days."

"Lucky me."

"There's the spirit. Come on in. What brings you over this way? Do you want some coffee?"

"You know I won't drink that swill. It's not civilized." Petra followed Marina inside the cabin and considered the best way to broach the topic at hand.

The inside of Marina's cabin was as cluttered as Petra's was clean. Every surface was covered with a patina of knives, books, newspapers, and clothes, but the one cushioned lounge in front of the window was clear of debris. Marina moved to the small potbellied stove and poured strong black liquid into a battered tin mug. She closed her eyes and sighed after the first sip.

Petra took in the piles of laundry and dishes, washed but not put away. "No one coming in here would ever think you were civilized."

Marina grinned and let the wild quality overtake her eyes. "We're monsters, remember. Monsters aren't civilized."

Something twisted inside of Petra. "We're not monsters."

Marina put her cup down too forcefully, and the coffee sloshed over onto a newspaper whose headline read: Gold Placer Found in South Platte River! "Gods, you're touchy. Our ancestors were exiled on Strophades and took every opportunity to act like foul animals. The best thing they ever did was lead the charge against Zeus, but that did not make them noble or civilized." Marina pointed her finger up and down Petra's lean mortal form. "You look civilized enough, but inside, we're still beasts stuck on an island."

Petra's shoulders slumped. Dora *would* have been the better choice. "We have monsters inside, but we don't have to let that define us."

Marina smirked and picked her cup back up. "Your problem is that you don't know how to have fun."

"Be serious."

Marina flashed pointed teeth at Petra. The harpy teeth looked menacing in her mortal mouth. Petra blinked, and Marina's teeth were again small and blunt. "I'm always serious about entertainment or a good fight." Marina's idea of a lively debate included punching.

The conversation was skewing too far from where Petra needed it to be. "Don't you ever wish you could just be something else and not be part of a cycle of violence and seclusion?"

Marina tapped the rim of her mug. "I don't know where this is coming from. We are what we are. There's no changing, just adapting to what is."

Petra struggled to find the words to explain how the ten years she had left to produce a daughter were like a weight around her neck, dragging her toward the repetition of a fate she clawed against. The gods had sought to control their vicious creation by both limiting them to one offspring per line and insuring the harpies spent most of their lives alone. They forced the continued existence of the harpies by tying the mother's survival to that of her daughter. The myths said that a harpy who refused to find a man to father their daughter or failed to reject their daughter when they came of age were sentenced to a cruel death. No harpy had ever been willing to test the truth behind the story.

Petra left her hesitation over having her own daughter alone and addressed the true reason for seeking out Marina. "I think I've been living like a hermit too long. My mother lived a completely secluded life in Venice, and I grew up thinking that was the way, but I'm tired of separating myself. You're more comfortable with people. Too comfortable, really, but..." Petra shrugged and looked at her hands. "I thought you might have some advice for me if I wanted to mingle with mortals more often."

"It helps if you smile occasionally. And talking also helps. Look, you already have some friends in town. Iris and Henry. You know other people. Just take time, talk to them, but mostly listen. Try Simon first. If you're ever going to learn to endure extended conversations, he's the one to practice on."

Petra groaned. Simon was the owner of Turning Creek's one mercantile, and he could hold a lively conversation with a wall. "I'm hopeless. It was a dumb idea. I'm fine the way I am." Petra put her forehead on the table.

"Don't beat yourself up. I've seen you take down a grizzly with nothing but your own hands. Making friends with mortals is not quite as hard."

Killing things was easy. That was the problem. Giving into the bubbling violence, lurking beneath the surface, was simple compared to walking down the street and having civilized conversations. Petra thought about working with James yesterday and the patience with which he had guided her through herding the cows. If she wanted to see more of him, she was going to have to overcome her self-exile and learn to be something more than a harpy.

Marina regarded her with unmoving eyes. "Why the sudden struggle with being part of society? I had you pegged as the one most likely to have your daughter and stay wrapped happily in your own territory, away from most people."

As a young harpy, newly expelled from her mother's home, Petra had enjoyed traveling and seeing new things, but now that she had found her place, she'd dug in. "I was thinking of branching out."

Marina drained the rest of her coffee. "If you're going to stay, come outside and throw knives with me." Marina stood and gathered some of the knives sitting on a shelf by the door.

Petra frowned. "I'm horrible with those."

Marina grinned. "I know. You make me look good."

Petra had nothing else to do, and it had been a long time since she had spent time with just Marina. Not all harpy generations were as close as theirs. Her mother had only visited her harpy sisters twice that Petra could remember. Her mother had spent too much time alone, and the wildness had eroded her. If Petra was ever to have a daughter of her own, she wanted her to have a strong relationship with the other harpies. Only since coming to Turning Creek and spending time with Marina and Dora had Petra begun to feel grounded, less feral.

"I'll throw a few times with you, but then I want to practice with my pistol. Using a gun draws less attention than all the weapons you prefer. You know it's not normal, even in these parts, for a woman to walk around dressed like that and armed to the teeth." Petra pointed to the knives she knew Marina had in her boots and the men's pants Marina had cut down to fit over her curves.

"A lady has to have some vices." Marina flipped one of the throwing knives in her hand and walked out the door.

The pair went outside. Marina handed Petra a set of throwing knives and fixed her grip before letting Petra throw the first knife. It went left of the wooden target. The second grazed the board and fell into the grass. Marina said nothing and handed Petra another knife. The metal was warm from the sun, and birds twittered in the branches above them. Petra narrowed her focus on the target. The noise and sunshine faded until all she saw was the weathered board with the bull's-eye painted in what Petra knew to be blood. She threw the last knife. The whack it made as it buried into the wood, just left of the bull's-eye, made Petra smile with satisfaction.

"That's the way." Marina threw one of her knives and it landed in the center of the target.

"Show off." Petra went to retrieve her knives. She bent over the grab one of the knives that had gone wide and then pulled the one from the board. She heard the whistle of a knife the second before it sunk into the wood a finger's width from her hand. Marina cackled behind her.

"You could have hit me."

Marina laughed harder. "I'm better than that, and you know it."

She was right, but Petra still wanted to wipe the cocky grin from Marina's face. The irritation awakened the channel of violence which always lurked below the surface. Petra swallowed it down. Marina was her sister, and she would not let something so small ruin the day.

Petra walked back to Marina and took her place before the target again. All the knives hit the target the second time, but none of them came close to the bull's-eye. She ground her teeth in frustration as Marina landed all three of her knives in the dead center.

Marina laughed again. "You know what your problem is?"

"I'm sure I can't avoid you telling me." Petra went to retrieve her knives. She would try once more.

"You have to embrace the violence, channel it. Like this."

Petra felt Marina's power shift. Her face darkened into the mask of something that swoops down on you in the night. The leak of violence swirled like a physical force around the two of them. Petra felt her own harpy rise in anticipation, wanting to be called to the surface. Marina swept around in a circle and let her knife fly toward the target without aiming. The knife thunked into the center of the board.   Marina blinked, and the harpy was gone from her eyes. "Easy as pie."

Petra knew then that Marina did not struggle with the duality of what they were. She embraced her harpy in a way Petra was unable to do; she almost reveled in it. Marina might be able to help her be friendlier with the people of Turning Creek, but she would not be able to help Petra with the way the violence of her harpy sometimes made her feel like she was drowning.

A shadow passed over them, moving too fast to be a cloud. Dora's brown feathers, speckled white, glinted in the sun. The white speckles on brown were reflections of the freckles which covered every inch of her human form. The harpy landed beside them and, in a blink, Dora stood before them with her auburn hair in a neat bun and her face alight with pleasure.

"What a great afternoon this is turning out to be." Dora's deep blue eyes sparkled, and Petra smiled in greeting.

Marina waved a knife in the air. "You're just in time to see me put Petra to shame again."

Dora chuckled. "Marina, no one can best you at knives. You need a new weapon to master so you will be less cocky."

Petra groaned and held up a hand. "Please, I beg you. Don't give her any ideas."

Marina rubbed her chin. "Too late. It has been some time since I used a sword. I should start practicing again." She dashed off into the house and came out brandishing a short sword with Greek lettering on the blade. She swiped the blade through the air.

Dora took a set of knives from Marina. "How long have you two been out here?"

Marina flipped the sword and caught the hilt. "Long enough for Petra to remember she is terrible at throwing knives." Marina cast a wicked grin in Petra's direction.

Petra stuck her tongue out at Marina. Childish, but it widened the grin on both her sisters' faces, so it was worth it.

"I have a proposition for you both." Marina waved her sword toward the bull's-eye. "We all throw for the target, you two with knives and me with a sword. The one who's is the farthest away has to make dinner. I have a rabbit ready, so no hunting required."

Dora tested the weight of one of the throwing knives. "Deal."

Petra knew she was going to be cooking later. "I think this is an underhanded way to gang up on me. Deal."

"Just to show I have faith in your non-ability to beat me, you can go first." Marina stepped nimbly out of the way.

Petra gripped the leather handle of the knife and centered herself. She pulled forth her harpy and all the darkness that came with her, and she pushed it into the motion of throwing the knife. Petra let the knife fly and sent a flood of power after it. The blade sank into the wood an inch from the bull's-eye. It was her best throw of the day.

Marina whistled. "That's the way. A little practice and you might actually hit something for real."

Petra was certain she would still lose, but she was pleased with her showing. "You're up, Dora."

Dora was average height, but slight. With her creamy skin, freckles, and blue eyes, she looked more like a doll than a creature of vengeance. She was every bit as dangerous as her sisters; she just hid it better. Dora's throw was true and her knife landed just right of center. She bowed to Marina. "Your turn, sister."

Marina made a show of taking her place at the line. She tested the weight of her sword as if she had not held it thousands of times before. She licked her finger and held it into the air, testing the slight breeze. Petra ground her teeth at the show.

Marina laughed. "Patience, Petra. Greatness takes time." In a flash, Marina threw, and the sword stuck in the wood in the dead center of the bull's-eye. She turned to Petra. "I look forward to the dinner you will be preparing us."

It was a nice night, so they made a fire in the stone pit outside and roasted the rabbit and some potatoes. In the end, all of them helped start the fire and cook, though Marina did not let them forget she had won. They finished the meal, but remained around the fire in conversation.

Marina waved a hand in Petra's direction. "Petra has decided to stop being a hermit and venture out some." Petra had been pleased that Marina had left this information out of the conversation thus far.

Dora turned towards Petra. "Why the change? Is it because you are running out of time to have a daughter?"

Petra picked a stick up and threw it into the fire. "My mother kept herself isolated, and I do not think it was good for her, or me for that matter." Her mother had let much of her morality go by the time she'd driven Petra from her home. "I want to be a part of the world so I do not forget my morality."

Dora nodded. "It's hard to find a balance in what we are." She pointed at Marina. "Some of us struggle less than others, but life was never said to be easy."

Petra threw another stick in the fire and watched it flame up. "Do you ever wish we could stop the cycle of our lines? Just choose not to have a daughter and die?"

Marina straightened up. "What in the name of the gods are you talking about?"

A crease marred Dora's forehead. "I know your mother was not kind to you, but my mother was nurturing, in her own way, and Marina's was not indifferent to her."

Marina kicked a stone on the edge of the fire. "Is that what this is all about? That harpies are terrible mothers?"

Petra pressed her lips together. Her mother had never ceased to remind her that she was the means of her survival and nothing more. The moment Petra had turned fifty, she had found her belongings in the street in front of their villa. "It seems cruel to have a daughter, knowing you can't love her."

Marina snorted. "Harpies aren't made to love. We're monsters, remember?"

"Stop. We're not monsters. We can choose to be something else." Dora scowled at Marina.

Dora wanted optimism alone to be the answer to their existence. Petra knew wishing alone did not make anything so. "But we don't have a choice. Not really." Petra poked a log in the fire and watched the sparks fly up into the night air. "Don't worry. I'll continue my line when they time comes. I just hate feeling like I don't have a choice."

They were silent for some time. Marina added another log to the fire and asked, "Do you ever wonder what it would have been like if Podarge's line would have continued with the others?"

Podarge, the lost and forgotten harpy, the harpy who was slain in the uprising against Zeus on the day Olympus fell. The myths portrayed her as the fastest and smartest of the four harpies, but Petra put little faith in the myths. In most of the stories, harpies resembled ugly, foul-smelling vultures. The descriptions did not come close to their bird of prey forms or the angular beauty of their harpy faces.

Podarge had been in the vanguard when the palace was overrun, and she had sustained more wounds than a harpy could heal by shifting between forms. Harpies lived a long time and were hard to kill, but they were not immortal. Podarge's body was not the only one that had been burned that night in the garden of the palace.

Dora twirled an aspen leaf between her fingers before throwing it into the fire. "One of the lost myths says her child lived."

Marina chuckled. "The lost myths also say Zeus preserved his soul somewhere until it could be resurrected by a Remnant of his line. The lost myths were lost for a reason. They're rubbish."

Petra watched the firelight on her sisters' faces and wondered what it would be like to have her family extended by one. "Besides, we all know the stories. Podarge hid her daughter, but there is no way the babe survived. The others searched for her for decades. After all these generations, we would have found them."

Dora looked at Petra over the fire. "Is there any other reason you have decided to take a more active interest in your territory?"

Dora's use of the word territory struck Petra differently than before. Harpies were territorial creatures, and they tended to guard what they considered their home ferociously. Though Dora and Marina lived close to her, they each lived on separate mountains.

Petra did not want to tell them about James yet. The possessive harpy in her wanted to keep the knowledge of him to herself, which in itself was ridiculous, especially as her sisters knew him at least by name. Part of her desired to keep James for herself. A secret she could deny or admit when she pleased. She would have loved to make them laugh over her adventures with the cows, but she hesitated to start the story. Once she started, she would have to continue to the conclusion, and tell them of meeting James.

"I suppose it is time to start looking after what's mine." Petra grinned and let the power of her harpy roll within her.

CHAPTER 3

When Petra woke up the following morning, she decided to put her decision to get more involved into action. She might regret taking Marina's advice, but a trip into town was her first order of business. Plus, she needed supplies, which would give her the opportunity to talk to Simon, and it had been some time since she had seen Iris.

Petra grabbed her running list of the items she needed from town from underneath a half-full jar of rocks on her desk, pausing wistfully over the keepsake. On her journey to this place, Petra had collected stones along the way. One from the street outside the house where she had grown up, one from the beach in New York when she had seen that teeming city for the first time, and one from the foothills of the Rockies, collected when she knew she had come home. Returning the jar to the desk with care, she gathered her traveling jacket and headed outside to saddle her horse for the trip down the mountain.

Petra would have preferred to fly into town. She rarely flew during the day in her harpy form. Even in this secluded area of the world, there were eyes to see her as the wind roared in her ears and slid over her wings. If she kept to the upper streams of warmer air, she would look like an over-large bird of prey, a trick of the eye, and be dismissed. In another time, however, her ink black, bird-of-prey body, too large to be any ordinary bird, with wings ending in clawed hands and an angular woman's face where a bird's belonged, would have been instantly recognizable. No longer. The time of the gods was long gone, and the true believers had passed into the arms of whatever lay beyond, whether Hades or heaven or another life.

While she could carry significant weight in her harpy form, she did not want to lug her supplies home on the wing. She saddled her mare and pointed her down the mountain. It was early in the morning, and the birds serenaded her as she traveled. Petra was not in a hurry and let the horse set the pace.

Turning Creek lay on the west side of the valley, surrounded by mountains with names like Atlas's Peak, Jolly's Folly, Baldy, Silvercliff, Lady's Favor, and Pikus Peak. Her path took her around the Lloyd farm, and Petra briefly considered making a detour, but she could not come up with a plausible reason for doing so. She did not turn her horse and continued on in the direction of town.

Three-quarters of an hour later, Petra heard the sound of a tree being chopped where there should not be any activity at all. Senses alert, Petra left the trail and directed her mare toward the sound. About a hundred yards off the trail, Petra came upon a clearing. The smell of freshly chopped wood permeated the air, and new stumps littered the ground. The frame and two walls of a cabin even smaller than her own stood in the clearing. A man, well over six foot and covered in dark hair, swung an axe with precision against the trunk of a tree. His shirt sleeves were rolled up, and Petra could see his muscles move as chips flew from growing wedge in the tree's middle.

The man turned and focused hard, dark eyes at Petra. "What do you want?"

Awareness of this man rolled through her like fire. Her harpy screamed danger, but she held herself still atop her horse. This man was a Remnant, and the predator in her recognized another of its kind. "Good morning. I live farther up the mountain. My name is Petra Celaeno."

The man shifted his grip on the axe, and Petra calculated how long it would take her to draw the gun holstered in her saddle. She was a fair shot, but not quick. She could change into her harpy and fly away faster than she could get to her gun. If he charged her, she might have a chance, but if he threw the axe, things could get dicey.

"Name's Billy Royal." He turned and went back to hacking away at the tree.

Petra pursed her lips. Her first encounter in this grand experiment was not going as she would have hoped. If this was how the rest of the day would proceed, maybe she should return home. She sighed. If she was going to make an effort, she may as well start here. She did not trust the power radiating from Billy Royal. If she was friendly with him, she could check up on him and make sure he stayed out of trouble.

Petra cleared her throat and let some of her own power leak from her. A mortal would not notice the subtle shift, but if Billy was as powerful as he seemed to be, he would know what message she was sending. "I'm headed to town. If you need anything, I could pick it up, since we're neighbors and all." *You are on my mountain and you should watch yourself*, she wanted to add.

The axe stilled. "I've got all I need. Have yourself a nice day, Miss

Celaeno." He drawled out her name and turned to smile at her. The expression stopped at his nose, leaving his eyes untouched. Billy returned to his work and did not watch as Petra left the clearing. She was not done with him though. She was a harpy, and while he was welcome if he did not cause trouble, she was going to keep a very close eye on him for a long while. He rubbed her feathers the wrong way.

Petra puzzled over her new neighbor and the unusual concentration of potential Remnants until she reached the outskirts of Turning Creek two hours later. While it was natural that sometimes Remnants would find themselves living in proximity to each other—the world was only so large—they did not tend to gather in large numbers. It was odd that Billy Royal, James, and herself, all Remnants, would end up on the same mountain near the same nothing town in Colorado. The moment she crossed into town, however, her thoughts on the matter ceased. Her encounter with Billy Royal and its attendant worry was eclipsed by the anxiety she always felt when she came to town.

Though Turning Creek was a small community, Petra still felt the press of humanity as she led her horse down the town's one street, Main Street. Most people lived scattered over the valley floor and mountains, but there were about ten families who lived in or on the very edge of town. On a busy day, there would be a handful of people walking between the stores.

Petra rode past Hughes Tailor shop, which was the last building on the north side of Main Street, and past the sheriff's office. She did not pass anyone on her way. Petra stopped at the mercantile and got off her horse. The storefront window displayed an odd collection of material, food stuffs, and tools. Marina had said this was the best place to start. If she could be patient through a conversation with Simon, she could listen to anyone. The real problem would surface when Petra had to hold up her own. Lucky for her, chatting with Simon did not require much interaction. Petra took a fortifying breath and opened the door.

The tinkle of a bell heralded her entrance and the head of a stocky, balding man popped up over the counter. Petra fished the list from the pocket in her skirt. "Good morning, Simon. I need a few things."

A welcoming smile spread over Simon's face. "I told the misses today would be a day of surprises, and here you are. Good morning, Miss Petra. How are you today?"

Petra looked at the ordinary mortal man holding out his hand for her list and blurted out what had been on her mind. "I met a new man this morning a ways down Atlas's Peak. Billy Royal."

Simon looked up from her list. "Mr. Royal was in here two days ago. He was not the friendliest man who's ever come around. He was polite enough, but cold. Very cold, yes indeed. He bought enough supplies for a month, so I doubt he'll be back in town anytime soon. I asked what he was doing in the region. I asked, and he said, well, he said he was looking for his purpose. It seemed odd, but people are sometimes odd. Especially if they've been alone in the mountains for too long."

And that was exactly the kind of oddness Petra wanted to avoid. For someone who talked more than he listened, Simon still noticed a lot. "He was not keen on having a morning chat with me."

Simon walked around the counter and began measuring out flour. "His loss, I say. Who would want to pass up a nice chat with a lady?" He closed up the bag of flour and laid it on the front counter.

Petra followed in his wake as he took things down from the shelves and added them to her growing pile, chatting all the while. "Did you hear about the recent discoveries by Russell and Jackson? They've had multiple articles in the Rocky Mountain News. They found gold pacers in two different places. In two places! Mark my words, Turning Creek is going to have an influx of people soon. Once the gold fever hits, men throw their whole lives aside to dig in the ground for the dream of finding metal."

The headline on the newspaper in Marina's cabin popped into her mind. "I think I did see something about that, but I do not know the details."

Simon waved a hand. "Details don't matter. Like I said, it's the gold fever that matters." He put one last bundle on the counter and tapped his temple. "I've read reports of other gold strikes. Sane men go crazy, and crazy men cause a ruckus. Just you wait. Things are going to get crazy around here. Billy Royal is just the first."

Petra sincerely hoped not. Her resolution to be more involved wasn't predicated on a bustling mining town. She knocked about for a response. "Turning Creek is far from South Platte. I doubt anyone knows we're even here."

Simon raised his eyebrows at Petra. "Just because we are in the middle of mountains doesn't mean we are in the middle of nowhere. Everywhere is somewhere, and people can always find a place when they look hard enough."

Petra did not know how to respond to that jumbled bit of philosophy, so she nodded sagely. "How much do I owe you?"

Simon rattled off a price, and Petra handed over the money. She packed her purchases into her saddle bags and tied them shut.

"Miss Petra, you come back soon. We just don't see you in town enough." He smiled widely up at her, genuine and kind. "I assume you are going to see Iris?" She nodded. "Good, tell her I got that paper she requested in a crate out back."

"No problem." Petra opened the door and the bell rang. "Have a good day, Simon." She waved and walked out into the sun.

Petra secured the bags to her mare's saddle. Her visit to the mercantile had gone well. On previous visits, she had tried hard to avoid Simon or extract herself from conversation with him as quickly as possible. Today, she had listened as Marina had suggested and the conversation had flowed easy enough. Perhaps living the life of a violent, grumpy hermit had not ruined her for society after all.

The frame of a two-story building was going up across from the mercantile and the mail depot. A canvas sign hung from the front of the structure: Daniel Vine's Fine Spirits, Serving Soon. Simon's prediction about the influx of people hit Petra in the gut. Petra narrowed her eyes and peered at the men hammering nails. Thoughts of overcrowding and men running amuck over her mountain caused the muscles in her neck to seize. She was ready to embrace society, but she did not want it reaching into every corner of her mountain home.

The harpy in her rolled with anxiety over the thought of a population influx. Petra should have reined in her darker side, but she let her anxiety turn to annoyance. She had to keep herself from stomping as she walked to the mail depot, a small storefront next to the mercantile, maintained by Iris. She opened the door harder than she intended, and it slammed against the wall.

Iris sat behind a counter made from half of a large log, polished and worn by many hands. Behind Iris were bird-hole slots, some empty and others filled with a variety of envelopes. One larger slot held a fist-sized package wrapped in brown paper. Iris was perched on a stool reading a book. She placed a finger on her place and closed the cover of the blue-bound book.

Like all Remnants, Iris held some of the power of her ancestors. She was descended from the original goddess Iris, the rainbow messenger of the gods, who held the power of prophecy and communication. The original Iris had been loyal to the harpies and had pleaded with Zeus to show them mercy after they drove the Argonauts from the island of Strophades. Her pleas were successful. Zeus had spared the lives of the four harpies, but then he'd cursed them to never find love or have more than one offspring.

The bond between the harpies and the messenger remained strong through the generations. The Remnant of Iris in each generation was born with the same talents as her forebears and given the name Iris. She watched over the harpies as her ancestors before her. There were many days Petra was thankful for the balm Iris provided to her stormy soul.

Iris looked up, clear blue eyes unstartled by Petra's abrupt entrance.

"Hello, bird. You seem to be in a mood." Iris put down her book and ran a hand over her cornflower hair. The cheeriness in Iris's voice cut open the bubbling emotions in Petra.

"Simon just told me about the placers found to the east. He thinks there'll be a flood of people moving in, and they're building a saloon across the street. In a blink, my town is going to be a crowded mess of mortals."

"Your town?" Iris raised an eyebrow at her. "Last I checked, America wants to lay claim to this plot of land. You are formidable, but you might lose that battle."

Petra snorted. The muted din of horses, people, and construction was the only sound in the room. Petra put her hand on the counter and drummed her fingers in an effort to create more noise. After wanting to be in town all morning, the need to leave was oppressive. She tried to still her spirit, but her harpy was too unsettled.

Iris's pale hand covered Petra's dark fingers, stilling them. The sight of their hands together, one pale and one deep olive, was a jolting reminder of what it meant to be the dark harpy and to control the power of the darkness. She had been named "the dark rock," Petra Celaeno, and though her mother had been fair skinned, she had inherited her darkness from the Romany man who had sired her. Petra concentrated on the warmth of Iris's hand and felt the tension drain from her.

Iris smiled. "All your scowling for nothing. You're too serious." Iris turned to slip Petra's letters into one of the slots behind her. None of the slots were labeled, and Petra had never been able to distinguish the filing system Iris used.

Everyone in the region knew Iris. From the mail depot, she operated what amounted to the only efficient mail delivery service in the region. The locals called it the depot. Colorado was still a territory, though with the mineral strikes to the east being reported in the papers, Petra knew it was only a matter of time before the territory was swallowed by the expanding states calling themselves America. The desire for land was as insatiable among men now as it had been when the gods had ruled all.

When locals travelled into town, they gathered letters from family and neighbors and took them to Iris. When they dropped off their packages and letters with her, they picked up whatever mail she had headed in their direction. Iris had a way of asking people to deliver things that made them want to do what she asked. Her delicate beauty did not hurt her influence over others. If a message needed to be delivered, it was sent through her. Consequently, she was also the best source of information in the region, although Simon was a close second.

"What brings you into town today?" Iris kept her back to Petra and continued filing.

"I needed to get off the mountain."

Iris nodded sagely. "They have a weight sometimes that's hard to bear."

"Marina also suggested I come into town more often."

Iris stilled and looked over her shoulder at Petra. "Marina seems like an odd choice for an advice giver, especially for you. I know you two let your anger get the better of you at times."

Petra crossed her arms over her chest. "Marina is touchy and in need of a slice of humility at times, but she is also the most sociable of my sisters." Petra uncrossed her arms and laid her hands palm down on the counter. "I am afraid of becoming a complete recluse, alone on my mountain. I'm tired of being in solitude for the majority of my time."

Iris turned and placed her hands over Petra's. "You've held yourself apart for a long time. I'm glad you've decided to try something new." Iris turned back to her filing.

Petra cleared her throat. "I visited one of my neighbors. James Lloyd, the dairy farmer."

Iris twirled around and her blonde eyebrows moved into the region of her hairline. "Did you?"

"I helped him herd his cattle the other day, and I stayed for the milking. And a meal."

"Indeed." Iris pierced her with a knowing look.

Petra squirmed. "It's not like that. I felt obligated to help." Petra swept her eyes down. "I may have scared the cows a few nights in a row while flying."

"You stampeded his cows? On purpose?" The corners of Iris's mouth twitched.

"Well, they looked hilarious scrambling around, mooing and hopping over bushes." Petra sounded petulant, even to her own ears, but the cows had been funny to watch.

Iris giggled. Petra smiled and laughed with her. "More than one night you did this?" Iris asked. Petra nodded. "What did you think of Mr. Lloyd?"

"James has the manners of a gentleman. He was friendly, but formal for the most part. The strange thing was that I would swear by the river Styx that he is a Remnant of some kind, but he never mentioned it."

"I have gotten the same vibe from him, but he has never said one way or the other, so I left it alone. It's not polite to pry in that direction." Iris asked.

Petra's cheeks warmed, much to her chagrin. "No." Petra ground her teeth, and Iris laughed. "His two hands are characters. Brothers from down south, but you probably already know that."

"I do. I don't, however, know much about Mr. Lloyd, other than how often he comes to town and how his dairy farm is doing."

"Does he receive no mail then?"

"You're awfully nosy, but not often, no. Twice a year he receives a packet from London, which causes his nice face to wrinkle up, but otherwise, no one writes to him."

"He does have a nice face." Petra clapped a hand over her mouth.

Iris clapped her hands with glee. "I knew it. It's past time. For all of you."

"I'm not looking for a mate. I'm not ready for the responsibility of a daughter. He's just nice. That's all. Besides, harpies don't keep their mates past becoming pregnant."

Iris made a noncommittal sound in the back of her throat. The muscles of Petra's neck solidified into a painful knot. She was not ready to find a mate and have a daughter. A harpy reached maturity at fifty, when their mother forced them from home. The daughter then had thirty years, until she turned eighty, to find a man to father the next daughter of her line. But Petra enjoyed the quiet life she had built. A lover and a child would complicate matters. Besides, she doubted James was the kind of man to enter into a casual affair. Pity.

"It's not my time, yet." Petra insisted.

Iris's eyes shifted to Petra's face. She picked up Petra's dark hands and held them tight. The shadow of something moved behind the blue of Iris's eyes and they lost their focus on Petra's face. The sun, which had been streaming in the window, was muted by passing clouds. Fear washed over Petra like water from the snow-fed creeks, and the hair on her arm stood up. The air in the room became heavy, and Petra struggled to keep breathing evenly.

"Your time is coming, Petra of the line of Celaeno. A time of sacrifice and pain. A wound in Gaia will reveal that which was lost. The power of thunder and lightning will be your undoing. You will be forced to sacrifice one who you love." Iris blinked and the shadow was gone from her eyes, but her eyebrows drew together in worry.

"Iris?" Petra turned her hand and gripped Iris's hand hard enough to feel the tiny bones of the messenger's hand crack together.

Iris shook herself and pulled her hands from Petra. "I'm fine, and I'm sorry."

"Styx, Iris. What did you mean the power of thunder and lightning would be my undoing? Am I going to cause the death of one of my sisters? What does it mean?" This was not what she had wanted when she'd come to chat with Iris.

The Remnants of Iris were not the only Remnants with the gift of prophecy, but the women of her line always foretold times of hardship and strife. The original Iris had foreseen the wrath of Zeus against the harpies and had known to intervene for them, though she had never been to Strophades herself. The original Iris had also foreseen the destruction of Mount Olympus and known the cost the victory would entail. Remnants of Iris had foretold plagues, war, and harsh winters. This was the first prophecy Petra had ever heard with her own ears, however.

"I don't know what it means. The gift is not always clear."

Petra snorted. "Not clear? You couldn't have been vaguer if you'd tried. Styx and fire. Damn." Petra kicked at the bottom of the counter and ran her fingers through her hair, giving the curled strands an excuse to break free from her braid. "I would never hurt my sisters or you."

Iris slid off her stool. She gripped the edge of the counter to steady herself and then walked around to the front. Petra towered over Iris, but Iris wrapped her arms around Petra and squeezed. The warm smell of vanilla and cinnamon covered her and released some of the fear left by the prophecy.

"I will not be the cause of anything that hurts you." Petra whispered. She heard the tremor in her voice.

"I know, bird. I know. The words are not always literal." Iris pulled back and tried to smile, but her eyes were heavy with moisture. Petra appreciated the effort the lie may have cost Iris. No prophecy from the Messenger meant sunbeams and rainbows. "I promise, whatever it is, you'll not have to face it alone. I'm here, and I know Dora and Marina will help."

Petra felt unsteady. "Great. Then you can all be witness to my demise as I throw one of you into the fire."

"It may not be so bad."

"Sounded fairly grim to me." Petra ran a hand over her face. She barely felt her hands over her skin. She was numb. "I need a drink."

"You're in luck. The building across from the mercantile is going to be a saloon. A new man by the name of Daniel Vine and his sisters are building it. Unfortunately for you, the bar's not yet open."

"I know. There's a sign up on the building."

Petra corralled her fear and anxiety. Whatever Iris's prophecy meant, it would not come to pass for some time. She would have days, weeks, and perhaps years to ponder the meaning behind the words. She could reverse her recent decision to take a more active role in the lives around her and truly become a hermit. If she kept to herself, she would not have to face the choice of bringing harm to her sisters or Iris. Petra knew she had time before anything came to pass, but she did not think that would help her sleep tonight.

"Do you have any mail headed for the Lloyd farm?" Petra tried to sound nonchalant, but Iris's face held a question. Thankfully, she kept it to herself. Petra forced her shoulders to relax.

"Yes. A letter for Adam and Robert arrived last week. You can deliver it, if you'd like." Iris handed her a thick envelope with slanted writing on the outside. Petra took it without a word.

Iris's voice stopped her before she could open the door. "Do you want me to tell our sisters?"

"If I'm the one who is going to be sacrificing one of us, I should be the one to break the news."

"I'm sorry, bird."

Petra swallowed several times. "Me too."

She let her feet carry her out the door and down the uneven boardwalk of Turning Creek. The boardwalk ended at Henry Foster's blacksmith shop. Henry was one of the few people Petra counted among her friends. He was a quiet man who did not mind a quiet audience. Petra never felt the need to carry on a conversation with Henry, which was why Petra considered him a friend. While she did not know what his favorite food was or whether he like coffee or tea, she did know he was steady and only spoke when he had something useful to say.

Petra went back into the forge area and sat in a corner, out of the way. The clanking of Henry's hammer, the hiss of steam, and the whoosh of the bellows allowed her mind to relax. The air was cool, but Henry was damp with sweat from his work and the steam from the fire. His brown hair stuck to his forehead and his muscles shone as he swung his hammer down. Henry was the Remnant of Hephaestus, blacksmith of the gods. The original Hephaestus had wielded many talents. Petra only knew that Henry was a fine and fair blacksmith by any standards.

Time meandered, lost to Petra. When Henry stopped his work, the sun was almost to the peaks for the evening. He wiped a hand across his brow, leaving behind a smear of grime.

"You been chewin' on something over there, Miss Petra. Can I help with anything?" Henry walked over to where she sat in the dirt. His limp was the only thing that marred the grace of his movements. Petra knew his club foot made standing for long periods painful, but it never kept him away from the forge.

She could not ask for help with a problem she was not sure how to articulate even to herself. Petra raised her head to look into Henry's face. His gray eyes held concern and affection. Henry was a good man. She tried to smile, but she knew it was at best an opaque imitation.

"Nothing right now, Henry. Thank you for allowing me to stay and watch."

"You're welcome anytime. It don't bother me none to have you." Henry hesitated. "You'll let me know, won't you, if I can help with whatever troubles you?"

Petra nodded, unable to trust her voice. Henry offered her his hand and she accepted his help to stand. His hand was rough and warm, although there was no tingle of awareness. Henry was her friend and nothing more.

Petra left the blacksmith shop with a lighter heart. The face of Atlas's Peak was bathed in the coming dusk. The top shone red, but the base was already wrapped in a blanket of darkness. The sky above the peak was clear of clouds, but the colors of the scene stole Petra's breath. This was her home. That was her mountain. Vague prophecies be damned. She would not run from her home because of some unknown tragedy in the future.

She gripped the reins tighter and kicked Merry into a gallop.

CHAPTER 4

The words of the prophecy hounded her the next morning. The sun shone in a sky so blue it hurt her eyes, but a cloud followed Petra. Unable to shake the wedge of gloom in her heart, Petra changed into her harpy form and flew in a circular pattern around the mountain. She could make out James's cows, but she did not fly close to his farm. She wanted to check on her new neighbor, Billy Royal.

With her first pass over Mr. Royal's homestead, she could see no movement around the cabin, which now boasted four walls and the frame of a roof covered with canvas. Piles of wooden shingles lay to one side of the structure. Mr. Royal had been busy. Petra circled around to get a better look at the area around the cabin.

An old path, a deer trail by the looks of it, wound to the west of the clearing. Petra slowed her wing beats so she could move slowly as she followed the trail. It passed by a rocky area where a gnarled tree clutched precariously to the top of a boulder. The trunk of the tree was half burnt, like it had been hit by lightning, but green springs of new leaves sprung from the half that had escaped being singed.

Mr. Royal swung a pickaxe into the mountain to the right of the boulder. He had hacked away a recess into the rock face large enough for a person to duck into. A pile of debris lay at his feet, and a larger pile of discarded rock was heaped on the other side of the clearing. Mr. Royal was building a mine on his land.

Petra frowned. The churning in her gut was disproportionate to the actions of Mr. Royal, who had every right to mine on his land. The idea of him digging here on her mountain struck her as dangerous, but she could not put into words why that would be the case. Petra shook her head and turned around towards home. Her anxiety over the prophecy was making her see doom where there was likely none.

It was too easy to let herself get wrapped up in the darkest of her emotions and fears. All her life, Petra felt like her harpy was a hair's breadth from taking over, and the prophecy had pushed her closer to the edge. Marina had called them monsters, but Petra wanted to be more than something ruled by violence and prone to isolationism.

Petra returned to her own cabin to the sound of a horse approaching. If it had been her sisters coming for a visit, they would have flown, not ridden a horse. She landed behind the small barn where her horse stayed in the winter and changed back into her mortal form. Not for the first time, she was relieved the change came with her clothes. When questioned about the physics of this, Iris had done some research and come up with the answer that their clothes and their mortal forms were somehow contained within a dimensional pocket which followed them and carried the essence of their mortal self and their clothes while in harpy form. Petra's harpy was better described as her soul, her essence, and it never left her. Her mortal form, clothes and all, was a costume for her real self.

Petra walked to the back of the cabin and grabbed an armful of wood. She made her way to the front of the cabin in time to see James emerge from the trees. Pleasure washed over her and she felt her face break into an inviting smile.

"Hello to the house." James grinned as he swung down from his horse.

"You're a welcome surprise to my day." Petra felt ridiculous flirting with an armful of firewood. Even with her arms empty she would have felt silly. She had just told Iris this was not what she wanted.

"Let me carry that for you." James reached to take the logs from Petra.

During the exchange she moved close enough to smell him, clean soap and warm male. Petra resisted the urge to lean in farther. Barely. "Thanks for the help. To what do I owe this visit?"

Petra led James to her front porch, which was spacious enough for one chair and the pile of firewood already stacked high. James laid the wood down and then went to the saddlebag tied to his horse. He pulled out a cloth-wrapped circular object. Petra smelled it before he placed it into her hands.

"I thought, in the spirit of being neighborly, I would bring you some cheese as a thank you for your help with the cows the other day."

"Thank you. I buy it whenever Simon has it in, so I know it's wonderful. Have your cows been on any more nighttime romps?" If she had to give back the cheese, she would never tell James all his trouble was because of her own nocturnal activities.

With his hands empty, James shoved his hands in the pockets of his work pants. "They have been in their pasture where they belong every morning." He shifted his weight from foot to foot. "Thanks, about the cheese, I mean. It's nice that something I labor so hard at is appreciated."

He appeared nervous and unsure of himself. Petra's stomach did a flip when the realization hit her. "It's almost time for the midday meal. I was planning on something simple with tea. Would you like to join me?" She waited for his answer without breathing.

His smile as he answered loosened something within her. "I would love to."

"You can tie or hobble your horse anywhere you'd like and then come on in." Petra suppressed the urge to skip into the house.

Petra stoked the fire and noticed her hand was trembling. She took a calming breath and laughed at herself. Styx, she was seventy years old and having a neighbor over for tea, nothing more. She needed to focus. Marina had said that all she needed to do was listen. She could do that.

A shadow blocked the light coming into the doorway, which Petra had left open, and Petra turned to watch James as he paused on her threshold. His face was in shadow, and his shoulders filled the frame. He stepped into her house, and her cabin suddenly felt smaller for his presence.

Petra busied herself filling the kettle and pulling things from the open cabinets on the wall. "Make yourself at home," she said, glancing in his direction. She kept an eye on him as he moved towards the only messy thing in her house, the bookshelves.

He traced his finger down the lines of books, pausing, then moving on. He was quiet for a long time. "You have an eclectic collection. Philosophy in Latin, German, and Italian. Milton. Pope. Bunyon. And *The Monk* by Lewis. That one is a surprise. I know Gothic stories are all the rage, but they have never been a favorite of mine."

"Tragic endings do have their appeal, now and then. Besides, if you really want to be particular, Milton and Pope both have their moments of tragedy."

"You have me there. No one reading *Samson Agonistes* would say it has a happy ending."

Petra laid two plates on the table and met his eyes across the room. "I like a variety of reading material. I was in town yesterday and have the newest copy of The Rocky Mountain News, if you want it. I haven't added to my personal collection for years. If I need something new, I borrow a book from Iris." Iris had the most complete research materials on Greek myths in the New World, but that was not a fact anyone advertised. Most of the information she guarded had been carefully kept and handed down from one Messenger to another since the time when Olympus had loomed over mankind. She carried other things, plays and poetry, that she did lend out on a selective basis.

"It seems Iris is a woman of many talents. Turning Creek is very fortunate to have her and the mail depot."

The kettle whistled, and Petra moved it from the stove to the round table where she had laid out the cheese James had brought, apples, berries, slices of smoked meat, and brown rye bread. She pulled a tin of crisps from the shelf. "Oh, I almost forgot. There is a letter there on the shelf for Adam and Robert." She gestured towards the table. "Please, sit down and have some tea with me."

Petra poured tea and sliced the bread, glad her hands had something to do. While she made preparations, she cast about for something to say or ask. If she opened her senses, she could still feel the small trickle of otherness about James. He was definitely a Remnant. She knew harpies let out more than a trickle of power, so there was no question he would know she was not mortal. Petra wondered why he had said nothing and tried to urge the conversation in that direction. "You mentioned before that you read Greek mythology as a child."

James's eyes lit up. "There are so many stories with different authors and origins. As the Roman Empire moved over the world, the names of the gods changed, but their essence remained the same. It's fascinating, almost as if the truth of the story could not be suppressed even as the conquering army swept its way through the land."

The kernel of truth could not be repressed because the Remnants remained after the dust had settled over the ruined Olympus. Oppression and bloodshed have a way of marking a land and its people so that even the generations that come after carry its stain. "The Greek myths do have a way of remaining part of the cultural psyche. They are full of violence, betrayal, and the abuse of power. The basis of all good tales. Do you have a favorite?"

James leaned over the table towards her. "I've always liked the tales of Zeus."

A weight, hard and fast, settled into her middle. "Zeus?"

James drummed a finger against his tea cup. "Zeus was the greatest of all the gods. He freed his siblings, founded Olympus, and created a renaissance of culture. Under his rule, Olympus was a power of light and learning in the world."

Petra swallowed the bile in her throat. Zeus had granted power to others, only to become threatened by the power later. He killed and raped his way across the land and people he ruled. The myths only held the smallest fraction of his deeds. The bloodiest truths were buried deep in the hearts of the Remnants. After Olympus fell, only a handful of the gods, goddesses, and creatures remained loyal to the fallen patriarch. In the end, even Hera had turned on him, having grown weary of the growing ranks of Zeus's bastards in her court.

Petra took a sip of her tea and considered her next words. She needed to know what James thought he knew. "Do you know what the myths say about what happened to Zeus at the end of his reign?"

James put his palms on the table and leaned closer. "There are stories, not even stories, but fragments of myths that talk about the lost Zeus. The stories say the other gods became jealous of his power and sought to remove him from the throne. Zeus knew the battle would be costly, so he stepped down from the throne and vanished, giving them what they wanted. I have been studying these fragments for years, and I am convinced Zeus came to the Americas after he disappeared."

Petra could not think. There was no way in any circle of hell James knew he was a Remnant—no one who had any memory of Olympus's fall would feel so enthusiastic about Zeus. All she had to do was come clean and tell him everything, to protect him from the wrath of other Remnants before he shared his perspectives with others—but she could not do it. She opened her mouth but closed it. Repeatedly, like a fish gulping air. James's views on the fall of Olympus were dangerous, but Petra could not put a crack in their new relationship, whatever it was. If she put a hole in the fantasy he had built, this would be their last conversation over tea.

A blush tinged James's cheeks and he leaned back in his chair. "I'm sorry. I can be obsessive about mythology at times, and I have no one to talk to about it." He stared intently at his empty teacup. "The boys have no interest in my theories and you are the easiest person to talk to I have ever met."

Warmth flushed over her face. "I've never been described as an easy conversationalist, but there's a first time for all things." Petra grinned with pleasure. She swiped her worry over James's ideas about Zeus aside. "Sheffield is a far cry from the Rockies. You could've had a dairy farm somewhere back east where transportation is better and there are more customers available."

James chuckled. The sound vibrated in her chest and Petra stilled to soak in the sensation. "I got off the boat, and I just kept going west. At the time, I wasn't sure why, but I knew I needed to keep going. After days of nothing but flat plains, the mountains were just there, looming larger and larger until I felt their weight and I knew I was home. It sounds trite, I know."

Petra covered one of his hands with her own. "It's not in the least bit trite. The mountains have a way of owning you. I searched for a long time before finding this place. The first time I saw the sun rise over the peaks of this valley, they glittered with snow. I had my sisters beside me, and I knew I'd never live anywhere else again." They had been flying all night with the smell of snow and pine in their noses. It was the first time Petra had known what her sisters meant to her. And in that moment she remembered Iris's prophecy—she would harm one of her sisters. Her heart constricted.

James squeezed her hand and the warmth of his skin on hers dispelled the fear of the prophecy. "I did not know you had any siblings."

Petra let her hand remain in James's a moment longer before withdrawing it. She laid it in her lap and enjoyed the leftover sensations sparking over her skin. "Marina Ocypete and Dora Aello. We are not related, really, but we were all only children and have become close over the years like family." It was as close to the truth as she could tell him without revealing everything. "Would you like more tea?"

"Yes, thank you." James rubbed a hand over his jawline. "Your surnames are peculiar. Celaeno. Ocypete. Aello."

Petra poured the tea and let him ponder the meaning of their names. She would not help him find a conclusion.

James straightened suddenly, and his gaze sharpened on her. "Your surnames match the names of the three harpies. Though I suppose an argument could be made for there being four harpies. Podarge is rarely mentioned in the official texts."

Current mainstream historians believed Podarge to be another name for Celaeno. It was mirage of the truth meant to conceal the facts, like the many myths where Zeus was concerned. Petra's shoulders slumped. Once James realized they were named for the harpies because they were harpies, he would leave. While he might consider flirting with her when she was a mere mortal, she did not think he would want to become closer to a monster. Even if she were easy to talk to.

"Remarkable. I wonder if your ancestors were believers."

"Believers?" Petra asked.

"Yes, people who remembered the glory of the gods and mourned the passing of Olympus."

Petra suppressed the urge to laugh. Her ancestors had been one of many to thrust a spear forged in the fires of Olympus into the body of Zeus to ensure he breathed no more. "Perhaps I do have a believer or a historian in my past. My mother never talked about her mother, her parents, I mean, so I know very little about them."

James looked out the window and a crease appeared between his brows. "It's getting late. I promised Adam and Robert I would be back for the evening milking. I'm sure I've already overstayed my welcome." He stood. "Would you like me to help clean up?"

Petra stood. She wanted to tell him that yes, she needed help with the dishes to make him stay longer. "I think I can manage two tea cups and two plates. But thank you."

James walked through the door of the cabin, and Petra followed him as he untied his horse. He turned to face her. "Thank you for the tea and the conversation. I hope we can do this again some time."

"Thank you for the cheese. It was nice to have company. You're the first person I've had here besides my sisters or Iris, and it was a nice change.

You are not what I expected of a gentleman farmer."

"How does the reality and your expectations hold up?"

Petra smiled. "I'm not positive yet. When I finish pondering over it, I'll let you know."

The look in his eyes shifted, and James took a step closer to her. He was not touching her, but she could feel the awareness of him pushing into her. He reached for her hand and bowed over it. He brushed her skin with his lips and Petra felt the feather-light touch as it traveled down her spine and into her toes. He stood up, the blush she was becoming familiar with spreading over his neck.

"I hope the puzzle suits you." James squeezed her hand before releasing it.

Petra blinked then returned his loopy smile with one of her own. "The thing about puzzles is you just never know what's going to happen next."

CHAPTER 5

Petra's sisters arrived later that night, flushed from hunting and high on mountain air. She heard them long before they made an appearance. They swooped in at dusk, screeching into her yard and scattering the chickens and goats. Marina cackled in her hoarse harpy voice as she chased the rooster from the yard.

"Animals. Go back where you came from." Petra wagged her finger at them.

In their harpy forms, Dora and Marina towered over Petra by a couple of feet, and Petra had to look up to scowl at them. Craning her neck caused her to lose the effect of righteous indignation. She gave up and smiled instead.

Marina walked over to Petra, her tan and brown feathers almost iridescent, and she leaned down so their faces were even. Depending on the version of the myth, harpies were said to have the face of a beautiful woman or a hideous hag. In reality, the face of a harpy was more angular and chiseled than that of a mortal human. Petra thought a harpy's face was sharper and on the verge of being masculine.

"Nice to see you too, sister." Marina's voice was low and scratched like sand over metal. The terrible beauty of a harpy did not extend to their voices, which were rasping and ruined.

Dora placed a large deer on the doorstep of Petra's cabin. Petra could still smell warm blood on the fresh kill. It seemed her sisters had brought a present.

"You've brought dinner. How kind." Petra crossed her arms over her chest.

"There's no need to pout. We came by and waited for you two days ago, but you were gone. Marina couldn't wait any longer. You know how she gets." Dora attempted to say the last part in a whisper but it came out sounding like a dying rattle. Marina shrugged and lifted off the ground, her wings kicking up dirt and scattering the few brave chickens who had ventured back. They squawked indignantly as they flapped away, again.

Petra must have been in town when they'd arrived, visiting Iris and receiving the bad news she would sacrifice one of her sisters. Petra rolled her eyes. "I dislike talking to you like this. Change so we can talk properly."

Dora turned in a circle and curtsied. She was brown with a patch of pristine white on her chest and a dusting of snow on the tips of her wings. "Do you not think I'm pretty, Petra of the line of Celaeno?"

At those words, the blood drained from Petra's head and pooled somewhere near her feet. She pointed a finger at Dora, who had frozen. Petra tried to still her shaking hand but the tremors only increased. Fear roiled in her and her harpy begged to be let loose. Strong emotions always brought her harpy to the surface.

"Why did you say that?" That was the way Iris had said her name during the vision or prophecy or whatever the hell it had been. Styx. She was going crazy. She needed to control herself. There was no reason to be upset yet, but she was losing the battle against the tidal wave of emotion. Petra stepped up to Dora until she could feel the heat coming off the harpy. "Why did you say my name like that?"

"What is it? What did I do?" The fear in Dora's voice was at odds with its harshness. She crouched beneath Petra's gaze.

Marina swooped down and landed heavily beside them. Her eyes were wide and her wings were folded completely back in submission. Petra was the oldest and most powerful of the three, and her sisters were right to fear her when she feared herself. Petra wondered who had more control over her life, her mortal side or the monster inside.

"What happened?" Marina asked.

The prophecy said she would sacrifice someone she loved. She loved her sisters, and helplessness ate a hole through her resolve. Rage tore through Petra. The myths were filled with terrible deeds of the harpies. Their anger was ferocious and unforgiving and Celaeno's dark violence was said to have been the worst of all. Petra's anger became a physical force and dark clouds gathered above them. Marina placed a tentative, but firm, hand on Petra's arm. Petra shook her off. The darkness continued to build inside her and was reflected in the air around them.

"Why did you say my name like that?" Petra demanded. Dora, though larger in her harpy form, cowered before the darkness of Petra's wrath.

Dora, covered her face before the gathering dark. "Please, Petra. I was only joking. Please, dispel the clouds and tell us what is going on."

In a darkening red haze, Petra felt Marina's clawed hand on her arm again, and she hesitated. The urge to change into her harpy form and rip something to pieces clawed at her. She wanted to scream and lash out because she had the power to do nothing else in the face of the nameless threat Iris had presented to her. Petra breathed deep and looked into Dora's scared blue eyes, which were the same color as her human ones.

She loved her sisters. She would not hurt them, prophecy or no. Petra gathered her fear and the darkness back into herself. The clouds parted and a ray of moonlight landed on the three harpies. Petra stepped back from Dora as she collapsed in the dirt at Petra's feet.

Marina removed her hand from Petra and squinted brown eyes at her. "What in the name of the gods was that about? I love a fight as much as the next girl, but I don't relish getting into fisticuffs with you."

Petra chuckled, breaking the tension. "Fisticuffs?"

Marina grinned. "It's a funny word. Besides, now you're smiling."

Petra rubbed a hand over her face. She needed a drink. There was a bottle of whiskey in the cabinet. She called over her shoulder as she walked inside, "It's a story best told with a drink. Preferably more than one. Change and come inside."

Petra poured glasses of whiskey and sat down with resignation. Dora and Marina sat and waited for her to speak. She told the story as quickly as possible, not skipping any vital facts, but not lingering over any details either. Hearing the words of the prophecy out loud again was like a noose around her neck. Dora asked her to repeat the prophecy a second time. Petra almost choked on the words, but she said them. "A time of sacrifice and pain. A wound in Gaia will reveal that which was lost. The power of thunder and lightning will be your undoing. You will be forced to sacrifice one who you love."

When she finished the retelling, the three sat in silence, sipping whiskey.

"Damn." Marina said for the third time.

"Indeed." Petra poured herself another glass.

"Damn." Marina said again and held out her glass to Petra, who filled it from the depleted bottle.

Dora glared at both of them. She slammed her empty glass on the table, "This isn't helping anything."

"Who cares? My fate awaits. Might as well have some fun. Apparently, I get to kill one of you. Honestly, I'm hoping it's Marina. She's the mouthiest." Petra drained her glass and poured another.

"If you can catch me. They don't call me the swift harpy for nothing. Cheers." Marina raised her glass with a sloppy smile.

Dora swiped Petra's glass from her hand before she could drink it. Petra tried to grab it back but her reflexes were slower than normal. Petra settled for scowling at Dora. It had worked out in the yard. If she called the dark again and drove them off, she could get roaring drunk and forget what was coming - for a few hours anyway.

"What did Iris mean by 'a wound in Gaia?' The earth? How is the earth wounded? What was lost? What is the power of thunder and lightning? How do you know the sacrifice is one of us? Why not Iris?" Dora's voice rose with each question until the volume grated on Petra's ears.

Gods, please let it not be Iris, Petra thought. Her sisters needed Iris. "I don't know." Petra had not meant to shout, but the words were roaring in her ears. "Styx. Don't you think I've been plagued by those questions for the past couple days? I've no idea what they mean. I wish to the gods I knew." Petra rubbed a hand over her face. She could not feel her nose.

"There has to be a way to fight this." Marina's voice was quiet but sure.

"Not everything can be solved with—what was the word you used?—fisticuffs. I can't fight what I don't understand." Petra said.

"Don't be such a coward. You're a harpy, for Hera's sake. Act like it." Marina took the last sip from her glass but kept her eyes trained on Petra's face.

"I think before I barrel in like an enraged bull, unlike you." Petra spat. Marina stood up and the chair she had been sitting in clattered to the floor. Her hands were fists at her sides.

Petra smirked. "See, always ready to fight, even when you should shut the hells up."

"Stop it. Both of you." Dora poked a finger in Petra's face. "You aren't handling this great at the moment, so stop making us feel small to appease your own fear. And you," she rounded on Marina, "stop looking for a fight at every corner. Just because we're harpies doesn't mean we're animals. Control yourselves."

They shrank under the censure. Petra dropped her head into her hands. Dora was right. She had let her anger control her, again. "What am I going to do? Sacrifice and pain, Iris said. Whatever is coming, it won't be pleasant."

"You won't be alone." Dora's warm hand was on her shoulder.

Petra reached back and took hold of Dora's hand, but she looked at Marina. "Forgive me." She loved her sisters, who loved her in spite of her darkness.

"Of course."

"The only thing to do is keep our eyes open and continue on like normal. If the prophecy comes to pass, we'll see signs of it in time." Dora took a sip from her glass, which was still three-quarters full.

Thankfulness for her small family flooded Petra, washing away the tinge of fear. Dora was the one who spoke peace and kept them sane. She handled the violence of what they were with grace. Her human form reflected this, pale skin covered by more freckles than expanses of white, and brown hair bordering on ginger.

Slightly unsteady from their talk over the whiskey, the three women dressed the deer and roasted some of the meat for dinner. The rest of the meat went into the smokehouse. As they sat down to a meal of greens and meat with berries for desert, a peace came over Petra. She had family, and she would not have to face her future alone. All would be well.

"Did Iris tell you there's a man named Daniel Vine building a saloon across from the mercantile?" Marina asked as she took a huge bite of venison.

"Yes. I know many will be happy to have a drinking establishment in town." Petra said.

Dora scowled at Petra and Marina. "Did you see his sisters with him?"

Marina snorted. "Sisters. I'm sure they're all blood related. Those ladies will be flat on their backs taking customers as soon as the walls are up."

Petra agreed but kept her opinion to herself. Prostitution was nothing new. As long as the women were willing and it was all above board, she had no problem with it. Everyone had to make a living somehow.

"I've taken your advice, Marina, about being friendlier. I had a visitor yesterday, my neighbor, James Lloyd. He stayed for tea." Petra tried to make the remark casual. She did not repeat the mistake of referring to him as James, as she had with Iris, and in so doing, give herself away.

Dora looked at her as if she had sprouted a second head. "The dairy farmer?"

"Yes."

"Was he nice?"

"He's very formal in the way the British often are but neighborly enough, though he might have been less friendly if I'd told him I was the one stampeding his cows at night." Petra felt a smile and a blush spreading over her face. Dora watched her.

Marina laughed. "That is a story you simply must tell."

Petra obliged, with some embellishments over the way the cows hopped and ran. She described the brothers in great detail, relaying some of their better stories. She made sure not to center her retelling on James, but it was delightful to share her impressions of him. She did not mention his misguided beliefs about Zeus. Petra hoped to change those with time, but she had not figured out how to do so without revealing all she was to him as well.

Marina's eyes sparkled. "I want to fly over the cows tonight."

Petra immediately knew she should have kept the story to herself. Petra did not want James's cows to become Marina's newest shiny object. Something else within her wanted to shout that James belonged to her, which of course, he did not.

"No. Go bother someone else's cows." Petra's hand clenched on her fork.

"Why not, after you just told us how much fun it was?" Marina crossed her arms over her chest. If she had stuck her lip out like a child, the picture would have been complete.

Petra sighed. "It was fun, but when I helped James, Mr. Lloyd, with the herding and milking, it made me realize how much extra work and worry my actions caused. The scattered cows are more susceptible to predators. Leave them alone, Marina."

Marina uncrossed her arms, but she stuck her tongue out at Petra. "Fine."

"You're such a child," Petra said with a smile. Relief that Marina would not be venturing into James's pasture and that they had not questioned her reasoning washed through her. Marina was beautiful, the way the ancient goddesses of Greece were beautiful, all dark eyes, light skin, and perfect curves. Marina's hair was curly where Petra's tended to frizz. Petra wanted to keep her far away from her new neighbor, and she refused to examine the truth of why too closely.

"We could still fly together tonight." Dora said. "It's been a long time since the three of us were in the air together."

"That's a wonderful idea." A flight was what Petra needed to get the remains of the day out of her system.

***

The waning moon hung over the mountains like an orb. Petra dove and twirled in the air. Her harpy form was ink black, and she disappeared into the shadows of the night. The beating of wings bore down upon her a moment before Marina dove at her from behind. Petra tucked her wings in and dove down, using speed to escape. Laughter, full throated and harsh, came from the three of them as they chased and danced through the air.

Not all harpy generations were this close. Petra had felt pulled to this place, and she had never questioned the reason once the mountains had taken up residence in her soul. Petra had known this was how it should always be between the harpies and Iris. As close as a real family, but with enough territory to seek seclusion when it was needed.

Petra did not know much about the mothers of her sisters or how they were raised, but her mother had not been a comforting maternal influence. Long after she had left Italy, Petra had come to understand her mother's aloofness and cool demeanor towards her only daughter was self-preservation. Her mother had not wanted to get too attached to a daughter she would have to reject when she came of age.

"Shall we fly over the Lloyd farm?" Marina's voice broke through Petra's thoughts.

Petra twisted to look at Marina. "No."

"We can always go help herd them up tomorrow." There was not enough moonlight to see Marina's face clearly, but Petra heard the laughter in her voice.

"It's too much extra work for James and his men. I don't think we should spend our time tonight chasing cows," Petra said stiffly.

"Not Mr. Lloyd then? James is it?" Marina cackled.

Possessiveness, strong and sure, surged in Petra. Today had been too full of emotions, and Petra was tired of keeping her harpy in check. The need to keep Marina from James was bewildering to Petra, but the rage she was familiar with. She knew, deep down, why she was acting territorial.

Petra turned and pumped her wings hard to gain speed. She tucked her head down and rammed straight into Marina. They tumbled through the air, Marina's shock and outrage loud in Petra's ears.

"Leave him alone, Marina. Do not meddle there."

Marina screeched. Feathers flew in all directions as the two harpies clawed at each other. She tried to flap her wings to regain altitude before they plummeted to the ground, but Marina had a claw in her back. This was crazy, but she felt unable to stop it.

The original harpies were said to have been violent, foul beasts, ruled by anger and vindictiveness. In her harpy form, Petra's emotions were always closer to the surface, and they had an edge she never felt when human. Marina's blood mingled with her own as they hurtled towards the ground. Petra reached for the part of herself still clinging to reason and grabbed it with both claws.

She had no claim to James and no need to defend him or his cattle. She was not in search of a mate, and, even if she were, harpies were not normally possessive nor did they care much about the men who fathered their daughters. He could be nothing to her. She couldn't keep fighting with Marina.

Petra filled her lungs with cool mountain air. She released the claw that gripped Marina's wing and turned away. This dark anger inside of her was overwhelming, but she swallowed past it. She was the dark harpy, but she did not have to let that define everything. Petra turned towards home and flew away from her sisters and the sound of Marina's outrage.

Remorse left an acrid taste in her mouth. She should go back and apologize, but she did not reverse course. If Marina were smart, she would stay away from James and his farm. Even though Petra knew it was not her place and she had no right, she did not want Marina anywhere near James. Marina was beautiful, and Petra would never be able to stand up under the comparison.

The mountains were looming shadows against the splash of stars in the night sky. There were more stars than Petra remembered seeing in weeks. She slowed her wing beats and allowed herself to glide on a warm current. She made a note of all the places she hurt. Nothing was badly damaged. Neither she nor Marina had been fighting to cause real pain. When she shifted back into her mortal form, most of the open wounds would close. The bruises would take longer to heal.

After some minutes of gliding, she heard another set of wing beats gaining on her, and she cursed. "Petra, wait." Dora was breathless.

Petra considered speeding home and barring the door, but Dora would just come again another night. She slowed and allowed her sister to come alongside her.

"What in the name of Hades was that all about?"

"I'm not sure I know."

"Are you honestly going to pretend that was a childish fight? It came out of nowhere. Are you all right?"

"I don't know." The bitterness in her mouth and stomach returned tenfold. "Is Marina alright?"

Harpies could not shrug well, but Petra heard the gesture in Dora's voice. "Harpies heal better than humans. She'll be fine in a couple days. You surprised her, though." Dora paused. "You surprised me."

Petra barked out a harsh laugh made all the worse by her harpy voice. "Styx. Something's wrong with me."

"If you want him for your mate, we'll stay away from him."

"I'm not ready for that. I think he's interesting, but that's all. I don't know what happened back there. I just lost control."

"Our harpies carry the rawest version of our emotions. We've been trying to overcome our origins since the beginning. Sometimes, I think the gods would have served us better if they would have ended our lines then and not allowed us to have daughters." Dora's voice was full of generations of loneliness.

"Then I never would have known you and tried to be better because of you. And because of Marina. You both make me want to be more than the one who calls the darkness."

The roof of her cabin was barely visible below them. There was a deep, burning gash on her back, and her heart was sore. She had ruined an evening of camaraderie with petty jealousy over a man she had no claim to. She would have to go to Marina tomorrow and apologize. Petra craned her neck to see Dora, flying below her and to the left.

"I'm sorry, sister."

"You're forgiven, of course. Go make amends tomorrow."

"I will. I promise."

CHAPTER 6

The gash on her back was scabbed over, but still bruised and throbbing when Petra stood in front of Marina's door the next day. She had rehearsed a few different things to say on her way over. Despite her black mood, Atlas's Peak had glowed a cheery orange and yellow in the morning light. Today, Petra had wanted the mountain, her mountain, to be dark and shadowed in clouds to reflect her mood. The singing birds had mocked her desire with their sweet voices.

Petra knocked again. Louder, this time. "Come out, you worthless harpy. I'm here to apologize."

The door swung open. A red mark spanned Marina's cheek and disappeared into the neckline of her shirt. Her right arm was in a sling. Marina glared at her through narrowed eyes. "Not exactly the way to start out groveling."

There was no excuse for her behavior. None. Marina was her sister and deserved better than what Petra had given her. Petra tentatively placed a hand on Marina's left shoulder. "I'm so very sorry. I don't know what came over me. Please, forgive me. I didn't mean to hurt you. I mean I did, at the time, but I'm sorry now. I was sorry the moment it happened."

Petra's confession was met with silence. She swallowed her pride. "Do you want me to grovel more? On my knees, perhaps?"

Marina's mouth twitched up. "I'd love to see that one day, but no groveling needed. I saw the signs and picked at you anyway. You know I can never leave well enough alone. I should've let James and his cows lie." Marina put a hand over Petra's and squeezed. Relief at the gesture flooded through her. She wanted to protest that her feelings for James were ordinary, but Petra was beginning to think otherwise.

"I don't deserve you."

"Of course you don't." Marina flashed a bright smile.

"How are you this morning?"

"I feel about as good as you look. Tired and sore. Want some breakfast?"

"That would be great."

"I want to go into town today to see Iris. Come with me."

Petra hesitated. Not enough time had passed since Iris had spewed forth the terrible prophecy. She cast about for a less cowardly reason to refuse. "Can you fly with that arm?"

Marina shrugged. "It's sore, but an easy flight might help. Changing forms eases the healing process each time."

Petra tried again. "I don't need anything in town."

"You can't avoid her forever."

Petra ground her teeth. Marina knew her too well.

Marina crossed her arms over her chest. "I'll revoke my earlier forgiveness unless you come with me."

Petra sighed. "Fine. Breakfast first."

***

They flew into town, but avoided flying over homesteads. Normally, Petra would have ridden a horse into town, but she had left Merry munching grass in the yard at her cabin when she had gone to see Marina. Marina did not keep an extra horse, so flying was their only option.

Flying under the morning sunshine was calming. Petra's ink black feathers absorbed the heat of the sun and warmed the soreness from her body. The fragrance from the last of the wildflowers filled her nostrils. It was a fine morning to be flying. It was unfortunate they were going to see Iris.

Guilt waged with foreboding in Petra. She loved Iris, but the prophecy terrified her. Sacrifice and pain did not sound hopeful, and the words were vague enough to be useless. Styx. Anything solid to point to would have been something. Now, Petra felt like she was waiting in fear of a cloud of smoke.

Marina, oblivious to Petra's anxieties or choosing irritatingly to pretend not to notice, was singing a bawdy tune she had picked up from the gods knew where.

"Stop grinding your teeth," Marina called from behind. "I can hear it over the wind. What's bothering you now?"

Petra considered lying, but Marina would just pester her until she had the truth. "I was thinking about the prophecy and how you were singing that song to irritate me."

"Worked, didn't it?" Marina laughed and Petra scowled. "You're doing it again." Marina laughed.

"Leave it alone."

"Fine. Be a grump. Look, this prophecy thing is bad, but we can't do anything about it now. Worrying will get us nowhere fast. We'll have to set down over there." Marina indicated a copse of trees to the northeast of town.

The shade under the trees was cold compared to the warmth of the sun and the exertion of flying. A rustling of the bushes almost under her feet caused Petra to jump back into the air. Cloudy brown eyes in a lined face looked up at her.

"Roger. Why are you sleeping under this bush?" Roger was a decent enough man two days out of five, but on the other three he lost his battle and drank anything he could get his hands on. Marina leaned over and pulled the man's blanket over his shoulders with human hands. She had changed faster than Petra ever had seen. "You know Henry will let you sleep in his loft over the forge anytime you want."

"I wanted to listen to the birds this morning." Roger's eyes were closed by the end of his sentence, and a snore punctuated his speech.

Petra changed and leaned over the sleeping form. "I did not even see him there. Do you think he'll remember he saw me?"

"Even if he does, who would believe him?"

Petra and Marina walked the last couple of miles into town. Petra used the time to shake some of the anxiety from her limbs. Each step loosened her muscles and opened up the tightness in her head and chest. By the time they reached the edge of town, she was ready to face anything.

When they reached Main Street, Petra saw the saloon was completed and open for business. There was no glass in the windows and the doorway held no door, but there were four walls and a roof. The saloon was not the only new building in town. The sheriff's office, which once held the distinction of being the last building on Main Street, was now flanked by the frame of another building, which sat next to a sturdy-looking canvas tent. A pole with a wooden shingle bearing a traditional caduceus, a single snake entwined around a gnarled staff, swayed in the breeze over the door of the canvas tent. Turning Creek had never had a doctor in residence before. They really were moving up in the world.

Marina jerked a thumb at the open door of the saloon. "I heard the proprietor has a European-style beer garden in the back and women are allowed to drink there during the day. It's not proper or some rubbish for them to be there at night. Let's go take a look inside."

"Why?"

"To have a drink, what else? Are you in a rush to see Iris?"

She definitely was not in a rush to see Iris. Having a drink, even at this early hour, suddenly seemed like a splendid idea. "Let's go see what Mr. Vine is serving in his fine establishment. Let's try not to get into any fights.

Yesterday was enough for me." Petra said. Marina rubbed her hands together and walked into the saloon.

The room was brighter than Petra expected, thanks to the open windows on the front side of the building. The tang of whiskey mixed with the smell of newly lumbered wood in a warm way. The anxiety melted further from her muscles and she left it at the door. A group of men sat at a round table, idly playing cards. There were a couple of loners sitting in their own areas. Two fierce-looking women in buckskins sat at one of the bench tables along the back wall. A well-maintained upright piano stood in the corner.

Petra followed Marina, who walked up to the bar and ordered two house whiskeys from an average-looking woman whose most striking feature was her large nose. Petra took a sip of the amber liquid the woman served them. It was warm going down, and she was left with a sweet, smoky flavor on her tongue. She had not expected something so refined to appear in her little town. Maybe the presence of some newcomers had advantages after all.

Marina nudged her. "They appear to be drinking the same thing we are. Let's get some to share and go visit."

Petra followed Marina's gaze out the back door to the two fierce-looking women sitting at benched tables in the back. If she was leaving behind her anxiety, she might as well leave behind her usual reluctance for chit chat too. "Half the people in here are drinking the same thing we are, but it appears that is the designated table." Petra sighed. "Lead on."

Marina ordered four more whiskeys and carried them outside. Petra followed in her wake. Both women looked up at them in the same moment. There was a calculating look in their eyes that Petra disliked, but it was too late to stop Marina, who was in the middle of introductions. The women were armed more thoroughly than was generally warranted for a trip into town.

The woman on the left spoke first. "Please, join us. My name is Atlanta, and this is my partner, Cyrene."

The hair on the back of Petra's neck stood up. Atlanta and Cyrene were the names of famous Greek dryad huntresses. In the myths, they were deadly to both animals and men, and their prowess was unrivaled. Marina seemed not to notice anything amiss, but Petra knew her need to find something new and entertaining overrode her instinct for danger. Atlanta and Cyrene's eyes followed them with the undisguised interest of predators stalking their prey. Petra was not often on the receiving end of that look, but she had given it often enough. Marina sat and dispersed the new glasses. Petra clutched hers tightly and sat down beside Marina.

"What brings you to Turning Creek?" Marina's question filled the silence.

Cyrene leaned back against the wall and leveled dark brown eyes at Petra. "We heard the hunting was good in these parts, and we decided to try our luck."

Marina nodded companionably. "This region has plenty of game. Mule deer, elk, bison. What're you looking for?"

Atlanta ran a finger over her small nose. "We just came from Kansas. Bison out there are easy pickings. We felt it was time to head farther west."

Petra thought it was strange for Atlanta to word it in that way, as if something was drawing them in this direction. She was being overly cautious. Petra gave herself a mental shake and took a sip of whiskey.

Atlanta leaned in. "Are y'all from around here?"

Marina answered, "I live in a high valley on the Twins and Petra lives up Atlas's Peak. We've been here for some time and know the area."

"It seems like an alluring place. The mountains are bolder here than out east," Atlanta said.

Petra agreed. She had stopped at the Smokey Mountains when she first traveled across the country years ago, and their weathered tops had paled in comparison to the rugged Rockies. Bold was just the word for the strength of her mountains.

"Do you two have a place to stay?" Marina asked.

Wonderful. Next, Marina would ask them if they wanted to move in with them.

"We've a camp outside of town. We don't like being too close to civilization." Atlanta took a sip from her nearly empty glass.

Petra lifted her glass in agreement. "I know exactly what you mean."

"I'm sure you do," Cyrene said, and Petra felt the trickle of power seep from the woman.

Marina sensed it too and sat a little straighter. The sense of power from another joined Cyrene's, and Petra recognized the feel of it. Marina was letting the huntresses know they were not ordinary women but harpies. Every instinct she possessed as a predator was screaming that these two women were dangerous. Petra was also going to have words with Marina about making new friends with scary-looking women in bars.

Petra's glass was empty. "We've a friend to see. It was nice meeting you two ladies." She only hesitated briefly over the use of the word ladies. "Hope your stay in town is pleasant. If you need to send word to anyone, see Iris down the street. She runs the mail depot and has a way of getting things delivered." Petra hoped they took the opportunity she offered. She wanted to know what Iris would make of these two.

Marina stood up, keeping her eyes on Cyrene. "Nice to meet you both." She shook both their hands and gathered the empty glasses onto the tray. "One more thing. This territory is ours. We don't mind if you hunt here, but you're guests, and I expect you to behave." Marina grinned at the two women in a friendly manner, but there was a flash of pointed teeth before she turned to go.

Petra gave the two huntresses a wide grin and walked to the door with her head erect. She resisted the urge to look back. She was not a creature who cowered. Marina delivered the tray to the large-nosed woman and the two harpies left the bar.

"That was interesting," Marina said as she fell into step beside Petra.

"Which part? The one where you made bosom buddies with the two huntresses who looked like they would love to have us mounted on their wall, or the part where you told them where we live, the better to hunt us down?"

Marina stopped and her jaw dropped. "What the hell, Petra? They weren't that bad. I'm sure we come across as dangerous to other Remnants."

Petra kept walking. "We are dangerous. Something was off about those two. Why would they stop here?"

"You're crazy." Marina's voice shook and she jogged a couple steps to catch up with Petra. "Why not here? There's nothing else for miles, and now we have a saloon and a doctor, if I read that symbol right."

"You did. Doesn't it seem odd, so many Remnants gathering in one place all of a sudden?" Petra thought of Billy Royal. She was going to have to tell Iris about him.

"What other reason would they have for coming to Turning Creek? And why now? You're being paranoid."

"Maybe. Let's go see Iris." Whatever Cyrene and Atlanta were doing here, it was sure to be bad news.

The door of the depot closed behind them and muffled the noise from outside. Iris was sitting in the same position as the last time Petra had come, though the book in Iris's hand was different. Her blue eyes sought Petra's first, and Petra felt a flush of guilt over wanting to avoid Iris, who had always protected her. Petra dropped her eyes.

"Good morning, my birds." Her eyes narrowed. "What happened to the two of you? It looks like you two were in a fight." Iris crossed her arms over her chest. Petra turned to Marina.

Marina shrugged. "Nothing, really. Just a disagreement over livestock. I don't have business in town, I just thought Petra should come in to see you."

Incredulous, Petra stepped up to Marina until she could peer down over her. "I needed to come in? You should stop meddling in other people's business, Marina Ocypete. Or did you not learn your lesson last night?"

Marina did not back down. Petra was simultaneously proud of her sister for her gumption and annoyed at her for using it against her.

Marina poked a finger into Petra's chest. "Iris might have some answers for you, now that a few days have passed. I thought you should come and ask, especially since you've been acting like a crazy harpy lately."

Petra rolled her eyes and stepped away from Marina.

Iris narrowed her eyes and looked from Petra to Marina. "What happened last night? It doesn't sound or look like a disagreement over livestock to me." Iris pointed to the marks on Marina's face and neck, which had faded to a sickly green and yellow.

"Petra laid into me while we were flying when I suggested we pay Mr. Lloyd and his cows a visit."

Petra was not sure which was more humiliating, that she had attacked her sister or that she had done so over a man and his dairy cows. She kept her eyes down, unwilling to look at either of the other two women in the room. There was no exclamation of surprise or reprimand from Iris. Just silence. Petra examined her feet with precision. Her boots were dirty and needed some waxing.

The silence grew heavy, and she lifted her eyes. Iris watched her, a frown and wrinkled forehead marring her pretty face. Petra had already apologized to Marina, she would not do so again for Iris's benefit.

"A package came for Mr. Lloyd on the stage yesterday. Will you take it to the farm for me?"

Of all the things Iris would say, this was the last Petra expected. A tongue lashing and guilt-inducing lecture would have suited the situation better than a request for a mail delivery. She cleared her throat. "Yes. I can do that."

Iris reached into one of the slots behind her and pulled out a slim package. "Good. I was hoping I would be able to give it to you to deliver." Iris placed the brown paper package on the counter. "What do you two think of all the goings on about town?" Petra relaxed when it became apparent Iris was going to leave the fight and the reason for it alone, for now.

"Finally, something exciting is going on here. I've not seen so much activity in town since Mary Mac married that Irish fellow five years ago. I thought her family would drink every drop of whiskey in town."

"They very nearly did." Petra grumbled. Mary's wedding had been rowdy and, eventually, obnoxious. About the time the men started singing bawdy tunes, she had retreated to the mountains. Marina had stayed to lead the chorus.

Petra felt a sharp pain as Marina elbowed her in the ribs. "Petra thinks the town is overrun with Remnants and that I'm too friendly."

"I got a strange vibe from them. Just be careful next time. Sometimes strangers should stay strangers."

"You're not very neighborly." Marina crossed her arms and narrowed her eyes at Petra. "I thought we talked about being more neighborly."

Iris looked from Petra to Marina. "Strange vibe from who?"

"Two women in the saloon. I bought them a drink so we could introduce ourselves. They seemed interesting to me." Marina shrugged.

"Two women whose main occupation is hunting and whose names are Atlanta and Cyrene. It can't be a coincidence, plus one of them leaked enough power so we'd know for sure." Petra jabbed Marina back and was gratified when she heard the air whoosh out of her. Petra slapped Marina's doubled over figure hard on the back and looked up at Iris. Iris's face paled and her eyes were wide. Petra stilled beside the wheezing Marina.

Marina straightened and caught sight of Iris. She flicked her gaze to Petra. "Both of you? I don't understand why all the fuss."

Petra ignored Marina. "Iris, what is it?"

"Did you see the new doctor's office on your way into town?"

"We did."

"Did you notice the sign he put on his shingle?"

Petra remembered the old fashioned caduceus with the single snake. The tingle in the back of her neck was back. "I saw it. You don't think he's one of the descendants of Asclepius do you? I didn't think there were any of them left." In the myths, Asclepius was a Greek physician who had been given power over life and death by Zeus. When Asclepius had dared to use the power he had been given, it angered Hades, who then appealed to Zeus to kill Asclepius with a blast from his thunderbolt. Zeus often granted power, then punished the use of it. He did not like threats to his dominion.

Iris ran a hand through her straw-colored hair. "I'm not sure if he is of the line of Asclepius or not, but he is definitely a Remnant. I met him two days ago. He said his name was Dr. Lee Williams. He seemed a nice enough fellow. His office looks legitimate, no snake oil in sight, though he did have a tank of brown and yellow snakes in the front room."

There was a ringing in Petra's ears. The worshipers and physicians of the original Asclepius had kept brown snakes with yellow bellies in their temples and offices. Dryad huntresses, Greek physicians, harpies, The Messenger, and who-knew-what others all in one town. This was not normal. Something was coming. A time of sacrifice and pain.

Petra swallowed past the lump in her throat. She gripped the edge of the counter to steady herself. "This many Remnants in one place. Does it have anything to do with the prophecy?"

"I don't know. Maybe it's unrelated." Iris did not sound sure.

Petra snorted. "Doubtful."

"I agree, but we shouldn't come to early conclusions. We should wait and watch and bide our time. Things have a way of revealing themselves. Until then, I can do some research and see if there has ever been a gathering like this since the fall of Olympus." The color was returning to

Iris's face, but her words still held the sharpness of uncertainty.

"Wait, says the woman who was not promised pain and a reckoning." Petra shifted her weight and wiped her hands on her pants.

Marina had been silent during the exchange. Her eyes had followed the conversation, but her mouth, blessedly, had stayed shut for once. Sometimes, Marina talked just to hear herself.

Marina's usual smile was gone from her face. "You both think something serious is happening here."

"Thanks for the summary." Petra spat.

"No need to take it out on her." Iris's tone warned. Iris protected the harpies, even from each other. It was part of her power and part of her burden.

Petra relaxed. "Sorry."

"Don't do anything rash. We don't know for sure why they are here. They may be here for the same reason we are, to live a quiet life. Let's give it some time," Iris said.

"What's the worst thing that could happen? This is a big place with lots of room. Neither of you are the land authority in the area." Marina crossed her arms and glared at them.

Petra placed a hand on Marina's arm. "Atlanta and Cyrene may just be here to hunt. Turning Creek needs a doctor and Asclepius was renowned for his skills. We just need to keep an eye on them. If they're here, there may be others who are not as harmless. That's all."

Marina relaxed. "Petra, you often assume the worst, but Iris, I'm surprised at you being so cautious of newcomers."

"Not everyone is as accepting as you, sister." Petra squeezed Marina's arm. "Speaking of newcomers, I have a new neighbor." Petra told them about Billy Royal.

"I think we should give him time too. Perhaps, he just doesn't like people. I'll let you know if I hear anything else." Iris shifted on her chair. "The prophecy has me spooked as well. Are you two staying in town tonight?"

Petra swiped the package off the counter. "I want to deliver this tomorrow, so I'd better head back today."

Marina waved in Petra's direction. "I'm following her lead, the gods help me."

"Don't stay away long. One of you or Dora come back in a few days to check on things in town."

Both harpies agreed and they took their leave. Petra picked up her anxiety in heavy sheets as they walked through town, past the saloon and the empty table where Atlanta and Cyrene had sat, and past the new doctor's office. They walked by the new buildings and left the smell of civilization and new wood planks behind them.

CHAPTER 7

Petra rose the next morning when the mountains were still shrouded in darkness. From the huge front window in her small cabin, she could see the morning mist obscuring the tops of the range. The sky was darker than it should be at this hour. Rain was in the future today. She would have to be careful crossing some of the ravines if it rained too hard. Flash flooding was always a danger this time of year.

Petra moved a chair onto the porch and sat with her hands wrapped around a cup of tea, the heat sinking into her palms. The chill in the air was pleasant, nothing like the biting cold it would be in a couple of months. She loved the movement of the seasons in the mountains. Even in the darkest of winter nights, the hulking peaks of the range was a familiar weight in her soul that said, "Home." There was no other place in the world she would rather be.

The brown paper package was its own presence on the tiny table inside her cabin. It added to the itching Petra felt to be off and moving towards the farm. She breathed deep and forced herself to relax and sip her tea before the cool morning air stole its heat. She did not want to interfere with the work on the farm, so she could not leave too early. She wanted to arrive during the midday break when James would have time to talk. For all her protestations, she did find James intriguing, and she enjoyed talking with him. More than that, she was unsure what she wanted.

***

Petra had timed her arrival perfectly. "Hello, the house!" she yelled as she rode up.

Adam stuck his head out of the door. He grinned and turned his head towards the inside of the cabin. "A pretty lady has come to see us, gentleman!" He swept open the door and waved her in.

"You're in luck today, Ms. Petra. Mr. Lloyd is cooking." Robert stood and held out a chair for her. James was standing by the stove, stirring a pot of something that smelled like beef and potato stew. He turned to face her when she entered the cabin. "Welcome, Petra. Would you like to join us for supper?"

"I don't want to be a bother." Petra held up the package. "Iris sent me with this."

His eyes lit up. "It must be the book I ordered last month. Will you place it on the desk there? I will show it to you after the meal, if you would like." He indicated a gleaming mahogany desk on the other side of the common room. Papers, inkwells, and quills were all precisely arranged on its surface.

"That sounds wonderful. Thank you." Petra placed the package on top of a stack of cream-colored heavyweight paper. She ran her hand over the cream silk of the paper. Not many dairy farmers would keep paper of such quality for everyday use. There were no personal touches on the desk, only the tools needed for writing and reading. Her own small writing desk in her cabin was littered with old letters, supplies, and books. She made a mental note to clean it up when she returned home. There was a bookshelf next to the desk, as tall as the ceiling, and filled two-thirds full with books of all sizes. All of them were well cared for, though some had threadbare bindings and looked worn by age or use or both.

James's cooking was, as promised, better than Robert's, though that was not a particularly hard standard to overcome. During the meal, James sat across from Petra and she kept sliding her eyes towards him. Once, he caught her looking and she glanced away. Heat crept up her neck. She did not know what was worse, that he had seen her looking or that she had blushed over it. James lips quirked up, but he said nothing. He was, if she knew little else, a gentleman to the core.

"While I was in town yesterday, I stopped at the new saloon, owned by a man named Daniel Vine. It was sparse, but there is a nice sort of garden in the back for women. The whiskey was surprisingly good."

"It's about time this town had something interesting to do." Robert said around a mouthful of food.

"I think our town is about to experience a boom. It seems we also have a doctor in residence now." Petra tore a chunk from her bread and used it to mop up the gravy on her plate.

James rubbed a hand over his jaw. Petra followed the movement with her eyes. "It seems our small valley will no longer be so hidden."

"A man has built a cabin in between our two properties. Have you met him yet?" Petra asked.

James shook his head. "No. What's his name?"

"Billy Royal." She wanted to warn James and the boys to give Billy a wide berth, but she had no justification for the request. Billy was gruff and unwelcoming, but the same could be said of her most of the time. "He wasn't inclined to be chatty at the time. He was working on digging some kind of hole."

James straightened. "A mine?"

"I'm not sure, and he was not forthcoming with information."

"So, boss." Adam cut in. "Can we have a night off soon, you know, to go and check on things in town?" Adam waggled his eyebrows at James.

"Of course."

Robert turned to Petra. "Miss Petra, you said there was a garden in the back where women could sit?"

Petra chuckled at the hopefulness in his voice. It must be hard to be young and live in such an isolated place. Robert and Adam made her feel every year she had under her belt. "Not many women are willing to go into a drinking establishment, especially the younger ones, so I am not sure you would find good company."

Adam's shoulders slumped a bit. "The pickings are few."

Robert slapped Adam on the back. "Look at the bright side, brother. If the town is growing, then there are sure to be ladies on the horizon who will need to be shown the ropes around town."

James waved an arm in a sweeping gesture. "I'm sure any young ladies who come to town will need a thorough tour of our one, short street." He smiled, pleased with his sarcasm.

Petra could not help but return his smile. "Maybe not so short of a street for much longer. Thank you for the meal. It was, as advertised, very good." Petra leaned back with a contented sigh.

James stood and started gathering dishes. "Boys, why don't you take some time off until we have to do the afternoon milking? I'll clean up in here." Adam and Robert escaped the cabin, glad to be free.

Petra gathered the silverware and cups. "Let me help."

"You're a guest. You shouldn't do the work."

"Well, I've already done work around here, and this is hardly my first time to eat with you. Surely, I can do some dishes."

James tilted his head. "Fine, you may help, but if you continue to show up at meal times on a regular basis, I'll have to put you into the cooking rotation." His delivery was stoic but his brown eyes danced.

Petra grinned until her eyes crinkled. "Deal." Petra wondered what it would be like to see James over every meal.

James took the water heating on the stove and poured it into the basin on the counter. "I'll wash. You dry and stack, then we can both put things away."

The counter was long enough to accommodate one person easily, but with two people working there, Petra was forced to stand close enough to James that her skirt brushed his legs. The next time she took a plate from his hand, she stepped closer and felt the heat from his body like a brand on her left side. His hand faltered as he scrubbed a plate. Petra turned her head to the side to shield her face and smiled in triumph.

"You're a good cook. Who taught you?" Petra took another plate from James.

He glanced up at her and then shoved his hands back into the water and washed a cup. "Neither Adam nor Robert is proficient at anything other than stews and roasting potatoes, and even those skills are negligible. I grew up in a house with a cook. After about a month here, I realized I was going to have to learn to cook something or else our diet would become less than tolerable." James pointed towards two books on the shelf above them. Petra read, *The Illustrated London Cookery Book* and *Miss Beecher's Domestic Recipe Book*. "I sent off for those. If you follow the recipes, cooking is not that hard of a skill to pick up."

"I have a cookbook, and I follow the instructions, but your cooking is better than mine."

"All it takes for any endeavor is practice and perseverance."

Petra took the cup he handed her and his fingers slipped over hers. She dried the cup, clutching it tight with a hand still tingling. "Did you ever think about doing anything else besides making cheese?"

Petra could see the question rolling around in his mind. She was beginning to understand what a deliberate man he was with everything he did. She knew he had not come upon this road in his life by an accident or poor planning. So much of her own life was moved forward by a tidal wave of emotions; his methodical approach grounded her, foreign as it was.

"It is always something I have known how to do. I grew up at the side of our head cheese maker. When I was not reading, I was in the cheese house. I never knew anything else, but when I was old enough to choose my own way, I found there was nothing else which appealed to me in the same way."

"It must be a very settling thing to know exactly what you want from life." A hair escaped from her braid and tangled in her eyes. She used a damp hand to tuck it behind her ear.

"You sound as if you have not figured out what you want from life yet."

Petra paused her drying and looked at James. The prophecy and the fear she carried melted away and she held nothing but this domestic moment in a rustic kitchen beside a man with warm eyes and a shy smile. It was an ordinary moment meant for an ordinary mortal woman. "I still have years enough to figure it out."

James put the last plate away and took the towel from Petra's hand.

His fingers brushed hers, and she tried not to feel the building heat in them. "Would you like to see the book I ordered?"

Petra nodded eagerly and walked over to the bookshelf. Reading was the best way to fill long winter days and nights. Some other, less solitary, ways to pass the time bloomed in Petra's mind. She tucked them away and cleared her throat. "You have quite a collection."

"You sound surprised." James gave her a mock look of hurt.

"How many dairy farmers do you know with the complete works of Shakespeare and a smattering of Donne, Yeats, and Beowulf?" Petra leaned over to peer closer to the shelf at waist level. "Pardon. Beowulf in the original Olde English." She straightened and cocked an eyebrow at James.

His laugh was full and deep. A zing of awareness started in her toes and built its way up her spine. "You have me there. I blame it on a childhood with few companions and aunts who cared naught where I was as long as it was out of the way. I had some tutors through the years, but nothing formal."

"You were raised by your aunts?"

The laughter faded from his face. "My parents and younger brother died when I was six. My father was an only child, so my mother's aunts became my guardians."

Petra placed her hand on James's arm. "I'm sorry."

Petra did not miss the bitterness when he replied. "It took me weeks to believe my parents were never coming home and I was stuck in a life with two women who loved me not. They did love my money, and the fine house my father's family had built, but they cared naught for me. My father was a gentleman farmer and our house, while not the largest in the neighborhood, was by far not the smallest.

"I tried for many years to earn their love, before I gave up. I spent most of my time in the library, the milking shed, or the cheese house."

Petra ached for the little boy he had been and the wound he still carried. "It seems we were both lonely children." She dropped her hand and looked at the shelves again to give him time to compose himself. She stopped scanning when she reached one collection of books. Clumped together were books she knew well, The Oresteia, Iliad, Aeneid, the complete volumes of the Metamorphosis, The Eumenides, and some collected works of Hesiod.

She touched the binding of the Hesiod. "You were not exaggerating your love of the old myths." It was a dangerous statement and a more dangerous question.

James stepped closer to stand beside her. His body did not touch her, but she could feel the heat coming from him. She had to stop her body from swaying into it. "They were all I took from my father's library when I left. He used to read them to me when I was small."

He was so close, one movement the right way and he could envelop her. "Serious stories for a child."

"Stories of courage, adventure, and morality are serious at any age."

"Well put. I know you are interested in Zeus, but do you have another favorite?" Petra was curious what he would say if he knew many of the myths he had heard as a child had at least a basis in truth, and parts of those myths still filled the world. She also wanted to steer him clear of Zeus. There were far less dangerous myths about which to be curious.

James reached around her and ran a hand over the books, his fingers lingering over them like a lover. Petra followed his movements and something warm uncurled in her belly. "I've always liked the adventure stories, like the Argonauts."

Petra snorted. Of course he liked the story in which her ancestors were foul-smelling, ugly beasts of torment. "What do you think of the story of Phineas?" As soon as the question was out, Petra froze. She should not have asked something so close to the truth.

"It's an interesting tale. I always wondered what the harpies had done to be exiled on Strophades." James pulled the copy of Argonautica from the shelf.

"Perhaps they had been unjustly punished by vengeful gods." Petra clenched and unclenched her fists. She willed herself to relax. She could feel the darkness of the old anger burning within her.

James rubbed his chin and flipped through the book. "Perhaps, though I find it hard to believe creatures as violent and vengeful as the harpies were completely innocent. Even we mere humans could not be labeled as innocent by any means."

The first harpies may have been violent, but the gods made them that way and then punished them for the very nature that had been created in them. They had been created to torture people on the way to Tartarus, the deep abyss of torment. They had done their job too well and been punished for it, much like Asclepius. It did not escape her that James had referred to both of them as human.

Petra crossed her arms. "I like Hesiod's version of the harpies much better."

"Hesiod was the only one who claimed the harpies to be beautiful women. The other historians described them as ugly and putrid." James took a step back from her.

Irritation flared within Petra. She could feel her darker nature swirling with the anger bubbling under her skin. She fought to get herself under control. "What if I told you the harpies had been sent to Strophades as punishment for the very job they had been given by the gods to do? That they had fulfilled their role as punisher of the unjust and were rewarded for their efforts with exile? What if the gods had been afraid of the power they had created and cursed the harpies to only reproduce once per generation, thus ensuring they would never rise up and rebel against their betters?" The words tumbled out of her before she could stop them.

James put the book back on the shelf, tapping a finger on the spine. "I would say that sounds like a nice story, but I've read all the Greek accounts and none of them match that particular version."

"Not everything in books is true, and not everything gets written down," Petra muttered.

"Quite right."

Petra was mortified at her outburst. James shifted from one foot to the other. She had turned a nice conversation into something awkward. Thunder boomed overhead, and the glass in the windows rattled. The storm, which had been threatening all day, was making itself known.

James picked up the paper-wrapped book and held it out to Petra. "Would you like to open it?"

Petra shook her head. "It's not often one has the pleasure of opening a package. I couldn't take that from you."

"All the more reason. Please, I insist."

Petra took the package and undid the string holding the paper in place. The paper crinkled as she peeled it back to reveal the unblemished leather cover of a new book. "*The Last of the Mohicans* by James Fenimore Cooper. I've not read this one."

"I thought it was time to add some American novelists to my collection."

"Which shelf would you like it on?"

James stepped closer to Petra again and his arm brushed hers. "There is room right here."

His hand indicated a blank space on one of the shelves, but his face was inches from hers. His smell reached her, a warm combination of male, leather, and hay from the barn. She inhaled again, letting the aromas roll through her. The desire that followed was sharper than she expected. Petra saw the answering flare in James's eyes, and she grinned. The universe shrank to contain only the two of them, frozen in front of the bookcase.

Thunder crashed above, rattling the entire house. Both of them jumped apart as if they'd been caught doing something wrong. Rain pounded on the wooden shingles on the roof. James opened his mouth to speak, but he was cut off by another boom of thunder and the front door crashing open.

Robert and Adam hurtled inside, slamming the door behind them. They stood in the entry, dripping and laughing. "That is one helluva storm out there." Robert shook out his hat. "Pardon, Miss Petra."

Adam stepped back to get out of the way of his brother's hat. "It's raining so hard the animals are startin' to pair up." Petra and Richard doubled over with laughter. "We put your horse in the barn, ma'am, when the weather started going south."

Petra wiped wetness from her eyes and grinned at Adam. "Thank you for taking care of Merry and for making me laugh."

Adam straightened and did a perfect impersonation of James bowing. "My pleasure, my lady." Petra and Robert burst into laughter again. James tried to look stern but gave up and chuckled.

"You two drowned rats take yourself off to the back and get into some dry clothes." James shook his head at their retreating figures. He turned to Petra. "You can't go out in this. Please stay here until the storm passes. The boys and I share a large room in the back. If you don't mind the company, we have extra beds if the storm does not pass before sundown."

"Is it proper for me to be staying here overnight without a chaperone?" Petra struggled to keep a straight face, but failed.

James shrugged. "I don't think any of the society dames of Turning Creek will descend upon us in the morning."

Petra reflected his wide smile back to him. When he smiled, his face lost its usual air of seriousness. She wished he would smile more often. Petra was not sure she wanted to stay in such close proximity to James overnight. The more time she spent in his company, the more time she wanted to spend with him. It was a circle of need she did not want to be caught in. He was fast becoming a kind of addiction.

***

The rain did not let up. If anything, the storm became fiercer as the afternoon wore on. After dinner, James made tea and the boys cleaned up.

James placed a steaming cup of strong brown liquid in front of her. Petra could see her shadow in the tea. She put half a spoon of brown sugar in her cup and stirred.

"I'm so glad you have not picked up the American habit of drinking coffee." Petra took a tiny sip. It was rich and perfect after a satisfying meal.

"Coffee is a bit strong for my palate, but the boys like it." James jerked his thumb towards Adam and Robert, who were putting away the dishes.

"Nothing will put hair on your chest like a strong cup of coffee in the morning." Robert threw a plate to Adam, who caught it and put it on the shelf.

Petra made a show of looking at her chest. "Mmm, I think I prefer to stay hair free, thanks."

Adam whooped with laughter. A faint blush tinged James face, and Petra wondered where his thoughts had gone. James cleared his throat and sipped his tea.

Petra mirrored his movements. "You said you spent a lot of time in the cheese house when you were growing up." It was not a question, Petra knew, but she wanted to know anything James was willing to share.

"Mr. Ferris was the head cheese maker on my family farm, and he was kind to me. I enjoy the science of making cheese, of taking one substance and creating something completely different with my own hands. It's not terribly complicated, but each cheese maker puts their own signature on the process.

"The environment also has a hand in how the cheese turns out. There are qualities in different regions, which can affect how a cheese tastes. The cheddar I make here is different than the cheddar I made in England. Better, I think. The mountain air enhances everything it touches." James's eyes bored into her as he said the words.

Her body answered with a surge of heat from her center. She tamped it down. She had an entire night to endure. Petra sipped her tea, trying to occupy her hands. Unfortunately, the action did nothing to still the wandering of her mind.

Adam cleared his throat, and Petra's face flamed in reaction. Everything in the room had faded under James's words. She traced a small crack on the side of her cup and kept her eyes down. She took deep breaths until she felt the heat of the blush fade. Adam and Robert made a show of keeping their backs to James and Petra and clanking the dishes together, which made Petra even more mortified.

"If you would like, I'll show you the process. You can even get your hands dirty. I know you don't shy away from work."

It would give her an excuse to stay longer. "I would like that."

Adam and Robert finished cleaning and sat down at the table with mugs of coffee. The smell of the strong liquid was pleasant, but Petra could not get past the bitterness of the beverage to enjoy it.

James refilled his cup from the teapot on the table. He added a touch of cream from the small ewer next to the sugar. "What about you? How did you come to be in Turning Creek?"

Petra decided to stick as close to the truth as possible without giving too many details. "My mother raised me in Venice. The city is beautiful, but crowded. I've never been comfortable with crowds. I left when I came of age and traveled around some. I ended up here, and now I belong to the Rockies." She shrugged.

"They do have a way of claiming people." James smiled in understanding. "Are you in contact with your mother?"

Petra remembered the violent ache of the day her mother had cast her from the only home she had ever known. Tears and pleading did not sway her mother from what she saw as her duty and the natural order, which was for Petra to strike out on her own and never look back. Her mother had nurtured her for fifty years and tossed her out as if she had been a worn-out garment. Petra could still hear the door slamming in her face. "No, we do not write. We parted badly."

James's warm hand covered hers and squeezed. "I'm sorry." His hand released hers and the air was cold where his hand had been.

Petra shrugged. "It's just the way it is sometimes. I'm used to being alone. The mountains suit me in that way."

"You're always welcome here."

Petra was not sure which bothered her more, that she was considering taking up the offer of hospitality more often or that she was beginning to dislike the idea of being alone. Before meeting James, she had reveled in the solitary nature of being a harpy, but now she was restless when left to her own devices.

Robert laughed. "Anytime you want to come do some work, please do. That way, I can go into town more than once a month."

"You just want to go visit the new ladies at Vine's." Adam jabbed his elbow into his brother's ribs.

"I hope you've not taken a fancy to the plain, large-nosed woman who served me yesterday. She was not too friendly, of course," Petra leaned over the table and waggled her eyebrows at Robert, "you could surely charm her enough to make her more pleasant to be around."

"I'll take that as a compliment," Robert said.

"As it was meant."

"He has his eyes on one of the other ones. Brown hair, big blue eyes. Tiny thing. No large nose in sight." Adam smacked Robert on the back. Robert returned the gesture just as Adam took a sip of coffee, causing Adam to inhale a good bit of the hot liquid. The table erupted in laughter as Adam choked and blew his nose into his handkerchief.

The storm abated by bedtime, but it was too dangerous to travel home on horseback in the dark after so much rain. The rivers and creeks would be swollen beyond their banks. Crossing them in the dark would be deadly.

James led Petra into the back room of the cabin. It contained two bunk-style beds and two single beds. The area around the bunks was cluttered with shirts and trousers hanging across beams and on pegs along the wall.

One of the single beds sat in the corner, a table to one side and a trunk at the foot. The bed was neatly made, and there was not a loose sock or stray shirt in sight. A single book and lamp sat on the bedside table. Petra had no doubt who slept where.

"The accommodations are spartan, as promised. I hope you will still be comfortable." James opened up the trunk on the end of the unoccupied single bed and pulled out a sheet and a worn patchwork quilt. Petra help him tuck the blanket around the mattress and spread the quilt.

"Anything is better than venturing out in all the wet." Petra had not slept in a room with another person for the last twenty years. Before that, she had only ever shared a space with her mother, who had been quiet and reserved. She went on hunting trips once or twice a year with her sisters, but they slept under the night sky. She had no doubt sleeping in a room with three grown men would be quite different. James would be only feet from her.

Normally, Petra slept in an old-world tunic and cotton drawstring drawers. They were back at her cabin. After some consideration, Petra decided to sleep in her clothes. If she removed her petticoat, she had less of a chance of becoming hopelessly tangled while sleeping. She plopped onto the bed and started unlacing her boots. She left her socks on and stood to untuck her shirt.

Her hands stilled when she saw she had three pairs of eyes fastened onto her movements. Adam coughed behind her, and James scowled in his direction. Adam and Robert lurched back into their own nightly routine. James continued to watch them. After some moments, he sat down and removed his own boots. He followed her lead by untucking his shirt only.

"I, uh, know this is awkward, but I appreciate the place to stay."

James had avoided looking in her direction, and when he did look, he fastened his eyes on her face. Petra wanted to giggle at his obvious discomfort. She was still fully clothed, even if her shirt was untucked. "I'd rather you be safe here than out on the mountain where flooding is likely after the day we've had."

The four of them crawled into their beds, and James turned down the lamp until the wick burned out. The mattress beneath Petra was stuffed with hay and herbs and the smell wafted up pleasantly when she moved. It was not as comfortable as her feather mattress at home, but the sheet was well-worn and soft and the blanket warm. She flipped onto her stomach and snuggled into the bed.

Petra lay still for a long time before sleeping. She could hear Adam and Robert snoring quietly in their bunks. The bed next to her rustled, and she longed to whisper to James and ask if he was awake. She bit down on her tongue to keep her voice inside. There were two windows in this room, one between the bunks and one between her bed and the one James slept in. If she sat up, there would be plenty of light to see James lying in his bed. Petra kept her head buried in the pillow.

It was a long time before she went to sleep. Her dreams were filled with thunder, lightning, and an approaching feeling of dread. The morning came too soon for her to recover from the foreboding of her dreams.

Petra knew as soon as her eyes opened in the morning light that the lack of sleep and dreams had grown a grump inside her. She needed to be up and away as soon as she could. She looked left and, to her surprise, she saw James's bed was already empty, the blankets pulled and straightened for the day. A glance at the other end of the room confirmed she was alone.

Petra did her best to smooth her hair into something resembling order, tucked her shirt into her skirt, and smoothed her hands over her skirt. Her appearance would not improve while hiding in the room. She took a breath and opened the door separating the back room from the front of the house.

Three chairs scraped back against the floor as the men stood. "Good Morning, Petra. There is a place here for you." James indicated the empty chair beside him. There were barely discernible circles under James's eyes, as if he too had been too plagued to sleep.

"Good morning. Please, sit and finish your meal. I need to get going. I've been away from home and tread on your hospitality long enough. I'll just go saddle my horse and be on my way."

James snatched a piece of toast from his plate of half-finished eggs. "I'll come with you and see you off."

"Bye, Miss Petra." Robert said.

"See you soon." Petra walked out into the sun with James on her heels. "You should have finished your meal." The heat of his presence was hotter than the sun beating on her head.

James's footsteps quickened and he moved around her to open the barn door for her. "I do not mind, and it would be rude of me to allow you to leave without seeing you off." Petra brushed past him. "Besides, this way I have a few more minutes in your company."

Petra resisted the urge to throw a smile over her shoulder and kept facing forward. This was not a flirtation she should encourage, as much as she was coming to enjoy it. She had no intention of having anything beyond friendship with James.

Petra walked into her mare's stall and ran a hand down the brow of the horse. James brushed against Petra as he moved into the stall. Awareness of the small space and man she shared it with kindled in her belly. She was not sure she could ignore this incessant heat he made her feel.

James lifted the saddle from the side of the stall and placed it on the mare's back in one smooth motion. He belted the girth and checked each buckle. When he straightened, his eyes met hers, and she saw the corners of his eyes crinkle in a smile. She found herself stupidly smiling back. She tried to craft something witty to say but the only thing she could think about was the way he was looking at her.

James broke eye contact first. "You should be all ready to go."

Petra nodded mutely and led the horse out of the barn. She wished one of the circles of hell would open up and swallow her. What was she supposed to say to a man she had slept a few feet from the previous night, a man she could not stop thinking about regardless of how foolish it was, and who was even now turning her thoughts to pudding?

Petra paused before swinging up. He stepped closer and even her thought about lack of thoughts disappeared into fluff. Her lips were tingling and her eyes riveted on James's lips. Her own reaction should have caught her by surprise, but she was long past being shocked at the wanton nature of her own body where James was concerned.

His eyes devoured her, but he held himself immobile. James was never going to presume to make the first move. She would either have to ask for it or do it herself. If this went on much longer, she may be begging for a kiss, but at this point she still had her dignity. She was not a beggar. The harpy within her rolled. The harpy was a hunter and never asked for anything. She only took.

Petra straightened and smiled. She let the greedy harpy in her show through her eyes, and James's eyes darkened in response. She closed the space between them and was engulfed by the clean smell of him. His chest rose and fell in ragged breaths and rubbed against hers with each intake. Her body tightened in anticipation.

Petra placed both hands on the wide chest in front of her and laid her lips firmly on his. The harpy in her soared with delight as she drowned in momentary heat. He was stiff at first then his arms came around her as he deepened the kiss. A moan escaped her, and Petra pulled back before her harpy took over. The point of this exercise was only to show she was willing, not to make a spectacle of herself.

She smugly noted the stunned look on James's face before she swung lightly up into the saddle. Petra wanted nothing more than to let her harpy rip through her and fly away with the tide of the moment, but she stayed human. She did not want to scare James away. She still had not solved the mystery of him, but there was time. Petra winked back at him and kicked her mare into a canter.

CHAPTER 8

It had been a couple of days since she'd laid eyes on James. Petra stopped her horse on the edge of the pasture and watched the three men release the herd back into the expanse of green summer grass. Her gaze went straight to James. From this distance it was a simple thing to admire his grace and economy of movement in a way that was impossible up close. Petra clenched her hands as the memory of what James felt like up close overtook them.

James waved a hand in greeting. He said something to Adam and then rode over to where she waited, a bundle of nerves and energy. "Good morning. You are an unexpected, but welcome surprise."

Petra felt the loopy grin on her face but did nothing to dispel it. "I'm going into town for a few things and to see Iris. I was wondering if you'd like to keep me company." She could have made the trip into town alone and on the wing much faster, but she was a glutton for punishment. She should have allowed herself a couple days to get used to the idea of kissing James, but here she was.

James shifted in the saddle, his eyes boring into hers. "We finished the morning milking, and the boys can handle the rest of the day alone. There are some things we need. Will you wait while I fetch the list?"

Petra nodded her agreement and followed James as he made a beeline for the house. She waved to Adam and changed direction to come alongside his horse.

Adam tipped his hat. "Mornin' Miss Petra. What brings you down the mountain today?"

"I need a few things in town and asked James to keep me company." Petra's neck warmed and she hoped it was only the sun and not the blush she thought it was.

Adam chuckled. "We've a running list. He's been in an uncommon good mood today, so he should be excellent company."

Petra smiled. "Has he now?"

Adam motioned for her to follow him toward the house. "Yes, ma'am. I hope you return him in high spirits. Robert wants to talk him into playing poker tonight. James is terrible at cards, and my brother is saving up money for a new saddle."

Petra laughed. "I'll do my best."

James emerged from the house with extra saddlebags and his duster thrown over one arm. He secured everything to his saddle and looked up at Petra. "Ready?"

"Yes, though I've been warned not to ruin your good mood."

James swung into his saddle. "I doubt that is possible, but why the warning?"

"Apparently, Robert has nefarious plans to take advantage of you." Robert rode up as Petra finished the statement.

He scowled at Adam and Petra. "You've ruined my plan."

James laughed and Petra clenched her toes at the sound. "I already said I would not be letting you fleece me at cards for a long while. I learned my lesson last time."

Adam smacked Robert on the back. "Better luck next time. Don't forget the nails, boss."

"It's on the list. I'll see you two tonight."

Petra and James set off down the mountain with the peaks looming at their backs. The blue of the summer sky was broken by wisps of clouds. The wind sang through the pine trees and the birds chatted around them. The path they followed was not large enough for them to ride two abreast so they rode in companionable silence.

Once the ground evened out, Petra moved her horse to ride beside James. He turned to look at her. "Our conversation about myths made me think about some of my early research on Zeus."

The hard weight settled in her stomach. It was too fine a day wreck it with a discussion about that oppressive overlord. "Did it?" She tried to smile but it felt like a tear in her face.

"Some of my notes are quite old. I was a boy when I started reading the myths about Zeus, but I did not start researching his disappearance until I read Thomas March's *Mythologia*. Are you familiar with it?"

Petra groaned inwardly. March was a pompous prick of a Remnant descended from one of the many bastards of Zeus. He had been determined to tell the truth of his ancestor's demise with some revisionist history, throwing most of the Remnants over the cliff as uncivilized revolutionaries. In the end he had been persuaded, with a little force and blood, by a harpy from Ocypete's line and The Messenger of that generation. The tome was mostly lies about the glory of Zeus's rule. Upon publication, they found he had slipped in one reference to the overthrown Zeus. His punishment had been severe and swift. "I think I've read it."

James's face broke into a grin. "Then you know how it ends. The last paragraph alludes to the fact that Zeus was not destroyed completely, but that a part of him remains to guard the mortal world, to be found when needed most."

Petra snorted. She could not help the derision in her voice. "Zeus was not some magnanimous ruler. He killed people. He raped women. He was cruel and viscous. If there is something of him left in the world, it would be for his own benefit and no one else's."

The excitement on James's face faded and was replaced by confusion. "Many of the myths do allude to the harshness of justice and rule, but that does not necessarily mean he was an unfair leader. Two days ago, you argued for the harpies. You said they were given a false retelling, though only one source holds your suggestions to be true. Why can't Thomas March be correct and the others wrong?"

All the reasons floated through her mind, and she could speak none of them without revealing what she was and what few mortals knew. She wanted to take a chance and explain everything to James, but the words stuck in her mouth. They melted and dissolved and she told him nothing. "I concede your point."

James nodded but he did not look pleased with his victory. "Another lost myth I found retold in a letter said Zeus buried something of value in a land far from Greece and the seat of his power. I theorized the land could well be America."

"I remember you telling me that." She could not think of a way to end this conversation, and she wanted it desperately to be over.

"I read over my notes again last night." His eyes sparkled. "I think whatever it is may very well be right here. In the Rockies. Maybe even in Turning Creek."

Denial was swift. "No. That can't be."

"Why not here?"

"Why not somewhere far, far away from here?" Anywhere else but this place she loved, Petra begged. Petra felt again the sense that James was a Remnant. She supposed he could be and not know it if the knowledge was lost. It had happened before.

"Where did you find these letters with the information about Zeus?" As far as most Remnants were concerned, Zeus died a bloody death at the Fall of Olympus. There was no record of any part of him surviving. Rumors, perhaps, but no evidence. Too many generations had gone by. Zeus was not a patient god. He would have made an appearance earlier if he were able.

"They were in an old journal in my family's library. I found them a couple years after my parents died. The journal and the collection of papers inside it belonged to an ancestor of mine, a few generations back. I did not recognize the name at the time, but I later discovered he was my five-times great-grandfather on my mother's side."

Petra stared at James and willed him to tell her now he was a Remnant of some minor god or creature without power or importance. It could not be a coincidence that his great grandfather five times removed possessed a journal containing information on Zeus, the real Zeus. "Would you be willing to show me the journal sometime?"

James hesitated. "Sure."

Surprise at the hesitation was replaced by the rub of hurt. She thought he trusted her. Immediately, all the things she was hiding crowded in her skull, and she looked away. "Why Turning Creek?"

The town loomed in the distance, but it would still be the good part of an hour before they made it to Main Street. Something looked off about the buildings from this distance. "This is as likely a place as anywhere else," James said.

The crisp mountain air was thick as Petra fought to breathe over her racing pulse. James was right. If Zeus had left a part of himself behind, it could be here; but it could be anywhere. Petra thought of the growing number of Remnants making their homes in Turning Creek and wondered if it was a coincidence or something else more sinister. Iris knew the most about the history of the Remnants and about the lost myths. Petra could talk to Iris while James was in the mercantile and see if his theory was crazy as she hoped it to be.

Decision made, she breathed easier. "Perhaps you are right. The Rockies are a glorious place. They would suit a god."

James was appeased by her statement and let the subject go. He swept his gaze over the peaks ringing the valley. "I never imagined anything so wonderful in Sheffield. The moment I was here, I knew this was where I always wanted to be."

Petra smiled, this time genuine. "I know exactly what you mean." She turned to drink in the sight of her mountain. "Atlas's Peak wedged itself in my soul. It's mine." Territorial pride unfurled within her, and Petra made no effort to disguise the harpy she knew shone through her eyes.

James watched her expression intently. "I have never met anyone like you before."

Petra's harpy preened and urged her to kiss James again. She did not want to make another move without seeing what he would do. It was not socially acceptable for a woman to be so forward, even if she did have a harpy clawing through her soul, yelling at her to take and take. Petra summoned all the willpower she possessed and stilled the monster within.

"I've never met a dairy farmer quite like you either."

"I would wager you had never met any dairy farmers before you met me."

Petra laughed, the tension of the previous conversation fleeing under the humor and heat in the eyes of the man riding next to her. "You would be correct."

"See, you have nothing on which to base your good opinion."

Another laugh. "Who said my opinion was a good one?" Petra kicked her horse into a canter and rode hard the rest of the way into town, with James laughing behind her.

Once they were close, Petra saw at once why Main Street had appeared odd from the trail leading into the valley. The edge of the road was lined with canvas tents, about ten in all. There were townspeople Petra knew walking around, but they were outnumbered by faces she had never seen. The majority of the newcomers were men with beards and fierce eyes. As far as Petra could tell, the newcomers were all mortal except for two, a mother and a young boy with straw for hair. She eyed Petra with a wariness she was used to from other Remnants. Petra nodded in acknowledgment but was careful to keep her posture non-threatening. The mother's shoulders slumped and she pulled her son away by his hand.

Sheriff Brant was leaning against a post in front of his office. His posture screamed relaxed, but Petra saw his eyes moving. He missed nothing in Turning Creek. It was a wonder he had not figured out something was not normal about half the population. Reed Brant was one of those mortals who eventually saw past the odd label most Remnants acquired to the truth below the surface.

Petra stopped her horse in front of the sheriff. He looked at her from under the brim of his hat. "Good day to you Miss Petra, Mr. Lloyd. How are you both doing?"

James halted beside Petra. "Fine. How are you?"

"Top of the world. What brings you into town?"

Petra pointed to James. "I was headed down and asked for company."

James turned to Petra. "Do you need anything from Simon?"

"Not today. I mostly came to see Iris."

"If Simon is in a chattering mood, my errand may take awhile. Can I meet you at the depot?"

"Of course." Petra watched him dismount and tie his horse in front of the mercantile. He sent a smile her way before he shouldered his saddle bags and walked through the door. "Sheriff, is it just me, or are there a lot more people walking around?" Sheriff Brant was a man to be trusted, and he was good at his job. She did not know if he liked coffee or tea or if he liked to read, but if something odd was going on, he would have some idea.

Brown eyes, lighter than James's, swept the street and returned to her. "You'd be correct. We've had an influx of late. Miners, most of them.

Looking for something better than where they were before."

"But the gold and silver finds have been miles east of here. That makes no sense."

"Neither does killing yourself digging through the dirt for the chance of something fleeting, but here they are." Sheriff Brant shifted his weight and bore his eyes into hers. "I know you live alone and far up the mountain, but be careful. I've had some problems with a few of the miners getting rowdy, and a woman alone is easy pickings for some."

Petra straightened in the saddle. The harpy rolled with a mix of eagerness and violence. This was her territory, and it was unwise to challenge a harpy in her own domain. "I can take care of myself."

Her words had just enough power in them that the sheriff examined her before answering. "I know that, but this is my town and it's my job to keep the peace. Just do me a favor and keep your eyes open. And don't go anywhere without a gun."

Only a fool went around in the mountains without a gun, though they were more likely to need it for wildlife instead of people. Petra had no need of a gun, but she carried one because it was expected. She had claws and teeth if it came to that. "Of course. Good day, Sheriff."

He tipped his hat as Petra rode down the street to the depot. The bell on the door signaled her entrance, and Petra paused on the threshold to breathe deeply.

"You must have known I was coming. I smell tea and fresh biscuits."

Iris laughed. "It never fails that one of you shows up when I have biscuits fresh from the oven. Can you smell them all the way up your mountain?"

Petra plopped herself down on a stool on the end of the counter. Two older men were playing checkers and discussing politics in the back corner. L.A. Smith and Johnny Pope were harmless, but they could be loud when they got enough liquor in them. They liked to play checkers in the depot because they thought their wives did not know where they were. Their wives knew Iris would not let them linger overlong and send them home in time for supper.

"I wanted to see you, and I stopped by James's farm to see if he wanted to ride down with me."

Iris's eyebrows rose. "You seem to be spending a lot of time with Mr. Lloyd."

Petra squirmed in her seat. "We're just friends. I like him too much to think about telling him all about...explaining things... It's not like that." Her face was hot.

Iris giggled. "You are a terrible liar."

Petra planted her forehead on the worn top of the counter. "I kissed him."

"What?" Iris squeaked. L.A. and Johnny looked up, frowned at the two of them, and resumed their game. Iris adjusted the pitch of her voice. "You did what?"

Petra did not raise her head and the wood muffled her response. "Kissed James. Day before yesterday. It was really nice." She raised her head to meet Iris's eyes. "And very foolish."

Iris stroked a hand over her hair. "Not foolish. Normal."

Petra plunked her head back down. "Nothing about this is normal. I can never have a normal relationship." Not with the man she chose to sire her daughter and not with her daughter. The closest thing she had to normal was the small, blond-haired woman beside her and two violent harpies. And according to the prophecy, she would be sacrificing one of them.

Petra raised her head and grabbed Iris's hands. "You, Dora, and Marina are the only things that matter to me. You three are the only normal I need."

Iris's blue eyes grew watery, but nothing fell. "Sweet bird. Why do you think yourself unworthy of something else?"

Petra sighed, a sound that came from deep in her soul. "Because this is the way the gods made us. To be violent and strong and not form attachments anywhere—or else forfeit my life."

Iris thinned her lips but said nothing. She poured Petra a cup of tea from the kettle on the counter and placed it with a rattle in front of her. She gave Petra two biscuits and then took the dozen or so remaining biscuits and walked them over to the men in the back. Petra crunched on the biscuit and ignored the conversation between the men and Iris. The biscuit was a gingersnap, one of her favorite.

Iris returned and sat down opposite Petra behind the counter. Petra waved the biscuit at her. "You knew I was coming."

Iris shrugged. "Perhaps. Why did you come?"

"Don't you know?"

"It doesn't work like that."

"Yep. It's all sacrifice, pain, and gingersnaps. No actual useful information though."

Iris wilted. "I'm sorry."

Petra crumbled inside. "Me too. I'm sorry for being snippy. I do love the biscuits, and I did want to talk to you."

Iris perked back up. "Something else about James?"

"Yes, but not what you're hoping for." Petra told Iris about James's preoccupation with Zeus and the morning's revelation about the journal, about Billy Royal, and Sheriff Brant's warning. "I think that covers all the particulars."

Iris refreshed her tea and refilled Petra's cup. "You're sure James would tell you if he knew he was a Remnant?"

Petra weighed the options. "I think he would if he knew. If he knew how to sense others, he would know I'm not mortal. Whatever he is, he's not powerful, but I am. There is no hiding a harpy. If he knew what he was, he'd know I was dangerous at least." She let the pleasure of her own power roll through her. It was wild and cold on her tongue.

L.A. and Johnny looked up. They were brothers, Remnants of nymphs or sprites or some such. L.A. met Petra's feral eyes. "Is there a problem, ma'am?"

"No. Sorry about the power leak." Petra smiled and reluctantly pulled in her power until it was a gentle hum under her skin.

Johnny winked. "No need to apologize. Women with flair are a sight to see."

Iris shook her finger at Johnny. "Don't start flirting or I'll have to tell your wife, and then she won't let you come here anymore."

"Sorry, Miss Iris. Wouldn't dream of it."

The bell broke the spell in the room, and Petra sucked all her power back in a rush. James stood in the doorway and paused before coming to stand beside Petra. He could have taken the stool a few feet from her, but he remained close enough that if she shifted slightly, she could lean against him. She kept a sliver of air between them.

"Good afternoon, Miss Iris. Gentleman." He waved to the men in the back and then turned to Petra. Their faces were close and for a moment, Petra could not breathe. "Ready? As it is, we will get back to the farm about sunset, and you still have an hour after that to travel."

"I'm done. Iris, would you check your books for that thing I was telling you about?" Petra tried very hard to look innocent and serious at the same time. Iris was right. She was horrible at lying.

Iris came around the counter and wrapped her in a hug. "Of course, bird. Come see me soon when you can stay."

"Thanks, Iris." Petra hugged her back hard enough to squeeze the air out of her lungs.

They left the depot. James's saddlebags were near to bursting. A bag she had not brought was slung behind her saddle. James looked sheepish. "I hope you don't mind. My list was longer than my ability to transport the goods home. It seems the boys added more things than I realized."

Petra swung into the saddle. "Not a problem."

"I hope you had enough time to do what you needed."

"I did, thanks."

The sun was on their left shoulders and making its trail towards the horizon. James eased his horse next to hers. "You came all this way to see Iris for tea. I didn't know you were that close."

The answer came easily. "She's part of my family. Dora, Marina, and

Iris are the closest thing I have ever had to a real family. Iris is good with advice and other things. She also makes excellent gingersnaps."

Petra looked at the bags behind James. She pointed to a wooden handle protruding from one side. "What did you buy at Simon's?"

James looked down. "This? It's a pickaxe."

The hard weight settled again in her stomach. "What do you need a pickaxe for?" Petra could think of many reasons he might legitimately need one on a farm and prayed he would not say the one thing she dreaded.

"I was thinking about our conversation on the way down here, and I thought, why not buy one? Why not see what I can find on my land? I may not find Zeus, but I might find gold or silver."

The acrid taste of bile flooded her mouth. Petra swallowed it down ruthlessly. "You are going to mine on your land?"

James shrugged, but there was a glint in his eye she had not seen before. "Why not?"

"You're a dairy farmer, James. You make cheese."

"And that disqualifies me from digging a hole in the ground?"

"It's dangerous," she spat. The harpy in her coiled in anger.

"Why?" he countered.

"You have no idea what you are looking for."

"But I do know. I'm looking for a god who sought to give light to the world. Every time I mention Zeus, you look like you have something rotten in your mouth. What do you think you know that I don't?"

Petra recalled the stories of blood and strife. She thought of the harpy who had not made it through the battle, Podarge, and she struggled with what to say to this man before her. "He may have had some good qualities, but the myths are full of his betrayals and mercurial moods, which made him do atrocious things."

"I do not think all of those stories hold the truth of his goodness." James's face was stony.

Petra cast about desperately. Her harpy was clawing to make herself known, and she would win the battle by force, but Petra knew this was a battle of wits, not brawn. "Why do you think that?'

"History is written by those left standing. Olympus fell and Zeus disappeared. The riffraff who took over were the ones who wrote his history, not the god himself. Whatever happened, it was not pretty, and Zeus had to disappear and wait."

"Wait for what?"

James shrugged, but it was a practiced move. He was lying. "I don't know."

Petra willed herself to relax. She quieted the violent cloud clawing to be free. "Zeus was a tyrannical bastard who crushed everyone but a precious few under his thumb. I would rather spend my life in an inner circle of hell than see him rule again."

"You have some mistaken beliefs about the Greek myths. I believe Zeus was meant to rule again and he left something of himself behind to see that happen. I'm going to mine on my land, and whether I find gold, silver, or the map to Olympus, it will be none of your business." James kicked his horse and sped past her on the trail.

"Styx and fire." Petra cursed and gave him his lead. She followed him in silence the rest of the way back to the farm.

When they reached the yard in front of the cabin, James got down from his saddle and looked up at her with stony eyes. "I apologize, Miss Petra. Have a good evening." He led his horse into the barn without glancing back.

Anger at herself for having mishandled the conversation so badly raged within her. The sky darkened overhead with her anger, and Petra had to concentrate on breathing deeply to keep the darkness from covering the sun completely. Adam came out of the barn a moment later, a question on his face. He froze when he looked at Petra. She knew the violence was visible in her eyes.

She licked her lips and ran her tongue over her teeth to make sure they were still flat. Petra spoke slowly and calmly to keep her voice normal. "Tell Robert I'm sorry. I ruined his good mood." She dropped James's bag of supplies, kicked her horse, and rode up the mountain without waiting for a response.

CHAPTER 9

In the morning, Petra's anger at James had cooled and morphed into determination. There was something between the two of them. Something that scared the feathers off her and also made her want to fly loops in the moonlight. It was something she could hardly define, but she was not going to let an ill-conceived belief about a lost Zeus get in the way. All she needed to do was convince James of the truth and prove his theory wrong. Preferably without dropping the harpy and Remnant secret in his lap as the *coup de grace*.

The conversation would go much easier if she were willing to come clean and tell James about herself. It was not as if the existence of Remnants was so sacred that no mortals knew. Plenty of them had been told over the years, but the numbers were few. Those who did talk were rarely believed and often thought crazy. The more Petra considered the idea of telling James the more certain she was that she would never do it. She was fierce, and she could call darkness on a sunny day, but laying this one truth at the feet of James made her blood freeze in her veins. She could not tell him the truth, and a part of her hated herself for it.

Petra also knew she needed to go and mend the fence with James. She could swallow her pride and apologize, but she would let him know her opinion of his undertaking had not changed. Being less isolated and venturing out into the world meant messy relationships. Petra wished her social skills were equipped to handle this kind of obstacle.

Still, Petra put off going to apologize to James. It was foolish and spineless, but she did it nonetheless. She flew straight to Bill Royal's homestead to say hello to her neighbor. Petra landed just beyond the clearing, where a now-completed cabin stood. The smell of new wood lingered in the air despite the breeze. The clank of metal hitting stone drew Petra across the clearing. She changed back into her mortal form and walked down a short path.

The path ended in front of a mine shaft. The darkness of the shaft hid the man inside, who was cutting a rhythmic swath through the mountain. The air here smelled like rock dust. The clanking stopped and was replaced by the crunch of a shovel and the plinking of stone into a pail. Petra licked her lips, unable to move. She had the sense to pull her harpy tight within her. She would only change if needed. She needed to talk to Billy Royal long enough to find out what he was doing.

The crunching of footsteps heralded Billy Royal's appearance, but they paused before reaching the sunlight. "What are you doing here, Miss Celaeno?" He emerged from the shadows. A pole was slung over his shoulders. Pails of stones hung from notches on the end of the pole. He did not stop but walked past her and dumped the buckets on the tailings pile.

"I came to see how you were settling in."

Billy Royal scowled. "I'm fine. I have work to do." He swung the pole with the buckets over one shoulder and turned to walk back into the mine.

He was not going to sit over tea and talk to her. Petra knew it was time for a direct approach. She released her power and allowed it to flow outward. "What are you digging for?" She gave each word a push to compel him to tell her. It did not always work. It was more persuasion than compulsion, and Billy's mind was not as weak as some.

He turned and put down the buckets. "Don't pull any of your tricks on me. What I'm doing is none of your business." He squared his shoulders and met her gaze without blinking.

Petra let more of her power seep out. "Oh, but it does concern me. This is my mountain. I know you are not mortal, and you know that I'm not either. Let's be frank, Mr. Royal. I'm a harpy." Petra paused. To his credit, his eyes widened slightly, but he did not back down. "I see you know what that means. I should tell you that I am not alone. There are others. Now. Who are you and what are you doing on my mountain?"

Resignation flared in his eyes, and Petra thought she had won. "I'm the Remnant of Bellerophon. I seek the lost myth of Zeus."

The earth under Petra shifted. "The lost myth of Zeus?"

"Are you familiar with it?"

"I have recently become reacquainted with it, yes." Pressure was building in her head.

"My family has sought the lost power of Zeus since the Fall. It will right the wrong the gods dealt us in refusing us entry to Mount Olympus. The first son of every generation spends his life looking for the seat of Zeus's power so that we may take our rightful place among the gods and rule as we were meant to rule." The fire of conviction rang in his words.

Petra was familiar with the line of Bellerophon. In the myths, Bellerophon, sired by Poseidon, believed himself to be worthy of admittance onto Mount Olympus. Athena gave him a golden bridle, with which he captured Pegasus. On the fabled winged steed, he tried to fly to the top of the mount, but Pegasus, knowing the futility of the endeavor, threw his rider and left Bellerophon for dead. In bitterness, Bellerophon wandered the earth, cursing the gods and vowing revenge.

"Why here?" It was the same question she had posed to James just yesterday.

Billy smiled, the first true one she had seen on his face. "Family secret, but this mountain is the place."

For the second time in two days, Petra found herself saying, "You have no idea what you are looking for." Billy smiled again, wider. Petra sucked in a breath. "You do know. You know and yet you search. All the destruction and bloodshed. Why?"

"Power, little harpy. The power I am destined to hold. I'm going to be the one to find it and return glory to my family."

"You're insane. By the River Styx, I swear you will never see that come to pass." She invoked the old oath so there would be no doubt of her intention.

He nodded. "So be it. I wasn't planning on being a friendly neighbor in any event. I'm still going to dig."

Petra wished she could kill him. He could not find anything if he was dead, but, unlike some of her ancestors, she had a healthy respect for life. He had found nothing, yet, and was likely to find nothing at all except a growing pile of dirt. She could not kill him on the possibility that he might, one day in the future, find something dangerous.

Her first concern was that Billy and James both had similar ideas about something hidden somewhere under the earth of Atlas's Peak. Either they were both crazy, or her mountain was hiding a secret. Both men would have to be watched closely in case they did find something. She would enlist Dora and Marina to keep an eye on Billy. She could watch James.

Allowing her harpy to take the reins, she changed in the clearing. She spread her wings to soak in the heat of the sun, and its light made her feathers glint ebony black and blue. In her harpy form she leaned over Billy, who took one step back. "Dig if you will." Her scratching voice dripped power. "But know this. If you ever do anything to threaten the peace of this valley, you will answer to me and my sisters. We are creatures of violent justice."

To his credit, he did not step back again when Petra jumped and took flight over his head. She craned her head to look at him one more time. He stood in the middle of the clearing watching her go. Petra prayed he would take her warning seriously. Despite her harpy's love of violence, she did not kill needlessly.

Petra turned toward James's farm. She needed to visit the other crazy man on her mountain. This next visit would contain less warnings and more apologizing. She would never convince James to see reason about the lost myth of Zeus if he would not speak to her. Besides, ever since the argument yesterday, a scratchy feeling had developed in her spirit. Petra found she did not like thinking James was angry at her.

Petra landed well away from the house and changed back into her mortal form. Much of her problem might be eased if she told James the truth, but she was unwilling to lose her growing relationship with him if he could not accept her. There was no one in the yard when she broke through the trees. After an internal debate, she approached the house first.

She had one foot on the wooden steps of the porch when Adam walked out of the house. He stopped short when he saw her. "Mornin' Miss Petra. Didn't think we'd be seeing you for a few days."

Petra looked at her feet. "I've come to mend the fence, as they say."

Relief crossed Adam's face. "Good. I'm not sure what went on yesterday, but he clattered around here like a thundercloud all last night and this morning. Burned all the damned, pardon ma'am, eggs." Adam looked back into the cabin, then closed the door. "James is in the cheese house, and Robert is taking his time this morning in the house. What do you know about this idea James has about mining on the backside of his land?"

Petra's shoulders slumped. "That's what we fought about yesterday. I don't think it's advisable."

Adam shoved his hands in his pocket. "I don't care what the man is looking for, but there is an unnatural gleam in his eyes when he talks about it. I've seen that look before, on men who yearn for something they know will eat them up inside, and yet they go after it anyway. I knew a cowboy in New Mexico like that about a woman. He ended up dead." Worry creased his face.

Adam's concern was similar to Petra's, though their reasons grew from different sources. "No matter how worried we are right now, James is a man grown and able to make his own decisions. It's just a hobby. However, keep an eye on him. If he starts behaving differently, we'll sit him down and have a talk with him. If we all share the same concerns, perhaps he'll listen."

Adam's shoulders relaxed. "Thanks, Miss Petra. We'll keep an eye on him. He's like family to us."

He looked so young in that moment, Petra had the urge to comfort him, but she did not move closer. "James is in the cheese house?" Adam nodded. "Wish me luck. I'm rubbish at apologies."

Adam smiled. "Luck to you, then."

Petra walked across the yard, aware of Adam's eyes on her back and the birds singing without care in the trees. She paused before the door and took a deep breath. Her knuckles rapped hard on the door.

"Come in." The muffled command came and Petra pushed the latch down and stepped inside.

James rose from a chair on her right. In his hands he held a broadsheet, The Rocky Mountain News. He must have bought it in town yesterday. He folded the paper, laid it aside, and bowed in greeting.

Petra colored at the gesture. Dismay over both her blush and the fact that they had moved back into formalities rose up. She ran a hand down her thigh and watched his eyes follow every movement. "I see you started making the cheese without me. You did promise to show me the process."

"Allow me to apologize. I did not think you actually meant to come again so soon." He sounded formal.

Petra opened her mouth to apologize, but the words stuck. She tried a small smile. "Will you allow me to intrude on your day?"

James checked the temperature on the vat. Petra thought he meant to send her away, but he looked up and smiled. "I have to warn you. Cheese making is not as titillating as you seem to think it will be. It's mostly waiting around for things to cook and set."

Petra relaxed. "It can't be as bad as all that. You'll be here, after all." She joined him by the side of the vat, stepping close enough that the sides of their bodies brushed. "Tell me where you are in the process."

He gestured to the cream-colored milk. "I added the rennet. It's a chemical from calves' stomachs that causes the milk to curdle. We get it from the calves. This batch is just about done with that step." James took a T-shaped wooden tool off the wall. Hanging from the crossbar of the T were knife blades set close. He handed the tool to Petra. The handle was smooth from use. "We'll use this to cut the curds into even pieces, like this." James closed his hands over hers and guided her as they dragged the knives through the thickened milk. The places where his skin touched hers tingled. She tried to concentrate as they made the horizontal cuts together, with the warmth from his body seeping into her own.

"Good, now go the other way." He moved away, and Petra had the urge to move with him.

The muscles of her arms strained as she pulled the tool through the vat. Petra felt his eyes on her, even as he checked on the temperature again, but she kept her eyes on her task and tried to find a way to apologize. His anger seemed to have cooled, but she owed him the words.

She lifted her head and met his eyes. She thought of kissing him again and focused on the task instead. "What's next?"

James blinked and thought a moment. He cleared his throat. "We maintain a low heat for thirty minutes." James checked the temperature again. "The temperature from the coals under the vat needs to be an even one hundred degrees. If you would please flip the hourglass marked with a thirty over," he said as he pointed to the brass and glass time keeper on a shelf behind her shoulder.

Petra did as he asked. "Now what?"

"Now we wait for thirty minutes before draining the whey. Would you like to sit?" James held out the other chair at the small table he had been sitting at when she had interrupted his reading.

Petra sat and rubbed both hands over her thighs as she gathered her courage. "I need to apologize to you."

James sat in the chair opposite. "No, I should be apologizing to you."

Petra ventured a smile. "I'll go first." She ran her tongue over her lips. "I should not have pressed it, yesterday. You should mine your land if you want. I was just concerned."

"Apology accepted, of course. I apologize as well. I should not have stormed off in such a manner. I knew as soon as you left that you were only speaking from concern and not malice. Please forgive my temper."

"Done. But you should know that I am a woman of many opinions, which I am likely to share often."

"Is that a warning that I may be accepting apologies from you more often as time goes by?"

Petra laughed. "You know me too well already." There was one more thing she needed to tell him. Not the information about her being a harpy, though, she was not ready for that. Petra fidgeted in her chair and James leaned back into his chair. "I've a confession to make."

"That sounds serious. This must be a morning of serious conversations."

She continued, "I think we're becoming," she hesitated, "friends or maybe something else, and I don't want to lie to you."

A cocky grin suffused his face for an instant then was replaced by a more subdued version. "I can't imagine what you would have lied to me about."

The list of things she had lied about was long, but she could tell the truth about this one thing. "When we first met, I told you I was a widow. I've never been married." She clenched her hands together on the table.

James scooped her small hands up in his own. "Why do you think that would matter to me, whether you had been married or not?" He squeezed her hands.

"I dislike lying to you. It's easier to lie usually. A widow gets certain liberties an unmarried woman does not." As a widow, she could travel alone and manage her own money in many places, though it was still frowned upon.

"Why are you alone? Where's your family? It's hard to imagine any family would let their daughter leave the fold and travel to another country alone." His hands did not leave hers.

Petra chose the truth. "I didn't know my father. My mother raised me alone, and she was not an affectionate mother. She did not kiss and hug me as I know some mothers do. She did what she thought was best, but it was a lonely way to grow up. As soon as I came of age, I left.

"People make assumptions of a woman traveling alone and most of them are unpleasant. I created the persona of a widow for protection. My travels brought me here, and I never corrected people, though it does not matter so much here in Turning Creek. Civilization is far away, and people are more forgiving here. The mountains are not harsh judges of our mistakes."

He gave her hand squeeze. "You were protecting yourself. I wouldn't hold that against you."

"Thank you, James." Reluctantly, she removed her hands from his and tapped the paper. "Anything interesting?"

"Not much. The Senate and House are embroiled in a battle over property and states' rights. I'm not sure if it will affect us much out here, but the arguments are getting nasty."

"There's been talk of Colorado requesting statehood soon. If that happens, whatever is happening in Washington will have more of an impact here, backwoods though we are," Petra said.

"Let's hope they settle their disagreements before then." James pointed to the timer. Petra turned in time to see the sand leave the timer. "The timer is up. Time to drain the whey. Come. I'll show you."

Petra stood and followed him around the vat. He pointed to some buckets below the vats. "These catch the whey as it drains from the vat." She watched as he turned a lever on the bottom of the vat. The dripping of the whey into the ceramic buckets gave the impression of rain on a metal roof. "We have more time to wait." James led them back to the table.

Petra sat, mind spinning, looking for a way to continue the conversation without taking it in a direction either would find uncomfortable. "You claim to have spent a formidable portion of your childhood in the cheese house, and yet you have very formal manners. Explain." She crossed her arms and regarded him with a challenge in her eyes.

He laughed. "I can never predict your actions." They grinned like loons at each other. "My family was wealthy and possessed a small title, so my aunts knew it would be possible for me to make a good match, once I came into my majority. Part of my tutor's duties included etiquette training. I wanted to please them, so I applied myself. I became rather better at exhibiting graces than they did at loving me." His words did not hold bitterness, but there was the lingering loneliness Petra had sensed before.

Petra's hand wound around his wrist. "Your aunts were fools." She could feel his pulse speed up as she left her fingers twined around his arm.

"I left them what they wanted. Well, almost." A sad smile graced his face. "I left them the farm, which, when managed correctly, provides a very nice income. I took everything else. My aunts were not as thankful as I would have liked."

"Perhaps one day they'll regret their actions."

"It matters not to me. I'm content with my life, and I have all I need." James rose and peered into the vat. "The draining is done. This next bit can be messy." James took a measuring cup and a bag from the shelf in the back of the room. "This is salt. It gets added to the drained curds." The metal measuring cup scraped against the salt as James scooped and sprinkled it over the curds in the vat.

Petra watched him as he worked. He caught her looking at him and paused to smile at her. A heat kindled in his eyes, and Petra was unable to look away from him, though he returned his focus to his task. James put the salt and cup away. From pegs on the wall, he pulled two smooth, wooden paddles down and handed one to Petra.

"Put the paddle in the curd mixture like this." He moved the paddle carefully through the vat. "You have to take care when turning the salt into the curds to keep from breaking up the curds."

A lock of hair blew in her face as she worked, and Petra blew it out of the way. "This is much more involved than when I make soft goat cheese."

James pointed to the large press in the corner of the room and they continued working. "After we do this, we will press the curds into wheels."

Like with milking the cows, they worked in an easy tandem. James showed her how to line the molds with cloth, pack the curds into the round molds, and set the mold on the press. They talked little during the process, but Petra found excuses to brush her fingers against his or stand close to him when she was able.

James moved the twenty pound press weight to fifty pounds. "Time for a break. There will be nothing else to do with the cheese now for twelve hours." They cleaned up the debris from the day and left the cheese house.

Dusk washed the sky. James held the door for her. "Thank you for helping today, again. It has been years since I had help in the cheese house, and it was nice to not be alone."

She waited for him for latch the door. "It was my pleasure. Thank you for allowing me to stay."

James stood close but his hands were behind his back. "Will you stay for dinner?"

Petra hesitated before replying, "No. I need to get back, but thank you for the offer."

James looked around the yard. "Where is your horse?"

"I walked."

"You can't walk home alone. It's nearly dark."

Petra's lips twitched in the ghost of a smile. "I can handle myself." She gestured to the gun she carried, small but serviceable. She would never need it to defend herself, but James did not need to know why.

James opened his mouth, but clamped it shut. He turned and walked toward the house. Petra gave him points for not arguing. She maintained an arm's length distance as she followed. She should say good bye and leave, but she felt compelled to follow.

He paused at the porch and turned to her. "Are you sure you won't stay?"

"I'm sure." Petra rocked onto the balls of her feet and then stilled. James was not close enough to touch and though she wanted to close the space between them, she could not. They had made headway after yesterday's argument, but she still hesitated. The next move would have to be his. She could not pursue him when she knew full well she had nothing to offer. Petra tucked a chuck of curls behind her ear and waited.

James paused at the edge of the porch and turned. He shifted his weight from foot to foot and Petra could see the indecision on his face. His eyes captured hers and did not let go. Determination hardened his gaze, and he closed the space between them.

His hands plunged deep into her hair, and he used his momentum to draw her into him. Petra had one moment to savor the feel of James grasping her before his lips touched hers. Her mouth opened to him without hesitation, and he kissed her with a burning possession. He was everywhere, and her body was aflame. Her harpy purred in delight, and Petra gave herself over to it.

Petra's fingers fumbled with the buttons on his shirt. She popped enough free to allow her to run eager hands over his chest. James rained kisses over her jawline and down the curve of her neck. His hand hovered over the buttons on her own shirt and Petra pushed her chest into the palm of his hand in an entreaty.

James laid his hand flat over her heart and his head on her shoulder. His chest heaved as if he had run all the way up the mountain from town. Petra's blood roared in her ears as she stroked a trembling hand over his hair.

"We're standing on the edge of the yard." The words were hoarse, and Petra stilled to hear them. "I would never... This is not the place... I'm sorry."

Petra lifted his head. "Hush." She kissed him gently, but firmly, on the mouth. "I'm not sorry." She gave him a saucy grin and buttoned up his shirt.

The smile he gave to her was shy at first, then confident. "You're like the gentian, blooming on the mountains, beautiful and wild. Can I see you again? Will you go on a picnic and a hike with me?"

Petra savored the sweetness of his request. "Are you requesting a formal outing?"

James's smile was radiant. "And if I am?"

"Even if you weren't, the answer'd be yes. The day after tomorrow?"

James took her hand and kissed her palm. Petra felt warmth spread from the base of her spine outward. "Goodnight, Petra."

His voice speaking her name struck a chord in the well of her soul. "Goodnight, James." She turned on her heel and walked into the darkening trees.

CHAPTER 10

Petra walked until she was no longer visible within the trees, and then she walked farther to be sure. The smell of pine and dirt did nothing to dispel James from her senses. Her scalp tingled where his hands had been. Unspent energy boiled within her. She could feel her harpy straining against the confines of her skin. She needed to fly.

Petra released control over her harpy and her true form burst over her with more violence than normal. She shook herself, aligning wings and feathers. The unbearable energy, which had felt trapped in her human form, rolled over her as power in this form. She spread her wings, darker than the coming night, and launched into the air.

Petra pumped her wings hard to gain altitude fast. When she was sufficiently high, she shot west over the mountains, putting Atlas's Peak and James behind her. The night air was cold up here, but it cooled the heat James had stirred up and calmed her agitated spirit.

She would be seventy tomorrow. It had been twenty years since her mother had forced her to leave Venice. She only had ten more years to have a daughter of her own. The prospect of her future crushed the buoyant energy from before. She had long ago decided to end the cycle by not siring a child, but she had not known James then.

Petra tried to imagine explaining to James that she was a mythological creature who only wanted to be his temporary lover until she became pregnant. Some men would think her crazy, but accept the no-strings-attached offer. James was not like other men. There was no way James, with his refined manners and sense of duty, would agree to any of those terms, though he would probably think she was crazy.

James had asked to call on her. No man had ever made such a request of her, but she knew what his request meant. He wanted to spend time with her because he meant to court her. She was both thrilled and terrified of the prospect of James pursuing her. James was steady and careful, but he had laid propriety aside for a few moments this evening to kiss her thoroughly.

For the first time in her life, Petra loathed what she was and the limitations of the curse put on her ancestors. The injustice of the solitary life forced upon the harpies was a raw wound, but she had never hated her harpy self. Until now. She had thought she would mourn most the loss of a daughter, of the continuation of her line, but it was something more. She wanted the love of a man. The pain of losing something she never wanted before pierced her soul. Generations of harpies abandoning their mates and their daughters had nurtured their selfishness and violence against others. The weight of all those generations pushed her down. Petra lost altitude.

She landed in a large cottonwood tree. Her claws gripped thick bottom branch and the tree shuddered under her weight but held. She folded herself as small as she could and sat. Her ancestors hid in trees and tormented people as they traveled through the forests. Often, they were given the task of harassing people as they made their way to the gods for judgment. They had rightfully earned their reputation for savagery.

This area was unfamiliar. Petra did not recognize the shape of the mountains against the night sky. She tilted her head to one side and the burble of a brook met her ears. It was just ahead, not far from where she perched. The air smelled the same as on her peak, fresh and cold, tinged with spruce. She could stay here and start over. If she did not tell the other harpies where she was, perhaps they would never find her, and then she could hide from the dilemma of James.

Petra sighed. That was a coward's solution. Besides, the bond between the three harpies and Iris would enable them to find her eventually. It could take years, but she could not escape them or her destiny. It would be easier if she could tuck her head under her wing, go to sleep, and wake up someone or something else.

The night was half over. It was time she headed back home. Petra left the tree and turned back towards her life.

***

Her dreams were not restful. The roll of thunder shook her body. Lightning flashed bright and hot on her heels as she ran across a rocky valley. There were no shoes on her feet, and she left a trail of blood in her wake. The pain in her feet lanced up her legs. She stubbed her toe on a rock and skidded to a halt, face-first on the gravel-strewn ground. She tried to change into her harpy to fly away, but she was stuck in human form. Helpless. She lay on the ground with the iron smell of blood and the tang of lightning before it strikes in her nose.

She curled into a ball, trying to make a smaller target for the lightning.

Thunder hammered over her again, filling her mind and making her teeth rattle. Someone was calling her. The thunder grew louder. Someone was pounding on the door. The door.

Petra sat up and swung her legs over the side of the bed. She squinted at the sun dancing through the window. She slammed shut her eyes and groaned. She groped her way to the door. The leg of the table connected with her little toe. The pounding continued and was echoed in her abused foot.

"Styx, that hurt. I'm coming. Do you know what time it is?" Petra yelled and yanked the door open. Marina and Iris pushed past her. Dora hugged her before following the others in.

Petra slammed the door and plopped into a chair. "Well, good morning to you too. Make yourselves at home and make me some tea." Petra rubbed her eyes.

Marina began unloading a bag she had slung over her shoulder. "I hope I don't look half as bad as you when I turn seventy. You look like hell."

"Thanks for the birthday wishes. It isn't polite to interrupt a woman's beauty sleep." Petra crossed her arms over her chest.

Marina snorted. "Beauty sleep, eh?" Petra swatted at her.

"We're here to celebrate with you." Iris arranged cinnamon biscuits on a plate and shoved them under Petra's nose. "Eat one. You'll feel better." Petra sniffed and put her nose in the air, but obeyed. If they wanted to waste all their good cheer and food on her, she would not let a decent biscuit go to waste.

Dora sat beside her. "You do look tired. Are you feeling well?"

Petra took a bite of biscuit to avoid answering. Cowardly, but effective. Sadly, it only held off the question for so long. "I went flying and got home late. I had disturbing dreams when I slept."

Iris's hands stilled in their task of spooning tea into the pot. "Disturbing how?"

Petra put her biscuit down and clenched her hands in her lap. "Thunder. Lightning. Being chased. Nothing unusual, really. I had trouble going back to sleep." Whenever she had gone back to sleep the dream had returned. She had spent the last hours of the night awake and staring out the window and wishing for the sun, but she did not need to tell them that.

Iris's steady gaze did not leave hers, but Petra refused to look away. She would not crumble beneath that azure gaze. Iris broke first and returned to her task of making tea. Petra kept her gaze steady on Iris, whose eyes misted.

Iris turned her back to Petra and put the tea kettle on the stove. "I'm so sorry the prophecy was one of pain and not joy. It breaks my heart to have brought it into your life." Her shoulders hunched inward.

Petra rose and went to her. She wrapped her arms around Iris and rested her chin on Iris's head. "It's not your fault. The strife would have been mine whether you had warned me of it or not. Today is my birthday, and though I was determined to mope and grieve my advanced age, I declare that there will be no more tears or sadness on this day."

Iris sniffed and nodded.

Marina clapped her hands. "I second that. Where's the whiskey?"

Dora frowned at Marina. "It's barely noon."

Marina shrugged. "I'll put it in my tea if that'll make you feel better about it."

Iris took Petra by the hand and sat her in a chair. "Sit, my bird, and I will braid your hair."

Petra relaxed and submitted to Iris's ministrations while Marina and Dora made noise in the kitchen while they cooked the noon meal. The pull of the large-toothed comb through her unruly hair, which she had left down yesterday, lulled Petra. Iris could always make her hair look less like a tangled bird's nest than she could ever manage.

Iris sucked in a breath and paused her combing. The lack of movement jerked Petra from the half sleep she had been enjoying. Iris bent over and examined her hair.

"Do I have fleas? Lice? A tick?" Petra attempted to twist around, but Iris clamped a firm hand on her shoulder to keep her still. For a woman with small hands, Iris was strong.

"Stay still." Iris pulled a lock of hair up from the mass of curls and held it to the light.

Petra tried to twist again and Iris's hand clamped down harder on her shoulder. "Ouch, Iris. What is it?"

Dora and Marina were crowded around now too. They were all looking at her hair. She should have felt worried, but it was anger driving her actions. Lack of sleep, troubling dreams, and James's peculiar behavior had used up what little patience she possessed.

"Am I growing a second head? It was a long night. Will one of you tell me what is going on before I kick the lot of you out of my house and resume my original plan of moping on my birthday?"

"You have a grey hair." Iris's voice was a whisper.

All the drama was over a grey hair. Relief, touched with exasperation, filled Petra. "Of course I have grey hair. I am seventy today, after all." Iris released her and she turned so they could see her roll her eyes.

"You're practically dead already." Marina smirked.

"Harpies don't age like mortals. They don't get grey hair from old age." Iris's voice was stronger this time.

Petra brought up an image of her mother. She felt a pang that it took a handful of minutes to remember the details. Her mother's hair was less curly than hers, but just as dark. She did not recall her mother having grey hair, even though she had been the ripe old age of one hundred and twelve when she had shoved Petra out the door.

Dora took the comb from Iris and resumed combing Petra's hair as though the tension in the room had not ratcheted up over the discovery "If not from age, then what?"

Iris placed a hand on Petra's shoulder. "Harpies only age if they have not yet given birth to a daughter by their eightieth birthday, if they have not removed their daughter from their house by her fiftieth birthday, or if they have formed an attachment not approved by their creators. It signals the beginning of their mortality and a quick death."

Petra chewed her bottom lip. "Stories could be wrong?"

Dora laid a hand on her shoulder. "There is the prophecy too. Maybe this and the prophecy are related?"

"I think she'll live for today, but I want to do some extra research and be sure. There are only one or two mentions of any harpy generations who are as close as the three of you. It might make a difference, in the long run." Iris took a section of Petra's hair and began to braid it.

"A difference in the prophecy or my impending death?" Petra relaxed again under Dora and Iris's hands.

Marina rummaged around in the kitchen and she clattered a pan on the stove. "We're all going to meet Charon on the banks of the Styx sometime." Meat sizzled as it hit the warm iron. "You said your dreams were bad last night. Did anything happen to set you off?"

A parade of images of the argument she had with James and the time she had spent with him yesterday went through her mind. She pushed down the miasma of emotions within her and kept her voice as level as possible. "James and I got in a fight after we left town the other day."

Iris's hands paused. "About what?"

Petra rubbed her hands over her thighs. "He wants to start mining on his land."

"That doesn't sound so bad." Marina flipped the meat.

"He thinks there is some evidence of the lost myth of Zeus in the Rockies." Petra twined her fingers together.

The other three women all spoke at once. Iris waved a hand and shushed the other two. "What is his reasoning?"

"He knows that Zeus was dethroned, though he does not understand why. He is a believer in the goodness of Zeus." Marina snorted and Petra continued. "He has a journal, passed down through his family, of research and fragments of information, which have led him to believe some part of Zeus escaped being destroyed on the top of Mount Olympus."

Iris came around and sat in an empty chair. "Has he said anything to you about being a Remnant?"

"No." Petra rubbed her face. She had let her growing feelings for James get in the way of the realization that there was something else going on. "Nothing. And I think he would have by now. We, well, we get along well. I think we are becoming close. He asked to come visit me, you know, like a proper visit, and he kissed me when I left yesterday." She said the last in a rush and closed her eyes to the shocked faces in the room.

"He kissed you?" Dora asked.

"He asked to court you?" Iris asked.

"How could he not know he is a Remnant if he has a book with research and legends?" Marina scowled.

Petra chose the easiest questions to answer first. "He did, and the kiss was more than I expected. He wants to court me. What do I say? Am I going to have to tell him the truth? How can I leave him behind? I can't stay here if I have his daughter, and he would never allow me to leave with his child." Petra plunked her head on the tabletop for the second time in three days. "What a mess."

"Those are all excellent questions, but it does not change the fact that he thinks that bastard Zeus was some kind of hero." Marina removed the pan from the stove.

Iris frowned at Marina. "Only you can decide how to handle your relationship with James."

Dora sat in the other empty chair beside Petra. "If you want us to leave Turning Creek, we could start over. As long as we are together, I would be willing."

Petra swallowed the tears in her throat. She had only been thinking of herself. Whatever she chose to do would affect all her sisters and Iris. Shame at her selfishness overwhelmed the good feelings Dora's declaration had stirred. "Gods, I don't deserve any of you."

"I never said I'd leave." Marina crossed her arms over her chest. Petra knew most of Marina's statements were bluster. The ones she meant were the ones that ended in someone getting bloody.

Petra took her time to answer. "Nobody's leaving. There has to be a way to figure this out. I want to get my hands on that journal."

"You sure you just don't want to get your hands on something else?" Marina batted her lashes at her. Petra felt her face heat.

"Either way, I don't think I have enough information to decide about either James or his mislaid belief in Zeus."

"Enough of this conversation. There will be time later. Now, we have a birthday to celebrate." Iris gave Petra a reassuring pat on the back, and they all sat down to eat.

CHAPTER 11

Petra grinned up at the peak above her cabin. The day was crisp and the sky clear. Atlas's Peak was as bright as her mood. Only good things could come on so fine a day. It had been pleasant to spend the day with the other harpies and Iris yesterday, and after the initial conversation, they had kept her from wallowing in her doubts about James. The night had ended with Marina practicing her poker skills on them.

It was too fine a day not to think good thoughts. While brooding was something she was more accustomed to, Petra chose to think of James with a smile. His wording had been careful. James Lloyd, the dairy farmer, was coming to court her, a harpy with a violent nature. There were many reasons Petra should have told James no when he asked, but she was tired of telling herself all the reasons she should not spend time with him.

An awareness settled over her. Someone was coming. Petra looked up. Dora's brown and white speckled form marred the piercing blue of the sky. Dora was flying fast and veered to dive straight into the small yard before the cabin. Petra's gut twisted and the chickens clucked and flapped wildly as Dora pulled up in the last second before she crashed into the ground.

"I need you to come into town with me," Dora said without preamble. The deeper pitch of her harpy voice gave her tone an extra urgency. Her angular face was pale, the freckles which usually dusted her face were muted in her harpy form.

Petra's anxiety at Dora's demeanor increased. Her harpy twisted in anxiety. "What is it?"

Dora shook herself but remained in her harpy form. "There's been some trouble. The new doctor, the one we thought was a follower of Asclepius, raised a little boy from the dead last night."

The twist of anxiety released. True descendants of Asclepius were said to carry the ability to call a person's soul back to their body. He had saved someone's life. That did not sound terrible, but there was fear sliding through Dora's eyes. It was not an easy thing for a harpy to feel fear. "Surely, you are not here because a boy is alive this morning?"

"Some of the people in town are accusing Dr. Williams of using dark arts to save the boy, and Iris was with him when it happened. The word witchcraft has been levied."

The metal taste of fear filled her mouth. "Iris?" It had not been that long since the fear of witches had run rampant through towns and villages in many parts of the world. Remnants with unexplained manifestations of power had often been caught up in the fever. Iris's grandmother had narrowly escaped being burned at the stake after predicting a storm that wiped out a nearby village.

"Yes, the sheriff has Iris and the doctor under surveillance until the hearing." Dora was afraid for her sister.

"Surely no one is listening to a few when they can be grateful a boy is back with his family." Petra thought of those who would accuse a man who saved a life and a woman who was the definition of kind to all. Fury wore away at her fear.

"At first no one was, but someone was able to whip them into a frenzy. A crowd seized Doctor Williams and Iris and dragged them down to Vine's saloon. Someone tied a rope to the banister. The sheriff showed up before they could get the rope around Dr. Williams' neck. He took them into custody and reminded the mob that everyone should have a chance to defend themselves."

Petra grabbed a bag from a peg by her bed and shoved some clothes into it. "What do we need to do?"

"The sheriff is worried that if the crowd becomes a larger mob, he will be unable to control them. He has a couple local men helping, but no deputies. We've never needed them before. Turning Creek has been a quiet place. It's been a few days since you were in town, but the size of the tent streets on the outskirts of town have doubled in the last week. Not all of the newcomers are exactly law-abiding. Iris told the sheriff we could help. He was dubious, but he agreed to let us be with her since we are what amounts to her only family."

Petra snorted. "It would be easiest if we just dispelled the mob. The emotions might be high, but with our three powers combined we might be able to do it. Even if we could, together, disperse a mob, how in the Styx does she expect us to stare down a mob looking like this," she waved towards herself, "and not like vicious vultures?" she pointed at Dora. "We can't just fly down Main Street in our feathers and teeth; though if it meant Iris's life, I would do it without regret."

"You know we still have some control over the violence of others, even in our human forms. We could help keep things from getting too out of hand. If things got dangerous, Iris would not be the only one in danger." Dora was softer than the rest of them. She lived in the light and felt things in a way Petra did not understand. Her empathy for the human condition was as deep as the well of black violence Petra found when she looked inside herself. She hated Dora for her humanity and loved her for reminding her not to lose hers.

"Do we need to get Marina?"

"She was in town when it happened, and Iris sent her to me. After she told me, she raced back while I came here. Iris figured if it came to a brawl, Marina was the best one to have on hand."

Petra tied her bag closed and slung it over her shoulder. "Marina is good for some things. I don't like getting involved, but we have to. It's Iris."

"I know."

Petra would do anything to keep her small family safe. "Let's go."

She got to the door, and then hesitated. "Wait. I need to do something before we go." She rushed back inside, grabbed some paper, and scribbled a note to James. Petra tacked it above the door where it would stay dry. "Now, I'm ready."

To save time, they flew as close as they dared to town before dropping below the trees. The rumble of angry voices grew as they walked down a side street. There were rows of tents on the back side of town where there had once been only scattered trees. Irritation at their haphazard placement flared within Petra.

The rumble of voices had turned into a roar by the time Petra and Dora turned onto the dirt boardwalk of Main Street. Petra's steps faltered when she took in the size of the crowd in front of the sheriff's office. She had not even known the town held so many people. Sheriff Brant, with his tall frame, was easy to see in the crowd. He stood resolute in front of the only entrance to the building where his office was located. He was joined by two men. Henry held a rifle like a baby in his large arms. The other man Petra recognized but did not know well. His name was Reggie Miller. He lived on the other side of the valley, on Pikus Peak.

"There's no cell in there. What did Sheriff Brant do with Dr. Williams and Iris?" There had never been a need for a holding cell. Before, anyone making mischief had been tied outside to a tree or left in a cellar until they sobered up or promised to move on. The tree was most effective in the middle of winter when there was five feet on snow on the ground. Turning Creek was not a place riddled with crime of any kind. Petra increased her pace.

"He's tied to a chair in the sheriff's office. Iris is confined to the office. One woman claimed the doctor would escape using black magic and kill them all in their sleep. Sheriff Brant offered to tie her in the chair next to the doctor."

"She sounds like a forgiving sort."

Petra gathered her power into herself and wound as much as she was able into a tight core before they reached the back of the crowd. Though her ancestor, Celaeno, had been created for violence, Petra did not often give into her darker nature by choice. It was too easy to let it take over, to let it have free reign over all her gentler emotions. Violence gave her an armor to hide behind, but it suppressed everything else in its wake. Petra rarely let it go completely because she was never sure if she would be able to bring it back into herself.

Sheriff Brant made eye contact with Dora and Petra then continued to address the crowd. "I understand you want to know what happened. I know you're scared, but I have Dr. Williams and Miss Iris under guard here. They're not going anywhere for the time being. Go back to your houses and we can talk about this in a civilized fashion tomorrow when everyone has a cooler head. There will be a formal hearing on the green."

The crowd was not pleased with this suggestion. "What if they escape?" asked a man in the back.

"I already told you. They are under armed guard, and they are not going anywhere unless I allow it."

"What if he uses his dark arts and compels you to free him so he can murder us in our beds? What if that woman has been spelled by him to do his bidding? What if she's a witch? We could all be next," yelled a woman in the front, her face red with anger. The word witch whipped the already high emotions into a frenzy. The roar of the crowd behind her increased in agreement.

These people were insane. While magic did exist, it was not rational to believe that a man who went to the trouble of saving a boy would then go on a murderous rampage. Petra had heard enough. She scanned the crowd with her other senses and felt that not quite half of them were Remnants. The number startled her. Those who were not mortal seemed to stand on the edge of the crowd, but they could be used to her advantage. The Remnants would know who, or more accurately what, was about to address them the moment she opened her mouth.

From the dark well of her soul, Petra pulled up her harpy nature and pushed as much of her power out into her human voice as she could. Using her violence in her human form was like pushing water through a small pipe. "Many of you have known Iris for a long time. She has only ever been kind. That's enough of this nonsense for today. You're all rational people. Go home. You can do no good here today, but if you stay, you might do something you regret. Do what the sheriff is asking and go home."

The noise of the crowd was diminished to uncomfortable shuffling. Dora filled the space beside her. "Dr. Williams will answer all of your questions tomorrow." She looked to Sheriff Brant for confirmation. He nodded. "The sheriff has said he will conduct a hearing to find out the truth. Until then, Dr. Williams and Iris will remain in his custody." The key to influencing a Remnant or a mortal was clear speech and repetition.

The power of Dora's voice danced up Petra's skin, and her harpy cried to be released into this crowd to wreck real violence. With her sister behind her, they would be invincible. Petra held it in check and channeled the feeling into her human voice. "Go. Home. Come back tomorrow in a calm, rational manner, and you will have the answers you seek." As soon as they could concoct some reasonable lie to feed them. The harpies and Iris could hardly tell the town of Turning Creek a good portion of their citizens were the leftover descendants of gods. As for the Remnants who were in the mob, Petra wanted to know why they were there at all. "Go now." Petra pushed more power into her words.

In twos and threes, the crowd began to melt away, kicking up dirt as they walked down the street. Some went through the doors of Vine's. Petra hoped a few rounds of Vine's brew would not embolden them further. Dora and Petra stood silent and glaring until the last person, the red-faced woman from the front, disappeared around the corner of a side street. She left a sour aura behind her. Petra was not certain what she was, but she was not a mortal.

Sheriff Brant sagged against the door frame when the woman was gone from sight. He held a rifle in white knuckled hands. He looked from Dora to Petra. "I'm not sure what just happened or how two unarmed, snippets of women just sent an angry mob on their way, but I'm going to accept it and say thanks. I've learned lately there are some things that cannot easily be explained."

"This is a mess," Petra nodded to Henry and Mr. Miller. "There were a lot of faces in that crowd I did not recognize."

Reed Brant shifted his weight and the gun in his arms. "People have been streaming into town for the last couple weeks. I'd swear the population doubles every couple days."

"Who's guarding the doctor and Iris, Sheriff Brant?" Petra asked.

"Please, you ladies saved my skin. You can call me Reed. Marina is with them. They already agreed to the hearing, so I trust neither of them will run. They were chatting quietly when I left. The doctor isn't a threat to anyone, and Iris would never hurt a soul. Henry, if you'll stay out front and look imposing, Reggie can sit by the back door. Hopefully, that is the last we see of the crowd until tomorrow. I'll show the ladies inside."

Petra reached out and gave Henry's arm a squeeze. He smiled but remained silent. Petra followed Reed through the door and heard Dora step in behind them.

The first floor of the building was one medium-sized room. A desk was off to one side with a large gun safe behind it. In the farthest corner, Marina sat on the edge of a cot. She held a six shooter in a loose grip on her thigh. Marina rarely carried a gun openly. She preferred to keep her weapons hidden. Across from her, a man sat tied to a chair with his back to the door. Iris sat in the chair behind Reed's desk.

Marina stood when she saw them. "What took you two so long? I tried to convince Reed to let me talk to the mob, but he didn't seem to think I would do much good." Marina winked. Petra rolled her eyes. Marina would have started a street brawl.

"Don't you take anything seriously?"

"Where's the fun in that? The doc and Iris were never in any danger. I could've gotten them away easy." Marina holstered her weapon, which looked natural on her hip.

"Easy, yes. In a fashion we could explain away, no." They could not say anything else in front of the sheriff. He was already looking at the three of them with a calculating eye. They would have to give him some kind of explanation. He was too smart to accept whatever excuses they could concoct to cover the truth.

The three harpies surrounded Iris. Petra spoke. "Are you all right?"

Iris offered a weak smile. "Shaken and surprised, but yes."

Marina made introductions. The doctor looked between the three women with a knowing look. "Not now, doc." Marina nodded in the direction of the sheriff, who scowled. Petra's estimation of him was correct. They would not be able to keep their secret from him for long if they continued to help him.

Dr. Williams was untied at the sheriff's request. "I know you won't go anywhere. Who needs some coffee?" Everyone accepted Reed's offer except for Petra.

They sat sipping their coffee and the silence piled on like a weight. Petra broke it. "Somebody better start talking about what happened yesterday or I'm going to start ripping out tongues." Reed choked on his coffee.

"There's that violent streak I love." Marina winked at Petra.

"That's enough." Iris shot them through with a look. "Margaret Meyers came in yesterday with Jeffery. He'd come down with a fever that had persisted. I took them to Dr. Williams. She was hesitant to go to him, but I assured her he was trustworthy." Petra read between the lines of Iris's words. The woman had gone to Iris first because not all Remnants were nice or benevolent. Some used their power to rule others or take advantage of mortals in the same way many of the gods had in the old days. The woman had gone to Iris first to make sure the doctor was of a benevolent nature.

"The boy was near death when they brought him to me." Dr. Williams picked up the tale. "From what the mother said, it was a simple cold at first, but the prolonged high temperature sapped the boy of strength. He died shortly after they arrived in my office. Miss Iris knows I have," here he paused and looked at Reed, "special skills. She begged me to do whatever I could. She assured me many of the people here would be understanding." There was accusation in his last statement.

There were enough Remnants in town who would guess at the truth and be grateful for his intervention. Normally, Petra would have agreed with Iris. Something else was at work here. "What happened then?" she asked.

"There's a woman, Angelica Brenner, for whom I did not perform the same feat. Her son died five years ago, and she has never forgiven me." Dr. Williams swirled the coffee in his cup and his eyes remained down.

Understanding hit Petra. "The woman in the front of the mob today. That was her."

A tired sigh escaped the doctor. "Yes. She has followed me to every town I thought to make a refuge and waited until I performed what she knew I was capable of to make her move. Her son was older and had already proven himself to be a selfish, arrogant swine who took what he wanted from everyone. I would not save him when she asked, and she has never forgiven me for it."

Petra knew without a doubt the man in front of them was a Remnant of Asclepius. Such men were compassionate, but were willing to withhold their healing ability to those who showed little or no respect for the lives of others.

"I had remained in the doctor's office and was still there when Mrs. Brenner burst in. The rest I think you can figure out easily enough." Iris reached out a hand to Dr. Williams. "You did the right thing."

"I have no doubts. Mrs. Brenner was bound to find her chance eventually. I deem myself fortunate that I have found some allies when she did." Dr. Williams patted Iris's hand and released it.

Petra stared at the doctor until his eyes caught hers. She let her harpy slip into her gaze and leaned forward. "We're happy to have a doctor in town, so don't take this the wrong way, but I'm here because of Iris. If she gets off, so do you. If Iris trusts you, then I do too, but I'm not here because of a warm feeling in my heart."

Marina grinned, but it had a menacing quality. Dora's frown reached to the ground. Iris looked disproving. Dr. Williams took in each of their expressions before replying, "I would not expect anything less than that from three such as yourselves."

Petra nodded in acknowledgment. Iris crossed her arms over her chest. Petra was certain there were words Iris wanted to say to her, but the presence of the sheriff kept them in her mouth.

"I get the feeling there are two discussions going on here." Reed rubbed his chin. His hand rasped against the day's worth of stubble there. "What I can't tangle out is how you two," he motioned to Petra and Dora, "dispersed a small but angry mob with nothing but words when I had been trying the same thing for almost an hour with no effect."

The five Remnants looked at each other and then turned to Iris. She paused. "Sheriff Brant, do you believe in unexplainable things?"

"Like miracles? I'm a believing man, raised in the church, if that's what you're asking."

Iris kept her gaze steady on Reed. It was hard not to trust her when she leveled that peaceful blue gaze your way. "There's a very good explanation for what you saw today and what happened yesterday, but it's not the time yet to tell you. I have to ask you to trust me, to trust us, and let us help you. If we tell you now, you might be called upon to lie tomorrow, and I would not ask you to perjure yourself."

Reed drained his cup and placed it on the desk without a rattle. "I want what I've always wanted, peace and safety for Turning Creek. I do trust you." Reed pointed to the harpies and the doctor. "The rest of you, I know well enough to know you would not outright lie to me, so if Miss Iris gives her word, I'll take it. If she says you can help me, then I will accept your help without questions." The relief in the room was palpable.

"Agreed," Iris said without hesitation.

"But," Reed pointed a finger at each of them in turn. "I want a promise that when the time is right, in the not-too-distant future, you will tell me what the hell is going on here."

"Deal," Marina said before anyone else could reply. Petra cast a questioning glance her way, but Marina was focused on Reed.

"Tomorrow, the hearing will be informal, but we will keep it serious. I will ask questions of both Dr. Williams and Iris and allow them to tell their side of the story. If the Meyers want to speak, I will allow them. If the mood of the crowd is friendly, we can allow some questions or statements, but we'll have to be very careful that does not get out of hand. If the crowd starts to get violent, I'll need Dora and Petra to repeat whatever they did this afternoon if possible."

Marina nodded. "It's possible. We should be able to keep them from erupting, but if there are too many, our skills will be less effective. We could keep them from real violence, but not control what they do exactly." Petra thought that was as delicately put as possible, for Marina.

Reed continued. "I'll accept that explanation against a future discussion. If after the evidence is given, I feel there has been an actual crime committed, I will have to retain both the Doc and Miss Iris until a judge of some kind can be summoned. Are those acceptable terms?"

"Yes." Iris and Dr. Williams said in unison.

A loud grumble erupted from Dora's middle. "Excuse me. I skipped lunch in all the commotion."

"My apartments are above. There's food enough for all of us. We might as well share a meal and talk about how tomorrow will go."

They followed him up the narrow stairs in the back to his sparse apartments. He had one small table and only two chairs, so they sat around in front of his pot-bellied stove on a worn, rag rug. Reed, it turned out, had a pot of roast and potatoes from the boarding house. It took no time to heat up the meal. Reed filled a plate for Dr. Williams and served him first. There was a kindness in him. Regardless of his position, not every sheriff would have stood up to that mob. Petra knew men gave up far more with far less provocation.

They took shifts watching the door so they could all eat. Henry and Reggie had gone home for the night, but they would return in the morning for the hearing. Marina was given first watch.

"I know some about these ladies," Reed waved his fork in the direction of Petra, Dora, and Iris. "but you, Doc, are a mystery. Where're you from?"

Dr. Williams chewed slowly and swallowed. "My family is from Philadelphia. I come from a long line of physicians. There are one or two in every generation. Both my sister and I have the skill." He shook his head. He had relaxed into his story and forgot there was a mortal among them. "We had the ambition to study medicine, I mean. She is a nurse in one of the hospitals in the city where we grew up. I came out west, both to escape my past and to serve those who I knew needed my skills."

"Why here? You could have settled in Golden City or Denver, but you chose to come here, a small town in the middle of the mountains. You could have lost yourself in the city and made a better living besides." Reed made the statement with a nonchalance that failed to hide the intelligence in his eyes.

Dr. Williams shrugged. "All I can say for certain is that I was drawn to this part of the country. I felt this is the place I should be."

The small hairs on her arms rose, and Petra looked to Iris to see if she had heard the implications of those words. No one else was concerned over the doctor's word choice, but it wedged itself into her brain. Her recent days had been filled with people doing things because they felt called to do so or compelled. Billy Royal was searching for something. James felt called to dig. Dr. Williams felt called to be here. There were more Remnants in Turning Creek than Petra thought had been gathered in any one place for generations. She, herself, was under a prophecy of doom and gloom. It could not all be a coincidence.

Reed finished his meal first and went below to relieve Marina. Her footfalls on the stairs announced her return before her face appeared in the stairwell. Marina plopped some roast and potatoes onto the remaining clean plate and sat with her back to the stove.

Marina popped a potato in her mouth before saying, "We have to tell him soon. Reed is smart, and I'll not lead him on for long. He's a good man who should know the truth."

Iris shook her head. "I agree, which is why I promised to tell him the truth when it would no longer cause him danger. There are many Remnants here now, and he is the peacekeeper. He should know."

"That's something I wanted to bring up. There were Remnants in the crowd today. They were mostly silent, but they were there. There were many more than I remember there being in Turning Creek." Petra put her empty plate by the basin in the kitchen.

A pinched line appeared between Iris's eyes. "In the past week they have been coming in from everywhere. Some have legitimate excuses, but most just say they were drawn to the place."

"That sounds promising." Marina's voice dripped with sarcasm, and she shoved a bite of meat into her mouth.

The familiar weight of the prophecy lodged in Petra's stomach. "It has to do with the prophecy and me. Something is coming."

Marina speared a bite of meat on her fork and waved it at Petra. "It's not all about you, darling."

Dora rubbed her wrists. "I think Petra might be right. There are too many strange things happening. It has to all be related. Doesn't it?

Iris rubbed her hands over her face. "My first reaction is to go check my books, but this is nothing I've encountered before. There are some texts I want to check, but it looks like it will have to wait until after the hearing."

"Wonderful. I'll be knee deep in prophecy dung before we know what's going on." Petra plopped onto the floor.

"Sounds like a party." Marina took another bite.

"What prophecy?" Dr. Williams asked.

"Nothing." Petra answered before anyone else could open their mouth.

Dr. Williams laid his empty plate aside and steepled his hands. They were long fingered and strong, a surgeon's hands. "Now that the sheriff is gone, I think I know who you three are," he indicated Petra, Marina, and Dora, "but I have not figured out who you are as yet." He fixed grey eyes on Iris, who met his gaze without blinking.

"We'll tell our secret if you tell yours." Dora issued the statement like a challenge, and Petra sat back, surprised. Dora was the least confrontational of the three of them. "We've risked our lives for you today, and we may have to again. I think we deserve to know what happened."

Dr. Williams placed his hands on his knees. "You're right, of course. My story, like yours, is long and, I expect, complicated, but I'll make it short. I know that we need to conclude our discussion before the good sheriff returns to us. My name is Lee Williams, and I am a follower and descendant of Asclepius. I discovered my heritage and followed the calling of my life to be a physician when I was young, as I have already revealed to you.

"That boy died, but I knew how to bring him back. A mix of magic and knowledge is the most powerful tool on earth. It was such a simple thing to remind his soul it was needed here for more time. Miss Iris asked me to help, and so I did. His heart and that of his mother's were pure." Dr. Williams swept his hand around the circle.

Dora broke the silence. "We are the Remnants of the harpies. Aello," she pointed to herself, then to Petra, "Celaeano, and Ocypete. We controlled the crowd today because they were riding high on the violence of their own convictions. Harpies are creatures of violence. It's our curse and our power. In mortals, we can meld their violence to fit our needs."

"And dear lady, who might you be? For I know you are no simple postmistress. There are too many truths in your eyes for that to be the case." Dr. Williams leaned forward in anticipation.

"I'm the Remnant of Iris, messenger of the gods and first of her name. I was the chosen in my generation to deliver messages when called and to be the guardian of the harpies."

Dr. Williams snapped his fingers. "Of course. Why did I not see it before? The original Iris had golden wings. Do you have them still?"

Petra had never asked Iris about her wings. The harpies had often gone flying, but Iris had never once asked to join them. Petra had never considered that Iris might be able to fly.

Iris worried a string sticking from the hem of her skirt. "No. There are no wings. I have dreams about flying, beautiful dreams where I skip over the clouds and float to the sun, but I always wake up on the ground, in my bed, alone." Iris pulled the string free and threw it into the fire. "I do have a birthmark on my shoulders. It's how my mother knew I was the chosen one."

Iris stood and began unbuttoning her blouse. She faced away from them and pulled her blouse off her shoulders. Petra's eyes darted towards the stairs. Now would be a very inopportune time for the sheriff to rejoin them. Petra's gaze returned to Iris, and she sat transfixed.

On Iris's shoulder blades was the outline of two golden wings. The color shimmered in the firelight and appeared to be on fire when Iris breathed in and out. Petra stood, compelled to touch what she knew was only skin. Iris had called it a birthmark, but they looked real, as if they would spring from her back at any moment, shining and terrible with their beauty.

Petra's hand was already outstretched when she paused. "May I?" Iris's eyes met hers and Iris nodded.

Up close, Petra could see each individual golden feather. If the greatest artist strove to create these wings, they could never be rendered with such beauty and precision. Petra's fingers stroked down the ridge of one wing and the warmth of skin met her fingers. The reality that the golden wings were only skin was a shock when her eyes were telling her something entirely different.

"Iris, they are the most beautiful thing I've ever seen." Dora had walked around to face Iris and cupped the messenger's face in her hands. "Why do you hide them?"

Iris's eyes pooled with unshed tears. "They are my burden and my beauty. They remind me of all I have given up, to be here with you, and they remind me of what I can never be, a true messenger." Iris pulled her blouse over her shoulders and began to button it.

Petra wanted to cry and ask to see the wings again in the same breath. To her, Iris had always been beautiful, but for the first time, Petra understood that she had never seen her real beauty. All of them, Iris, Dr. Williams, and the harpies, were living shadow lives of what they once were, what they had been under the gods. As terrible as that time had been, their ancestors had been fully themselves with their full range of power. An undefined ache filled Petra's heart.

Iris finished buttoning her blouse and sat back down at her place in the circle. "They remind me that I could fly once. Not in this life, but in another. It was a life where I had power and danced on the clouds. They remind me that we are stuck here, on a broken earth, in a broken world, and we must find beauty where it comes and be thankful for the people we love. We only have each other, after all." Dora wrapped Iris in her arms and held her.

Petra loved flying. The sound of the wind roaring in her ears drowned the scream of violence in her soul like nothing else. If she could not fly, she would be lost. Her heart broke for Iris, who she loved like a sister. A hand found hers and twined their fingers together. The smell of summer grass told her it was Marina next to her. Petra squeezed Marina's hand tight enough to rub the bones together, but Marina did not protest. The warmth of Marina's hand in hers kept Petra from feeling this was all more than she could bear.

The doctor closed the distance in a few steps and stopped in front of Iris. "Messenger, you have honored me beyond measure by sharing this with us. If your actions last night and today had not already won it, you would have my unequivocal loyalty. I hope one day to be able to return the gift you have given." Iris smiled at Dr. Williams.

After that, it was time to sleep and prepare for the even longer day that would come with the morning. Somehow, they would have to convince the town that Dr. Williams was a normal man who had worked a normal, scientifically explainable miracle.

CHAPTER 12

There was no building in town big enough to fit everyone for the hearing, so they gathered in the empty yard near the well on the south end of Main Street. It was where the yearly Aspen Jubilee Festival was held in the fall. The Jubilee was the only major social event in the valley, and everyone came.

Reed set up chairs for Dr. Williams and Iris in the middle of the open area. Henry and Reggie were off to the far side of the clearing with a table where Reed had declared all firearms would be kept until the end. Dora, Marina, and Petra were dispersed strategically throughout the crowd. Marina was closest to the front. Petra was to the left of Iris in the middle of the crowd. They had all followed Reed's no weapon rule outwardly, but Petra knew Marina had a knife or two hidden in her boots.

The people of Turning Creek came in trickles and clumps. Petra knew some of them, but there were many she did not. A tease of power here and there told Petra there were Remnants scattered amongst the humans. With this many people, Petra had trouble separating the Remnants from the mortals. The people brought blankets or simply sat in the short grass and whispered to their neighbors as they waited. Petra eyed each set of newcomers and waited for one of them to step forward and do something deplorable, but they all sat there as if settling in for a stage drama. Petra admitted to herself that if Iris had not been involved, she might have come as a spectator as well.

Reed cleared his throat and lifted a hand for silence. The effect on the crowd was immediate. The birds continued to sing in lilting tones accompanied only by the wind. The peaks loomed over them and Petra wished for an instant that she could solve this problem with tooth and claw instead of words.

Reed's voice cut through her thoughts and the silence. "Thank you for coming. Grave accusations have been made against this man," Reed moved to stand behind Dr. Williams and then shifted to stand behind Iris, "and this woman."

The crowd was silent.

"We'll hear his accounting of what happened and then hear from witnesses. After that, we can discuss what we've heard, but I'll have the final say in what happens here today. You, the entire town, asked me to be sheriff, and I take those responsibilities seriously. I will not, at this first testing, back down and allow justice to be circumvented by emotion. If the majority of you disagree, we can elect a new sheriff. Later.

"First, some rules. We'll hear from Dr. Williams, Miss Iris, and the witness. You'll listen respectfully and without comment, or you'll be asked to leave, with force if needed. After the testimonies, we'll discuss. You'll abide by the decision made here today and go in peace."

Heads nodded in agreement. Mrs. Brenner, who had secured a place up front, crossed her arms but her mouth remained shut. If she opened it, Petra would shut it for her. A small part of her wanted to come to blows today. Petra called forth that anger and grasped it tight. She might need it later. She eyed the woman with the crossed arms and waited.

"Miss Iris, you're first," Reed said.

Iris stood. Her eyes appeared wide in her pale face. She twined her hands together. "Mrs. Meyers came to me yesterday, with Jeffery in a cart. I could see he was not doing well. We're fortunate to have a doctor in town now," she paused to smile at Dr. Williams. Her voice gained strength as she continued. "I urged her to take the boy to the doctor. I have spoken with him a few times. He came to visit me soon after he moved into town, like you all do." Iris smiled to the crowd. "I thought he seemed like a nice man. She agreed, and we took her son to the doctor.

"Jeffery was not doing well when we arrived. The doctor had us bathe him, but his fever continued to get worse. At one point, Jeffery stopped breathing. Dr. Williams tapped on his chest in a rhythm, not unlike a heartbeat. The boy woke up. It was a miracle. We were lucky, Dr. Williams knew what to do."

"Thank you, Miss Iris. You may sit." Reed turned to the doctor. "Dr. Williams, please tell us, in your own words, what happened yesterday."

Dr. Williams stood and straightened. He took a deep breath and started. "Mrs. Myers brought her son Jeffery to me yesterday. He was running a fever. His poor little body was burning up. I tried to bring down his temperature by sponging him down. His mother and Miss Iris helped." He looked the audience in the eye as he talked, unashamed and with nothing to hide.

"His breathing was labored, and he had developed a rash." At the mention of a rash some people squirmed in their seats. Rashes could be a small portent of something much more dangerous, like small pox or measles. Dr. Williams put out a hand, palm down, in caution. "Not that kind of rash. He had developed a rash due to his prolonged fever. The fever itself was caused by the cold the boy had been battling. His breathing became more and more labored. After some time, his breathing seemed to ease, but then the boy stopped breathing altogether."

The crowd leaned forward to hear the next words. Petra scanned their faces and saw mostly curiosity, not animosity. Perhaps they would get Iris and the good doctor out of this trial in one piece without coming to blows. The exception to the general mood was a cluster of people in the front. In the middle of them sat Angelica Brenner, her face twisted in bitterness.

The doctor continued. "Alarmed, I waited for the breathing to resume. When it did not, I tapped on the boy's chest, which can loosen the congestion and encourage the heart to beat. I would tap, then wait, tap, then wait. After a few attempts, I was about to give up when his eyes opened and he woke up."

A sigh went up from the audience. Collectively, people were ready to be manipulated by a good story with emotion. The woman yesterday had whipped them into a frenzy as easily as Dr. Williams had made them anticipate his triumph over death. Mortals were too easily controlled by the emotions of others.

Sheriff Brant walked from behind the doctor and angled himself so he could face Dr. Williams, Iris, and the crowd. "Was there anyone in the room with you when this happened?"

"Yes, the boy's mother, Margaret Meyers." The doctor pointed to a handsome young woman sitting with her arms around a tow-headed boy who was no more than five. A man with salt-and-pepper hair and two other children snuggled together with them.

"Was there anyone else in the room at the time besides the boy's mother and Miss Iris?" Sheriff Brant pressed.

"No, sir."

"Thank you, Dr. Williams." The sheriff turned to face the Meyers family. "Mrs. Meyers, would you be willing to tell us what you saw yesterday morning in the doctor's office?"

The woman stood and brushed grass and leaves from her skirt. She faced the crowd. One hand gripped a blue shawl tighter around her shoulders, and the other sought and found the hand of her husband. "I took Jeffery to the doc because Miss Iris said he could help. Jeffery was having so much trouble breathin' and he was burnin' up. Doc put him on the table and took a wet rag and had me help him rub him down. It seemed to help and then," her lip trembled but she continued, "Jeffery started strugglin' for air. I thought he was going to die." Tears slipped down her cheeks and dripped from her chin. She did not wipe them away, but left them, a testimony to her fear.

"He stopped breathin' and the doc tapped on his chest and listened, then would thump again and listen. I prayed to the Lord for a miracle. I didn't want my baby to die, and the Lord heard my prayer. Johnny drew a breath, then another, then another, and then his eyes opened and he looked at me."

The front of her shawl was wet with tears. She pointed to Dr. Williams. "That man saved my Jeff's life. Nothin' evil happened in that room. He's a good doctor. Miss Iris was there out of kindness and concern, same as she would do for any of you. The Lord saved my baby, not whatever nonsense you've heard." Mrs. Meyers stared down Mrs. Brenner, who seemed to shrink before the censure. "We're lucky to have such a good man here. Anyone who says otherwise will have to go through me."

"Thank you, ma'am. You may sit." Sheriff Brant paused and a beam of sun shone on his sandy hair. "Is there anyone else here today who'd like to say something?"

Petra moved her weight to the balls of her feet. If there was going to be trouble, this would be when it erupted. Petra sent small tendrils of power into the crowd to better gauge their emotions. The Remnants closest to her sat up straighter and looked in her direction. She backed off and made herself relax. The tension stretched and grew, but the crowd remained silent. The woman who had stirred the crowd into a frenzy the day before had her lips pressed together in a line. She stared intently at her lap. Petra willed the woman to look up so she could stare her down, but the woman did not comply.

Simon stood. "May I speak?" The sheriff nodded. Petra relaxed and choked off a sigh. If Simon started speaking, they could well be here for hours. "For years we've waited for a doctor to settle here. We've watched our loved ones and friends suffer from illnesses and maladies which could've been healed had we a proper doctor. Now, we have one and we want to send him off for doing the very thing for which we've prayed. Dr. Williams, I ask that you forgive us for the behavior exhibited yesterday. We hope you'll choose to stay past this day and know you have friends here."

Simon's eyes bore a hole in the back of the woman's head, who seemed to shrink even more. Her circle of supporters, so tight with malice at the beginning of the proceedings, had, by degrees, moved away from her so she now sat in a small clearing alone. The tide had turned against her. Simon regained his seat. Petra had never heard him speak so succinctly. Miracles were possible, it seemed.

"Thank you, Simon, for your words. Anyone else?" The trilling of a songbird was the only response the sheriff received. "Well, then. Unless there are objections, I find nothing foul or dangerous about Dr. Williams's actions yesterday regarding the Meyers boy." The mood of the crowd broke and people smiled. A relaxed exhalation went up into the air. "If, in the future, one of you would like to bring charges against one of our own, I ask that you would do so in a calm manner and refrain from vigilante justice, which is not something I permit in my town."

The audience, chastised, rose and milled about the field. Some people went to the doctor to shake his hand and talk. Others approached Reed, who had dropped his official sheriff demeanor and tried to look relaxed.

Petra had lived in Turning Creek for over eight years, and she had never been included into the fold the way Reed and Dr. Williams were now. If it took a near lynching and a miracle to gain their trust, Petra would pass. She crossed her arms and squeezed them close to her body.

A hand grabbed her arm, and Petra jumped. Marina tilted her head and regarded her with calculating brown eyes. "Where did you go?"

"Nowhere."

Marina's eyebrows rose and she let the lie slip by. Petra was grateful. "Dr. Williams has invited us to his house for supper. Will you join us?"

"Only if Iris is going. I have the urge to keep her in my sight." Petra walked to the knot of people surrounding Iris. It was cheating, but she sent little sparks of power in front of her to suggest to the crowd they should move.

Petra walked through the opening and felt Marina behind her. Dora was already standing by Iris. Petra wrapped her arms around Iris and tucked her head down so her mouth was by Iris's ear. Petra whispered in a voice pitched only for Iris. "I'm thankful all was well today. I would have torn them to pieces for you. We need you."

Iris returned her hug. "I would never leave any of you. Who else would keep Marina out of trouble?"

Petra released Iris with a smile on her face. "Let's go celebrate."

Dr. Williams offered Dora his arm, and she accepted it with a pink blush. Interesting. Petra's eyes followed them. Marina and Reed walked side-by-side without touching. Marina's arms gestured wildly and a booming laugh from Reed caused Dr. Williams to turn behind him before continuing on.

Iris came up next to Petra and offered her arm. "Come, my bird. Let's walk together." Petra took the offered arm, grateful for the unquestioning acceptance.

"Usually, after a day like this, I just want to go flying." Petra cast a sideways glance at Iris. "I wish you could fly with us."

Iris was silent and Petra opened her mouth to apologize, but Iris cut her off. "Sometimes I forget they are there because I can't see them, and other times my heart breaks because I want them to be real. I know you struggle with your harpy. I know how the violence and anger of that form threatens to overcome you. I know you're scared that one day it will and that you'll no longer be Petra but the animal inside, neither woman nor bird of prey, but something vicious and terrible. Something in between." Petra's steps faltered and Iris increased her grip on Petra's arm until their steps resumed their natural cadence. Petra had never admitted her fears to anyone. She barely examined them closely when she was alone.

"I know because that is how I feel about my wings. I don't deliver messages because I want to. I deliver the words of others because I have to. The need to carry the words of others is a desire so deep within me that if I denied the need, it would burn me up. I wake at night with my shoulders aching with the need to fly, but the gods left us here and my wings are gone."

There were no tears on Iris's face but they filled her words. Petra stopped and took Iris in her arms and squeezed her until her arms hurt. "I love you," she whispered in Iris's ear.

"Thank you," Iris breathed back. They linked arms again and increased their pace to catch up with the others.

CHAPTER 13

Petra stayed in town for a few days to make sure things had truly settled down. She helped Iris flip through books and scan parchments, looking for mention of harpies aging or the lost myth of Zeus.

Petra reached the last page of the book she was reading and closed the book. "Nothing in this one. I'm getting frustrated by our lack of finding...anything."

Iris's lips twitched up as she ran her finger down a parchment. "You lasted two more days than Marina."

"We've only been looking for two days."

"I know. She never was very good at research."

Petra rubbed at the aching spot between her eyes. "I don't think I'm much cut out for this either. I need to get back to my cabin. I will stop by and see James on my way home. I told him he could come and see me and then I disappeared for days. I don't want to send him more mixed signals than I am already." Petra placed her book on the stack of items they had already combed through.

Iris left her finger on the line she was reading. "And are you sending him signals?"

Petra chewed her bottom lip. "Yes, I think, maybe."

"All he asked was to come and court you. You didn't agree to anything more binding or complicated. There is nothing wrong with getting to know him better or spending time with him. Relax and see where it goes. Perhaps he will surprise you."

Petra stood and paced the length of the room. "I think the surprises in this relationship will be the ones I have to spring on him if I ever tell him the truth."

Iris left her stool to come and stand beside Petra. "I'm not saying it's not complicated, but don't start trying to solve problems you don't have yet.

One day at a time." Petra nodded. "Same with the prophecy. Don't borrow trouble, yet."

"How did you know I was worried about that?" Petra had tried to keep the growing weight of dread and fear to herself, especially after the way Iris had responded on her birthday.

Iris gave her a hug. "I know you. I know when you're worried and brooding."

"According to Marina, I'm always worried and brooding," Petra grumbled.

"It's a fine line, I'll admit. You harpies do love to brood. I know you're worried about how the prophecy will affect all of us, but remember that prophecies are not straightforward. The words do not always mean what you think or come to pass in the most obvious fashion."

"Yet another reason to rejoice."

Iris tucked some hair behind her ear. "I also know you, Marina, and Dora decided not to leave me alone for awhile."

Petra tried washing her face with a look of innocence. "I have no idea what you are talking about."

Iris wagged a finger in her face. "I'm not an idiot, and I know the three of you too well. It's my job to watch over you, not the other way around."

"That may be the case in your mind, but you are our family and thus ours to protect. I know we have not been as territorial as our mothers in terms of land, but we would do anything for you. Just agree to let us keep you safe just as you try to do for us. You aren't going to change our minds."

Iris laughed and pulled down Petra's head and kissed her cheek. "As you wish, my bird. Now go. Fly away and go back to the mountain you love. I'll stay here with the books and find answers."

Petra went home first. After being gone for a few days, there was work to be done, and she did not make it down the mountain to see James until the next day. The note she had left was gone, so she did not worry about the extra day. Robert and Adam walked out of the farm house as Petra approached.

She smiled in greeting, but here hello faltered when she looked at their faces. "What's wrong?"

Adam turned to Robert. "Go get started with the cows. I'll talk to Miss Petra and join you in a few minutes." Robert tipped his hat to her as he walked past them. Adam gestured to the table in the yard. "Will you sit a spell with me?"

"Of course." Petra sat, swallowing the ball of worry in her throat. "Where's James?"

Adam took his hat off and rubbed his fingers through his hair. "He's up at the mine."

Petra had to force the words out of her dry mouth. "The mine?"

"After you left the other day, we've only seen him when he comes home to sleep."

An insistent buzzing noise filled her ears. "What does he say when he comes home at night?"

"Almost nothing. Robert asked him about it the first night, and he clammed up. We confronted him last night, and he threatened to give us our wages and send us on our way." Adam placed his hands flat on the table. "Something is not right about him."

James loved his farm, and if Petra knew him at all, she knew he would never abandon it. She also knew he cared about Adam and Robert and would never send them away without just cause. Petra suspected something else at work and thought of Billy Royal. He was digging in a place only miles from James, and they both sought something similar. Petra did not think it was a coincidence.

"Has James said what he was digging for?" Petra asked.

"That's the thing. When Robert asked him if it was gold or silver, he laughed, but it was...wrong. He has been reading through this journal over and over. I searched his book case for it yesterday, thinking it would give some clue, but it was gone. I think he's keeping it with him."

"I'll talk to him, but I can't promise anything. I can't imagine he would listen to me when he behaved with anger toward you and Robert. He cares about both of you." Petra stood.

"He does care for you. You're the first person he has made friends with since we started the farm. He cares for you more than he's admitted. Wait here." Adam went into the house and returned a few minutes later with a parcel. "Mister Lloyd skipped breakfast. Here's some food for him. Will you come back down? Let us know how it went."

Petra took the parcel. "Thank you. Of course I'll come back down."

Adam tipped his hat and walked toward the barn. Petra looked at the mountain behind the house. Something unearthly was causing problems on her mountain and in her town. She needed to start finding some answers. With steps heavy with determination, Petra hiked toward the mine.

She found the shaft easy enough. It was a large maw in the side of the mountain. For a handful of days of work, James had made more progress than she had thought. Adam had not been exaggerating about how much time James had spent at the mine. A large tailings pile was off to the side of the mine. James was moving dirt by the bucketful, but he was not sorting through the dirt he was dumping or doing anything more than simple digging. Adam had been right. James was not looking for gold or silver. Petra knew he was looking for something more dangerous.

A steady thunking sound came from the black mouth of the tunnel. She leaned into the opening. "Helloooo." She heard her voice stretch and grow as it bounced down the tunnel.

She waited for some moments, and then James's voice bounced back up to her. "I'll come up. Stay there."

James shielded his eyes when he stepped out of the darkness. He blinked like an owl. "Good morning, Petra." James paused and turned his abused eyes towards the sun, which was already past its zenith. "Or should I say afternoon? I tend to lose track when I'm underground. This is a pleasant surprise."

"Will you come take a break? I brought you some food from the house. Adam said you've not been down there all day." Petra did not succeed in keeping the worry from her voice.

James shook his head, as if to clear it, then said, "That sounds like an excellent idea. I'll admit when I had not seen you for a few days, I thought you might have gone into hiding. I found your note, though, so my mind was eased."

Petra led him to the shade of a nearby tree. The presence of the mine was an itch between her shoulder blades not unlike the watchful eyes of a stranger in a public place. She sat so that the mine was situated to her left. She did not want the mine at her back. James sat directly across from her, but he was careful to keep the mine in his line of sight, Petra noted.

"Why would I go into hiding? Did I commit some heinous act I have no recollection of?" Petra smiled and started unpacking the parcel from Adam. She had missed this easy banter while she had been in town.

James's stomach growled.

"Hungry?" she asked.

"Famished." James rubbed his hands over his knees and looked at the ground between them. "I thought perhaps you had changed your mind about letting me come to visit you in a more formal manner. I thought you had gone home and changed your mind about letting me pay my respects to you." His neck turned a delightful shade of pink, which deepened as it spread to his cheeks.

Petra reached across the space between them and laid her hand over one of his, still resting on his knee. His fingers twitched under hers, but she grabbed his hand and squeezed. "Our time together has not been one of the regrets of my life. I was kept away by some events in town."

Petra grabbed a slice of cold beef and cheddar and put it in the hand she had been holding. "Eat." The tang of cheese and the smokiness of meat filled the air. James took a bite and stifled a groan. Petra raised an eyebrow at him but said nothing. He ate as if he had not eaten in days. He polished off the food in his hand greedily and grabbed for more. He stopped, noticing he had her attention.

"Please," she said, "don't slow down on my account." He slapped another slice of meat and cheese on a chunk of bread.

"You said there had been some trouble in town?" he asked in between bites.

"Dr. Williams saved a boy's life. It turns out there is a woman in town who holds a grudge against him, and she got enough people to believe he had performed some kind of witchcraft that they tried to string him up. Trouble was, Iris was there when it happened, and she got caught up in the mess."

James swallowed and sat up. "Is Iris all right?"

Petra's heart melted at his concern for her friend. "Yes, but I think it went better because she was involved. While people do not know Dr. Williams much yet, they know Iris, and they know how big her heart is. Even so, there was an angry mob. We held a hearing. Nobody died, so all ended up fine." Petra shrugged and turned her smile on him.

James stared at her, transfixed, until she looked away. James brushed crumbs from his lap. "I'm glad Miss Iris is well. I can honestly say that this is the first time I have ever had a woman use an angry mob to excuse her unwillingness to spend time with me."

Petra laughed. "I couldn't have made up a better excuse if I had tried."

James's eyes darted to the mine, but his lapse of attention was quick, and then he focused back on her. She was not sure why, but she sent her awareness out from her, searching for that small trickle of power that marked someone as other than mortal. When Petra had first met James, his aura was a whisper of something "other." It was faint, a tease of a smell on the breeze. Today it was stronger, more pronounced. Terror sped up her heart. His eyes bounced back to the mine.

She picked at the waist of her skirt. "Adam says you've been spending a lot of time in the mine. How's the digging going?"

James moved his eyes to rest on her. "I'm sorry. I was distracted. Could you repeat that?"

The terror was a weight pushing her into the ground. Her harpy was ready to respond in anger. It wanted a fight, but Petra had nothing to fight with but a pile of stones. "I asked how the digging was going."

James turned a proprietary eye on the mine. "Wonderful. I've made some amazing progress."

"That sounds great." In an effort to shift his focus, she asked, "I was wondering if I could look at the journal you were telling me about the other day. I mentioned it to Iris and she was very keen to see it. You know she collects writings on Greek mythology, and I thought you might let her borrow it." James had not begun digging in earnest until he had read the journal again. Petra wanted to know what it said.

James rubbed his jaw. "It's a family heirloom, but I trust you. It is on my desk at the house. You can borrow it if you'd like." James's focus went back to the mine and stayed there.

Frustration welled within the pool of dread in her belly. If she changed in front of him, he would cease to look at his mine. His focus would be consumed by the monster in front of him. Petra suppressed the urge to be overly dramatic. "Do you want to go back to work?"

James's eyes moved from the mine to her, but they took a minute to focus. "Would you like to come and see it?"

While going underground was not her first choice, she wanted to see if there was anything otherworldly about this hole in the ground James had dug. She pasted on her best effort at a smile. "I'd like that."

James stood and held down his hand to her. His hand engulfed hers in warmth as he lifted her to her feet. He kept her hand in his as they walked to the mine, and Petra felt the need to fly, but this time from something other than rage. The feelings that James evoked within her were equally wild and untamable, but they left her breathless instead of out of control.

At the lip of the mine, Petra hesitated. James tugged her hand. "Come, there's nothing down here but earth." Petra hoped he was right and made her feet take her into the darkness of the mine.

The tailings pile did not do the depth of the mine justice. Petra had trouble believing James had dug this far in a few days. The shaft was well-formed and went down several feet into the side of the mountain.

"This is amazing. I can't believe you've done so much in so little time."

James stopped and turned to her, a look of surprise on his face. He blinked and the expression was gone. "I'm surprised myself." He stopped at the end of the tunnel, where the wall of earth was jagged from his pickaxe. It was dim, but he lit a match and held the flaming end to the candle laying on the ground. The wick caught and James shook the match until the flame went out. The smell of sulfur and burning wood mingled with the damp earth.

James picked up his pickaxe and started working. Petra took a step back and watched him swing and listened to the thunk of the metal as it dug into the earth. James's concentration was on the wall in front of him. Petra thought it was like he had forgotten she was there. She took another step back.

She had only known James well for a small span of time, but he was a rational man. His behavior this afternoon did not reflect what she knew of him. Petra centered herself and pushed her questions aside. She gathered her power and sent it out into the cave.

Nothing. What she felt from the cave was nothing. Frustration boiled up within her. There had to be an explanation for James digging this mine, on this particular spot, but Petra could sense nothing. She thought if there was something of Zeus involved it would leave a trace or something. There was some quality of the mine itself that was affecting James. He continued to hack large chunks of the wall aside and paid her no attention. Petra was unsure he even remembered she was there.

"Perhaps you should take a break from digging." Petra laid her hand on James's shoulder.

He paused, mid-swing. "No."

Petra considered her options. It was not so dire that she needed to drag him bodily from the mine, yet. "Please, James. Something is not right here. You must feel it."

James did not turn around. He continued to swing the pickaxe in to the wall. "I will not stop. You have no right to ask that of me."

Hurt crumpled her features, but she rearranged her face into a mask. "This isn't right. You love your farm, the cows, and making cheese. Something is wrong. Talk to me. This isn't like you."

"How would you know what I'm like? You barely know me. You have no right to demand things of me. It's my land, and my choice. You have no right." The pickaxe shook in his hands as he faced her.

She did have the right. Rage flared within her and she embraced it. "You're wrong. We are becoming something more than friends, and I have the right to ask when I see you doing something destructive to yourself."

"It's my land. Mine. What lies beneath the earth is mine. I'll find it, and everything will be different. It'll be better. You have no right to stop me or make demands of me."

Something flashed in his eyes, but it was gone before Petra could categorize it. It left her unsettled. Petra swallowed whatever retort had risen on her lips.

His words sliced through her. "Please leave. I have work to do."

The pain was quick and sharp. Petra felt her harpy roll close to the surface. James took a step back. She scrabbled and dragged the hurt and rage into a ball and pushed it into a dark place she could take out later and examine. Hurt flowed into the void left by the rage. "I'm sorry to have intruded upon you." Her words were clipped and formal but it was better than the violence raging in her head.

Petra turned and started toward the light at the end of the tunnel. The sound of the pickaxe drowned out the crunching of her footsteps.

***

Petra went to the house first. She ground the twisting hurt and anger under her feet as she walked. The journal was where James said it would be, sitting on his desk. The brown leather was stained, but it in good condition. Petra rubbed a hand over the cover. Something in this book had sent James on a journey into the earth and away from sanity. Petra wanted answers.

James's words had wounded her. He might as well have sank the axe into her chest for the pain running through her. He had sent her away as if she meant nothing to him, and there had been a moment when something else had flashed behind his eyes. Petra was more and more certain something was not right with James and his mine. She rubbed the cover of the journal as she walked.

She went to the barn in search of Robert and Adam. The door of the barn opened the moment before she touched it.

Adam jumped. "Miss Petra, you startled me." His brows knit together. "It looks like your conversation with the boss didn't go well."

"If he gets worse, send a message to Iris. She'll be able to reach me, though I'm not sure what good it'll do. He's made it quite clear he wants nothing to do with me or anything besides the mine, for that matter. Styx and fire." Her hands were shaking. She slapped them against her legs in an effort to keep the shaking from spreading to the rest of her body. If she did not leave here soon, Adam was going to get a very ugly, firsthand lesson in Greek mythology. "Send word if you need."

She escaped before Adam could reply.

CHAPTER 14

Petra did not cry. Anger was far easier to handle than the hurt. Her harpy had wanted to rip something up, preferably James himself, but Petra was not so far gone as to consider it, good though it might feel.

She half ran to the trees until she was concealed within them, and then she ran in earnest. The argument with James replayed over and over in her head. It had gotten out of control too fast. Something was wrong, something more than a newfound interest in mining.

The earth, Petra thought as her legs propelled her through the trees. She was not far away enough from the farm to fly. Her harpy cried to be released. Not yet. The earth. A mine in the earth. A hole in the earth. A wound. A wound in the earth.

Petra stumbled and caught herself on a tree. Bile rose in her throat. A wound in Gaia. The prophecy was coming true. James's mine was the wound in the earth. The wound which would reveal something lost. Fear, acrid amongst her anger, twisted. James sought Zeus or something of him, and Petra was afraid of what he would find at the bottom of his mine. He needed to stop digging.

She sunk down to the earth. The scent of pine needles rose from the ground beneath her knees. He was unlikely to listen to her now. He had sent her away.

She was such a fool. She had begun to wonder, to breathe hope into the idea that she could find a place here in Colorado where she could build a life that looked different from the life her mother had taught her. Petra had started that life with her sisters and Iris. She had begun to hope James might be included in some way in this new life.

Petra was not going to let this disappointment drive her from her home. If James did not want to see her, then she would not see him. The mountains were big; she had been here for years without seeing him, she could go many more years without seeing him again. Anger at his rejection was easier to bear than the hurt. Whatever he found at the bottom of the hole was no longer her concern. If only she could believe her own lies.

She would have to tell the others of her suspicions. If James was truly seeking something of Zeus, then all the Remnants and mortals in the region were in danger. Her ancestors had stood against him once, they could do so again. Petra fervently wished her fears were groundless.

Petra released her harpy, and it ripped through her. The release of the violence was a relief. She clutched the journal in her talons, and with a cry, Petra leapt into the sky. Birds scattered from the trees as she tore over the tops of the aspens. It felt good to see the small birds scatter in fear. The wind in her face and the power of her anger drenched whatever tender emotions she had felt.

In her foolish dreaming, Petra had forgotten who she was and mislaid the true darkness of her soul. Her mother had never allowed her to forget. She was ashamed at her recent behavior. She would not make the same mistake again. It would be a long time before she forgot again what being a harpy meant.

Marina and Dora were waiting for her in their harpy forms when she landed in front of her cabin. Petra reigned in her tornado of emotions. She loved her sisters. It was not their fault she was in a foul mood. "What is it?" She knew from their expressions something had happened. Dora was serious, and Marina's eyes snapped in excitement.

"Strange things are happening in town." Even in her harpy form, Dora managed to appear calm. Petra did not understand how Dora kept her harpy so reined in.

"There was a brawl at the saloon last night and this morning. A miner drug himself into town, telling a story about two women who are offering money to any man willing to be hunted." Marina rubbed her clawed hands together. Her desire for excitement was going to give her strife one day.

Petra wanted nothing more than to be left alone with her anger. "Saloons have fights all the time. It's what drunk people do. Wait, if the men are hunted, how does that make them money? You can't spend money if you're dead." Petra pinched the bridge of her nose. Her claws were cold on her skin

Marina's laugh sounded more like a hoarse cough. "If they reach the drop point before being killed, they keep the money. It's brilliant."

"It's barbaric." Dora scowled at Marina, the expression forbidding on her angular face.

Marina's feathered shoulders went up and down in a semblance of a shrug. "If the men are stupid enough to make the bargain, then why can't I enjoy the farce of it?"

The pressure in Petra's head increased. She needed a drink, many drinks. "What does this have to do with me?" Petra's anger was morphing into apprehension. She would not like the answer to her question.

"Reed wants our help. He knows we have a way with crowds. Marina and Iris agreed we could offer some extra help until things die down. Marina also offered her services as a tracker to find the women responsible for the hunts." Dora was unable to meet Petra's eyes, but Marina grinned.

Petra did not think much of Dora's answer. "Well, I didn't offer my services. I didn't want to get involved last time with the doctor. I only did that for Iris. What makes you think this will be any different?" Petra rose to her full height and struggled to keep from calling the darkness to them. It would serve Marina right if she called forth her power and made her sister cry for mercy.

Dora's voice calmed her. "There's some reason why all these things are happening. Iris thinks it has to do with the Remnants who have been arriving in the last few weeks. It's time we started taking a more active role in our territory. Iris thinks we should help if we can. This is our home, Petra. We shouldn't stand by and let things like this happen."

"Why the hell not?" It was hard for her to care about some fool miners too blinded by greed to avoid certain death when she wanted to figure out the problem with James first.

Dora changed into her human form. The freckles on her face were as plentiful as her pale skin. "We aren't animals."

Petra hated it when Dora appealed to her humanity. "You're right," she said. Dora's posture slumped in relief. "We're going to have to tell the sheriff the truth, though."

Marina's predator eyes glittered, and her smile revealed pointed teeth. "I want to be there when you tell Reed. I want to see his face."

Petra rolled her eyes. "You enjoy the strife of others too much."

"A girl has to find amusement where she can."

Petra argued with herself and blurted her fears out before she could think better of it. "I think all the strange things going on have something to do with the prophecy. The prophecy said, ' A time of sacrifice and pain. A wound in Gaia will reveal that which was lost.' I think the Remnants coming in and the violence erupting in town is all related."

Marina's eyes, for once, did not gleam with anticipation. "I think you're right. We should talk to Iris when we can."

Petra took a deep breath. In for a penny, in for a hundred pound weight around her neck. "There's something else. James is digging a mine on his property, and there's something...off about it."

"It could be nothing," Dora said.

"It could be the calf eyes you've been making at him are clouding your judgment." Marina added. Petra clenched her fist to keep from slamming it in Marina's face.

Dora glared daggers at Marina. "Now's not the time for a fight between us. Let's solve the problems in town first. Talk to Iris when you can."

Petra did not like putting James to the back of the list, but she nodded and held up the journal. "I'll give this to Iris while we deal with the other problems. Maybe she'll find some answers to help us by the time we are done."

Dora changed back into her harpy, and the three sisters left for town. Petra did not think they would find anything good once they got there. After some discussion during the flight, they went to the sheriff's office first instead of going straight to Iris. The sheriff's desk was empty, as were his quarters upstairs. Marina led them back out onto the street.

It was midday. The sun was warm enough to keep the chill in the air at bay, and people were going about their business, dodging horses and carts as they rattled up the dusty street. The crack of gunfire halted traffic.

Marina took off in the direction of the saloon. The shock of hearing gunfire within the town limits froze Petra to the spot. Dora was hard on Marina's heels before Petra could get her feet and mind moving. Marina pulled out the gun she had tucked into her belt as she ran. She always had been one to shoot first and ask questions later, as long as nothing else caught her attention.

Marina reached for the door and it flew open. Marina was not quick enough to get out of the way of the door, and it struck her arm. Bone pierced through the skin. Inventive words spewed forth from Marina's mouth. Petra was impressed with the variety. A black-haired man with a profusely bleeding, bulbous nose came barreling out of the saloon.

Another man was propelled through the door, with Reed holding the collar of a shirt that had seen better days. It was surprising the fabric was holding up under the assault of the sheriff. Reed deposited the second man on top of the first. Petra did not think the sheriff needed their help for this fight and stepped back.

Marina slumped against the building, away from the door. Her skin was tinged green. Marina had her broken arm pinned to her side at the elbow with her good arm. The splintered bone must have cut a blood vessel. A pool of blood grew by drips in the dirt at Marina's feet. Her breath came in little gasps. They needed to get her off the street so she could change and heal her arm enough to ease the pain and stop the bleeding.

"If I catch either of you in the saloon again for anything else but a well-behaved, solitary drink, you'll be run out of town or I will lock you up. I would prefer to never see either of your ugly faces again. Consider this your first and last warning." Reed swiped his forearm across his mouth, smearing blood on his shirt.

The sheriff's warning had been enough, but Dora stepped up to the two men who were struggling to their feet. Two were better than one, and Petra joined her sister. The pull of Dora's power tickled her senses, and Petra dug into her soul and added her own darkness to Dora's.

The daylight continued to shine on Main Street but a chill that had nothing to do with the coming fall descended upon the area in front of the saloon. The men struggled to their knees in front of the harpies. Their eyes widened with a growing realization the sheriff was not the thing they needed to fear in Turning Creek. Even mortals could sense the power of a Remnant when faced with the unequivocal truth of it, and these two were not mortal.

Dora's blue eyes were hard, and her voice could have frozen water. "You will not cause trouble again, or you will face much worse than banishment or a jail cell. Do you understand?" Dora looked like an innocent maiden, but her voice held the steel-and-nails quality of her harpy voice.

"Yes, ma'am," the men nodded and babbled in unison. Dora bore her icy eyes into them while they stumbled over each other in an effort to get away from the diminutive woman who appeared to want nothing more than to rip them to shreds. Petra had half a mind to chase them down the street.

Reed swung Marina into his arms, careful of her broken arm, and walked toward his office. "I can walk, you oaf." Marina's protest lacked conviction.

"If you say so."

"Put me down."

"I will. As soon as we get to my office." Reed spoke over his shoulder. "One of you go get the doc and meet me in my apartment." He did not wait for confirmation, but instead increased his pace.

The ice went out of Dora's eyes and she looked at Petra. "I'll go. You follow them. Make sure she doesn't kill him."

Petra snorted. "I'm not getting in between her and anything she wants to do when she'd wounded. You know how she is." Petra dropped her voice. "We have to tell him. There's not a way to explain this away, and Marina needs to change to begin healing."

Dora ran a hand through her hair, pulling some of it free from its binding. "I know. I know."

"Go. Bring Dr. Williams. And please, be quick. I won't tell the sheriff anything without you."

"Should we get Iris?"

Iris would have to be told, but with Marina wounded, time was not on their side. It would be better if they could explain some things to Reed before Marina had to change and heal. "Yes, but let's get this sorry business over with first."

Dora nodded and ran off in the direction of the doctor's office. Petra jogged in the direction Reed had taken.

She had never before told the secret of the Remnants to a mortal. All the mortals she had met who had known had been told by someone else. Petra was unsure how to break the news to Reed gently. The world he lived in was a bit more complicated than he imagined.

Petra heard Marina shouting as soon as she went through the office door. She took the stairs two at a time and hoped she could make it before Marina shed any blood.

"Stop fawning over me. I'll be fine. I just need to be alone for a moment."

Marina was propped up in Reed's single bed. Reed glared down at her with his hands on his hips. Petra smothered a laugh, and Reed turned at the sound.

Marina pointed with her good arm. "Tell him to leave me alone and go away. It's not so bad. I can fix it." Her other arm continued to bleed onto the towel Reed had placed underneath it. An unhealthy paleness had replaced the green on Marina's face. She had lost a lot of blood.

"Fool woman. How are you going to fix your own broken arm? That door must have hit you on the head." Reed leaned over and ran his large hands over Marina's head, feeling for lumps.

She batted his hand away and tried to move her head out of his reach. The sudden movement jostled her broken arm and her skin turned the color of the sky before a storm. She lay back on the pillow, panting. Petra looked around the room for a bucket or basin in case Marina lost the contents of her stomach. There was a chipped ewer on a stand with a rag. Petra wet the rag and put it in Reed's hand.

"Christ, woman. Be still before you do yourself more harm." Reed put the rag on Marina's forehead, and she shrank into the bed.

Dora came in, followed by Dr. Williams, who was holding a black medical bag. He knelt by Marina and placed two fingers on the wrist of her good arm. He spoke to her in low tones. Marina gasped when he touched her broken arm.

The doctor finished his examination and stood up. "The two lower bones of the arm and a few of the bones in the hand are broken. When your arm broke, one of your vessels was cut, and you've lost more blood than is good for you. Setting the bones will be painful and difficult. I can't guarantee you will have full use of it if I set it. How much will you heal if you change?"

"Enough to get the bones set, the pain eased, and make the bleeding stop. It'll be tender for a few days, but it'll heal fine if I change." Marina said through clenched teeth. "But I'd prefer for that to happen sooner rather than later. I'm starting to see stars."

"What do her clothes have to do with any of this?" Reed demanded.

Petra exchanged a look with Dora. It was time to tell the sheriff. "Sheriff, what do you know about Greek myths?"

"What the hell does that have to do with anything? You three women make no damned sense." Reed clenched and unclenched his hands.

"Just answer the question, please," Dora said, always the diplomat. Petra would have shaken him by the shoulders first. Marina, if she were feeling better, would have punched him.

"The basics, I suppose. Zeus and all his wives and children."

"He only had the one, and she was not the kind who enjoyed sharing her husband." Marina's answer was thin, but steady.

"I only stayed in school long enough for the basics. The intricacies of Greek myths were not taught," Reed said. "What do myths have to do with Marina's arm?"

"Sheriff, you have trusted us to help you protect the town, now we need to ask you for something more. What we need to tell you is not exactly a secret to some, but it is not well known. Can you keep a secret?" Petra asked.

Reed's eyes landed on each of them in turn before he nodded.

"Remember when Iris asked you if you believed in unexplainable things? What if we told you myths weren't exactly myths or reality, but something in between?" Dora, the least intimidating of the three harpies stepped closer to Reed. "The gods were real, but when their believers died out, their power did too. Before they faded from this world, they enabled the lower creatures and minor gods and goddesses to remain on the Earth as Remnants. We blended with humans, some more than others, and over the generations, we have come to live mostly normal lives except that we are not normal."

"We?" Confusion warred with understanding on Reed's face.

"We," Petra indicated her sisters and herself, "are descended from the three original harpies, Ocypete, Aello, and Celaeno."

Reed opened and closed his mouth several times. "You're harpies? Actual harpies? I thought harpies were foul, ugly-faced birds."

"Who says we aren't? We fly and everything." Marina answered from the bed.

Reed glared at her. "Well, that explains your sunny temperament."

To her credit, Marina laughed and then winced as her shaking moved her arm. "I think I like you, Reed."

"Don't get too attached. You make me crazy." The sheriff spun on his heel and pointed a finger at Dr. Williams. "And you? Are you a myth too?"

"We are called Remnants, and yes, I'm one of them as well. I'm descended from Asclepius, who was punished by the gods for bringing a boy back to life."

"So you did bring that boy back to life?" At the question, Dr. Williams nodded. Reed continued, "If this is all true, what happened to the gods, like Zeus, Hera, and Hercules?"

"Some of them were killed in the Fall of Olympus," Dr. Williams said, "which is a story for another day. Some faded from history because they could not stand to be part of a world where they were no longer worshiped. They not only needed the belief of others to retain their powers, they also needed to be worshipped to exist emotionally and spiritually. They were an egocentric group."

It was time they got this conversation moving where it needed to go. Marina was looking worse. Petra spoke up. "We can prove what we say is true. Marina needs to change into her harpy form to help her arm heal. It won't heal all the way immediately, but it'll speed the process and prevent complications."

Reed swiveled and looked at each of them in turn. Petra could see when his decision was made; a calm steadiness took over his features. "Do it."

"Thank the gods. This arm is killing me." Marina closed her eyes. The change was swift. Three blinks of an eye and one would miss the sprouting feathers and sharpening of the face.

Marina had risen from the bed as she made the change, and now she shook herself out, spreading her wings and taking up a large amount of space in the small room. Petra felt her own harpy cry to be let out. After the display in the street and then the drama of this room, she wanted nothing more than to let her baser emotions run free. Petra tramped them down. There would be time for that later, she hoped.

The sheriff was a tall man, but his head barely reached the top of Marina's tan-colored chest. He took several steps back and craned his neck to see Marina's new form. Marina, instead of showing apprehension as Petra would have done, preened under his scrutiny. Petra envied Marina's confidence.

"What do you think?" Reed jumped at her voice. Marina twirled like a dancer. The effect was more macabre than graceful.

"You sound different, like Dora in the street earlier."

Marina's laugh was like glass being ground under a boot. "Your observation skills are outstanding. No wonder we asked you to be sheriff. Harpies are prone to violence. We've a voice to match our nature." Reed glared at her, no small feat since she could disembowel him with a flick of her talons.

The sheriff seemed to be taking the news in stride. He was, if it was possible, too comfortable with the disclosure. Petra said, "Now that you know, you'll also understand why we were able to help with the crowd at the hearing. Harpies were made to torment and control people with violence and fear."

Without a word, the sheriff stalked to the cabinet above the kitchen area. He pulled a bottle filled with brown liquid from a shelf; the only other occupants were some glasses. Reed left the glasses alone and swigged a hearty amount from the bottle itself. "Anyone else want some?" Marina waved her clawed hand, and he passed it to her, careful to avoid touching her.

Reed rubbed his chin. "This does clear up a few questions I had, and honestly, it is more probable than any of the crazy ideas I concocted on my own. The one thing I don't understand is why my town seems to be going crazy. Do you know that fight you saw me break up was the third one today, and it's not even noon yet? I got a report before I had to go to Vine's that there's a pair of women hunting men for sport up on the other side of Atlas's Peak."

Petra and Dora exchanged a look. "We heard about that. Marina, do you remember those two women we met back in Vine's?"

Marina cocked her head, a natural gesture for a bird, but not entirely normal for a human. "Oh, those two rough women you did not want me to drink with, Atlanta and Cyrene?" She looked down at the sheriff. "Petra is never any fun, but she is right. It's probably them."

"I need an explanation in words someone who is not descended from gods can understand." Reed rubbed his forehead.

"We're not descended from gods. We were created by them. Pay attention." Marina indicated the doctor. "He, on the other hand, is actually descended from Apollo, who was a god. The original Asclepius lost favor by displaying too much power."

"Cyrene and Atlanta were famous huntresses during the time of the gods. Sometimes Remnants retain the nature of their ancestors, and sometimes that nature is twisted over time. Their desire for difficult hunting has likely changed Cyrene and Atlanta from their original nature and stolen some of their morality." Dora went to the stove and stoked the fire. She filled the kettle with water and placed it on the top to boil.

"So I have two crazy huntresses up in the mountains killing men. Great. Why all the fighting at Vine's? Are Remnants rare? Why don't more people know about this? Is it common for so many Remnants to be in one place?" If Reed rubbed his forehead any more, he was going to rub in permanent indentions.

Dora answered the easiest questions. "Remnants are rare, but not as rare as you think. Mortals, normal humans, don't often know of our existence, but some do. Like mortals, Remnants sometimes marry and have children, which often necessitates the disclosure of certain things. Remnants don't usually congregate together in the same region. I think Turning Creek is rather unique in that respect."

"So Remnants and humans can have children together?" Reed asked.

Marina took up the explanation. "The gods had children with mortals all the time. Zeus never could keep his pants on. Sometimes there are limitations. A harpy, for instance, can have only one offspring, a daughter. Each generation of harpies has the ability to find each other, if they choose. Some generations see each other infrequently, others, like us, live in close proximity."

Petra only half-listened to the discussion with Reed. There was some piece they were missing about Daniel Vine. He could be the root of what was going on in the saloon, and not only because he owned the drinking establishment, but that would not explain the huntresses.

"What do we know about Daniel Vine?" Petra interrupted Marina telling the sheriff how they had come to be in Colorado. "He's a Remnant, but I'm not sure if he's powerful or not."

"Which means he is harmless or very dangerous," Marina said.

The group took the interruption in stride. "He owns the saloon, and he makes his own liquor and beer. Doesn't seem the type to stick his neck out for others. He was not the one who called me about the fights. It was Iris, who can see the brawls when they tumble into the street." Reed said.

"Three women live with him who do not appear to be connected to him either romantically or by familial ties. Though there were rumors when they arrived, the women are not his whores." Dr. Williams offered. Petra looked at him when he spoke. She had forgotten he was there.

"Fights keep breaking out in his saloon," Dora concluded.

Petra turned to the sheriff. "How does Vine react to the outbreaks after you show up?"

"He seems unconcerned, even amused by the arguments. His amusement was what angered me most. He did nothing to control the situations before they got out of hand. By the time I was called over, fists had already flown. The doc here patched up some of the men from an earlier argument."

Petra pressed the others. The bartender may not be the only piece of the puzzle, but he was one she could solve now, unlike James. She knew she was right about Vine. "Who makes his own brew and has a band of women following him around who have the ability to unhinge men? In the myths, they tore apart men with their bare hands."

Marina flapped her wings. "Dionysus. Of course, who else could it be?"

"I thought he was a god. You said they died off." Reed took a sip from the bottle Marina held out to him.

"Daniel Vine is not the actual Dionysus. He's probably a great, great, great, great, great-grandson or something. Whatever he is, though, he retains enough of his ancestor's power to be dangerous." Marina took the bottle back from Reed.

"He's very clever, but he doesn't hide his nature as well as he thinks." Petra felt smug at knowing the answer before the others.

"I'm not sure he cares enough to hide," Reed said. "Dionysus is the one who caused people to drink in excess and go into rages of ecstasy, right?"

"Right." Marina's eyes gleamed.

Petra punched Marina in the shoulder. The effort was lost on the harpy, but the words were not. "You could pretend to act like you care that our town is going crazy."

Marina stuck out her tongue at Petra. "Since when do you care about your territory? Is this about James?"

As soon as she could get Marina alone, Petra was going to kill her.

"James Lloyd, the dairy farmer?" Reed asked.

"Yes," Marina replied.

"No." Petra crossed her arms over her chest and glared daggers at Marina. The heat of a fierce blush cascaded over Petra's face, and the effect of her anger was spoiled.

Dora stepped between them and brushed a lock of Petra's hair behind her ear. "It's greyer today. Did you know?"

Petra shook her head. "I've not looked in a mirror in a long time."

"Whatever he's doing, it's making you more empathetic, which is good. Unfortunately, he's also making you possessive and grumpy." Marina ruffled her feathers. Reed stepped back to get out of the reach of her wings.

A spike of anger at the truth behind Marina's words shot through her, but she let it go. Marina wanted her to react, so she would not give her the satisfaction. Petra focused on the sheriff and ignored Marina. "What do you want us to do? We'll help in whatever way we can."

The sheriff looked at each of them, considering his options. His gaze stalled on Marina, taking in her tan and brown feathers without any of the apprehension or fear Petra had expected. She had always considered the sheriff to be competent and friendly, if firm. She added unflappable to the list. It was an excellent quality for a sheriff.

"Can two of you handle Atlanta and Cyrene alone? With things getting so out of hand in town, I'd like to stay here and keep an eye on everyone. I'd also like to go have a conversation with Daniel Vine about the kind of behavior he allows in his establishment. One of you can stay here with me in case things deteriorate."

"I'll stay and help Reed." Marina said. "I'm the best tracker, but the fight with those two will be very hands on, and I do not have the full use of mine. If I stay here, I can just scare people into submission."

"You'll have to change back. While I think you are very intimidating like that," Reed waved an arm at Marina, "I think you'd alarm most people."

"I was hoping you'd be more alarmed."

"Sorry, sparrow. It takes more to startle me." The sheriff delivered the line deadpan. Petra did not ever want to play poker with that man.

"Did you just call me sparrow?" Marina harrumphed. Dora snickered, and Petra full out laughed. "I'm a bird of prey, dammit."

Petra laughed again. It was not every day the harpy met a tongue as quick as her own. Marina needed to be put in her place. Petra was glad she did not have to do it.

"Petra and I will leave now. There's still enough daylight to get into the mountains and find their trail." Dora grabbed her rucksack. "We'll check back in two days or send a message. If you don't hear from us, send Marina to find us."

The sheriff nodded. "Wait. Before you go. I can't deputize you, as we're not officially a territory yet, though I hear it won't be long now before the United States brings us under their wing." The sheriff smiled at his own pun. Marina rolled her eyes. "You won't be working in an official capacity for the city, but it also means you have more leeway when dealing with the hunters. I don't care how or even if they come in. I just want them stopped, understand?"

"Crystal. In all honesty, Sheriff, I think we have the easier end of the bargain." Petra grabbed her pack and turned before reaching the door. "You're the one who has to work with the sparrow."

She gave Marina a wicked smile and walked out.

CHAPTER 15

They did not make it past the boardwalk before Beth Kramer, Simon's wife, ran into them. Her hair was disheveled and her eyes were wide. She composed herself and then grabbed Petra's arm.

"He's been gone all day. He went out and never came back. I thought he had gone for a walk before getting the water. He loves the sunrise, but he never came home, and now, now I think he might be dead." Her frenzied entreaty contained more words than Petra had ever heard her speak in eight years.

"Who's gone? Simon?" Dora asked in a smooth tone.

Sarah nodded frantically. "I got worried after he missed the midday meal. Something is wrong. I asked the trees." Sarah looked back at Reed, who was hovering behind Petra and Dora.

Petra turned around to give him a look and then returned her focus to Sarah. "The sheriff knows a little, but not all. You can trust him." Petra knew Sarah's power was weak.

"I am the Remnant of a minor nymph. I can sense the things on the air or listen to the talk of the trees. Nothing too exciting. But the trees are agitated. Something bad is coming." Sarah's face was bald with fear. "I'm afraid for Simon."

Petra was uncomfortable witnessing so much fear when she was struggling against her own, but she did not look away. "Dora and I are headed into the hills. We'll keep an eye out for Simon. Marina is staying here with Sheriff Brant, and they will look here. He wouldn't have gone far. He loves you too much."

Reed shouldered Sarah's hand. "Go home, Mrs. Kramer. I promise to send word if we find anything." Sarah nodded and turned to go.

"Gods, I've got a bad feeling about this," Dora said.

"Two days. If you don't see us, send Marina." Petra walked off the boardwalk and made a beeline for the trees, where there was enough shelter to change and get away.

***

They found the site of a kill before the darkness claimed the peaks. The body was fresh, less than two days old. The stench of blood and fear had been easy to locate in their harpy forms. Harpies could smell fear and violence like a hound could smell a rabbit. They found blood spatters amidst a grove of golden aspens. The leaves rattled in their quiet way, and Petra drank in the scent of the man's death like wine. It was intoxicating.

Most days, she worked hard to keep her violence in check and deny her true nature, but James's behavior and his angry dismissal of her made Petra reckless. Thinking of James sent an unpleasant sensation through her chest. The pain was bearable, but it needled at her and wore her down. The scent of the kill site dulled the pain she had felt since yesterday. Petra breathed deeply.

Dora walked in slow concentric circles around the blood on the forest floor, widening her circuit with each loop. The only sound in the area was the leaves above them and their breathing, deep and even, engaged, searching. There was pleasure in the hunt, and Petra could see it reflected in Dora's face.

"This site is only a day old." Dora paused and leaned over a series of blood drops. She sniffed, her harpy face lost in concentration. "He was afraid when he died. His fear is...delicious." Her voice wavered, and for the first time, Petra knew that Dora, always so controlled, also struggled with the violence in her heart. It made her love her sister all the more. The weight of everything—the smell of violence, the prophecy, the hurt from James—pressed into Petra's skin, and she flapped her wings to release the pressure.

Dora looked up from a broken branch. "Is something wrong?"

"No. The smells here are making me antsy." It was not a complete lie, but antsy was the wrong word. It was not strong enough. The feeling inside Petra was savage. It wanted to rip into something. Dora pointed to the body. "They killed him here, but then went west, around to the pass." Dora knelt and turned the dead man's head over, revealing a missing ear. A trophy.

Petra was annoyed at their lack of originality. "You think they have a hideout somewhere near the pass?"

"Makes sense, I think. It would give them easy access out of the valley if they needed to escape, and it would be a good vantage point for getting around to the other peaks."

"Then it's west we go."

Newlywed's Pass was a thin track wedged between the solid mass of Atlas's Peak and Jolly's Folly. According to local legend, Newlywed's Pass was so named after a couple became trapped in a cave on the pass shortly after their wedding. They proved that one cannot live on love alone. Their bodies were found months later. Love is not good for much when the snow is piled high and you are starving.

Marina had a place on the backside of Folly, and the harpies were well-acquainted with all the nooks and crannies in the mountains around their homes. The two huntresses had picked the wrong valley as a base for trouble. Petra's nerves hummed in anticipation. This hunt was going to be fun. She needed the distraction.

They flew on and dipped down twice more to check the trail. The huntresses were cocky. Petra pointed to an obvious trail of footsteps and broken branches on a well-used path leading to the pass. "They did not even bother to hide."

"They either think they're safe from being found or they think they can handle whatever comes."

Petra flashed her pointed teeth at Dora. "They're in for a nasty surprise on both counts. We should wait and continue on once it's dark. They won't expect that. We can reach them within a couple hours."

"You have an idea of where they are."

Petra preened. "The cave up at the mouth of the pass, the one we stayed in two years ago when we hunted that bear. It's big enough and hidden unless you know where to look."

"Let's get going, then."

The women were exactly where Petra had predicted. She'd hoped for a better chase from two famed huntresses. Petra and Dora hung back from the mouth of the cave and watched the two women dance around their campfire. A man was gagged and propped against the wall of the cave opening, his head lolling. His closely cropped black hair was matted with blood from a blow to his temple. They were lucky Simon appeared to be alive. It might be the only thing that would save the two huntresses once Petra got her talons into them.

They watched as Atlanta and Cyrene became increasingly drunk, dancing and passing bottles of Vine's liquor between them. Petra and Dora stayed in their vantage spot until the festivities seemed to be winding down. Petra motioned to Dora, and they inched away from the glow of the cave and into the blackness of the night.

Petra crept away and then maintained silence until they were a good distance from the area. "Any ideas on how to go in? My plan is simple. Surprise them and take them with brute force. They are no match for us in harpy form, especially in their current state."

"Can you call your darkness into the cave itself? We could use it to confuse them when we attack."

Petra did not often call the darkness to her. It was a physical reminder of what she thought her soul must look like, a large gaping black thing without light to penetrate it. The last few times had been uncontrolled, and it had happened as a reaction to her unsettled emotions. It would be a change to use the thing she hated most about herself to do something worthwhile.

Petra nodded. "We can sneak up on them, one from each direction. I will darken the cave and then we will rush them. The darkness will not be complete, but it should cause some confusion. You take the one closest to the west, and I will take the one on the east."

"Are we going to try to take them in alive?" Dora's nose wrinkled with the question. Dora, for all her fierce demeanor, had the softest heart of them all.

"If we have to kill them, then we shouldn't hesitate, but I want to make an example of them. If Remnants are going to keep coming into Turning Creek, they have to know that this is our territory and they are only welcome if they behave."

Until she said the words, Petra had not been sure of her reason for wanting them alive. She questioned why she was on this mountain at all, hunting down two women who were dangerous and a tad crazy, but she was sure now. Turning Creek was her home, and this was her place. She'd spent years keeping herself separate from the people here, but she could no longer remain at a distance. Her distance had almost cost Simon his life. As much as he'd plagued her with chatter, the town needed him—and she was beginning to think she needed the town.

If she was going to live in Turning Creek, she must accept the people in the same manner in which she embraced the mountains. They were hers to protect and to defend. Duty was not meant to be a walk in a flower garden. It was more like bumbling through a thorn thicket.

"Agreed." Dora laid a hand on Petra's arm, breaking her out of her reverie. "Stay safe. Fly true. See you in the middle." Dora sank back into the shadows. With her human eyes, Petra lost sight of her within moments.

The buzz of the hunt filled her veins. The smell of the mountain night, a mix of cedar, wood smoke, and chill, was sharp in her nose, and it filled her brain with alert focus. It had been far, far too long since she'd hunted. Atlanta and Cyrene had chosen the wrong territory in which to hunt. They would soon find out the truth of their folly at their end of her talon.

Petra inched as close to the cave mouth as she could while staying hidden. Once she transformed into her harpy, there would be no hiding the bulk of her form behind a boulder or tree. She settled in to wait. She wanted to be sure Dora had plenty of time to get into position.

Petra measured the time with even breathing. The celebration within the cave had cycled down. The huntresses were sitting, one on each side of the campfire, holding a bottle. Snippets of their conversation carried out to her.

"...be moving on soon... good pickings over near Boulder City. So many miners... no one to miss a few here and there... Couple of days... this one was no fun."

Injustice burned in Petra. She was a creature of violence and vengeance, but that man had done nothing to deserve his fate. The violence of a harpy served a purpose, to punish the wicked and lead others where they needed to go in the afterlife. Petra knew her soul was black, and she lived with the darkness inside, but she only unleashed her worst onto those who truly deserved it. She did not torment people for her amusement alone.

Petra concentrated on the light from the fire first. The moon overhead was small and would not lend much light within the shelter of the cave. Firelight was harder to dispel than daylight. During the day, Petra could simply call clouds and have them do the majority of her work for her. At night, things were different. A small light on a dark night held great power. Lightning in a dark night sky could be seen for miles on a night like tonight, with a weak moon and a cloudless sky.

Petra gathered her darkness like a ball in her chest. She spun it around and wound it tight. Perspiration beaded on her forehead and goose flesh danced on her arms. She spun the sphere of darkness until she could add no more to it, and then she flung it, into the cave, straight at the fire. The cave was plunged into darkness.

The instant the sphere left her, she changed, her harpy ripped from her. She hurtled herself into the mouth of the cave. Her claws dug deep into Cyrene, who had been sitting on the west side of the fire. The woman screeched in pain. There were similar sounds in the darkness on the other side of the fire where Dora was attending to her own huntress.

"Be quiet." Petra dug her claw in deeper into the flesh around Cyrene's collar bone. The chest would have been her first choice, but she did not want to take the risk of puncturing a lung or heart and kill Cyrene by accident. The woman squealed. "Quiet. Listen." There were hiccupping sobs coming from Atlanta. "Dora, you good?"

"Yes. I have her."

"I'm going to release the darkness now."

"Do it."

Petra released her hold on the darkness that had covered every crevice of the cave from the mouth to the very back, where only the sightless animals lived. The darkness had not affected them at all.

The fire whooshed up, and the harpies were exposed by its light. Dora's speckled form was spread over Atlanta. She had one set of talons around Atlanta's slender throat and one was digging into the fattest part of her thigh, dangerously close to where the femoral artery ran. Petra smirked. No wonder the woman had not made so much as a peep since being overtaken.

Cyrene, on the other hand, flailed like a spawning fish in springtime when she saw what was holding her down. Petra moved one of her talons to Cyrene's gut and pricked in, enough to draw blood, but not enough do serious damage. She leaned down and bared her pointed teeth to the huntress and hissed.

"Hell. Harpies. We didn't bargain on harpies." The voice came out constricted because Dora had left Atlanta little room to breathe.

"We didn't know we were in your territory. We don't want trouble." Cyrene's voice was high-pitched with fear. Petra tightened her hold on Cyrene's shoulder. Cyrene was also a disappointing negotiator.

"We aren't going to kill you." Dora's voice was flat. Cyrene's eyes widened until Petra thought they would pop out of her skull.

Petra leaned over once again, touching her sharp harpy nose to Cyrene's crooked one. "Yet." The woman whimpered, and Petra threw back her head and barked a hoarse laugh.

"Petra, stop playing with your food." Dora's comment sent Cyrene into a keening sob, which made Petra laugh even harder.

Atlanta did her best to turn her head towards Cyrene. "For the love of all that's holy, shut up. Why I travel with you is beyond me, you worthless sack. If they wanted to kill us, they would've done it already. They want something." Petra stopped laughing to glare at the woman pinned under Dora. At least one of them had a backbone.

"Maybe I just want to play with you before I eat you." Dora ground her talon into Atlanta's thigh, but the woman made no sound. "Isn't that what you plan to do to that poor man there?" Dora flipped a wing in the direction of the body propped against the wall.

"Harpies don't eat humans." Atlanta spat.

"I might make an exception for you." Dora hissed back. "Besides, you aren't strictly human."

Petra enjoyed it when Dora lost control. It made her feel better, in a twisted way, to watch the gentlest harpy give way to her violent side.

"As fun as scaring you has been, we do want something from you." Cyrene was silent as Petra talked. "You hunted in our territory. You hunted innocents."

Harpies only hunted those who deserved violence as a just return for their deeds. Even in their violence, harpies would offer repentance if it was requested with a pure heart. They were created for that very purpose, to torment a soul until they repented.

"You're not welcome here. We're working with Sheriff Brant in Turning Creek, and he told us we could do whatever we wanted to make sure you got the message." A soft whimper escaped Cyrene. Petra showed her a mouth full of pointed, inhuman teeth.

"You'll leave this region and not return here," Dora said.

"Feel free to spread the word. Remnants, or mortals for that matter, who seek to cause trouble here will find themselves on the wrong end of our wrath. You two were far less sport than I'd hoped, so if anyone doesn't believe your story and wants to try for us themselves, send them over. I'd like a bit of a challenge next time." Petra released her hold on Cyrene's shoulder but ran a talon down the woman's face. Blood welled up and ran down the woman's cheek. She would have a scar to show at the end of her story.

Dora moved off Atlanta one talon at a time. Her eyes never wavered from her prey. Her concentration was a palatable thing. Petra saw a flash of silver, and Dora tumbled back into Atlanta. A ball of flailing limbs and feathers rolled through the cave as Dora and Atlanta struggled over a knife. Atlanta got one decent slash in, and Dora hissed. Before Atlanta could strike again, Dora bit into Atlanta's wrist and the knife fell to the floor. Petra dove for it.

"Styx. Where did she have that hidden?"

Drops of blood fell from Dora's right leg. "Doesn't matter if she can't use it."

Atlanta shrugged. "I had to try."

Petra and Dora nodded in understanding. Atlanta was a true hunter.

Petra turned her focus from Cyrene to Atlanta. "Do not come back here. Stop hunting people regardless of whose territory you are in. Go back to hunting animals. I hear there is big game in Africa, and wide spaces in which to hunt them. You should look into it."

Atlanta turned her head and bore her eyes into Cyrene. "We'll leave and head east until we can find a boat to Africa."

"I'm glad we understand each other." Dora stepped off Atlanta and moved a few feet away from her.

Petra mirrored her movement. "Leave at first light. Don't go through town. Find a different route. It's still early enough in the year, you should be able to get over the pass."

"Your word that you'll go," Dora demanded.

"By the River Styx, I swear we will leave and not return." Atlanta inclined her head in submission.

"Both of you," Petra prompted.

"By the Styx, I swear it," Cyrene repeated.

"Good. Sleep well, ladies. You've a long journey ahead of you," Dora backed out of the cave without looking away from the women.

Petra hopped over to Simon. Careful not to touch his skin, she used her claws to slice through his gag and the rope binding his hands and feet.

Petra picked him up in her wings and hopped him out beyond the mouth of the cave. Flying him back was the fastest way, but the least comfortable for him. Petra leaned into Simon's ear and whispered, "I'm sorry, friend. You can double charge me on my next visit."

Petra hopped on top of him and grasped his belt in her talons. Before she could heave off, Dora said, "Bury that man you left on the trail before you leave." She did not look back but launched in a wave of power and wings into the air. There was no doubt the huntresses would be gone by morning, and the cave would have a new ghost to haunt its caverns.

CHAPTER 16

Clouds obscured the light from the moon, so Petra and Dora were able to fly into the yard behind Simon's house at the edge of town. There was no perfect way to go about dropping Simon to the ground. His feet and arms hit the ground first, and Petra pumped her wings hard to maneuver him so he rested on his side. With effort, she uncurled her talons from his belt and stepped off the shopkeeper. Tingles of pain traveled from her talons and up her legs. She had carried game before, but never so far.

Dora changed beside her. "I'll go get Sarah. You two can move him in while I get Dr. Williams."

Petra changed. The tingling was replaced by a pressing exhaustion. She nodded, but Dora had already turned toward the house. Petra bent over and uncurled Simon. She felt for his pulse and felt the warm breath coming out of his nose. He was still very much alive, but the swelling on his head had not gone down. Dangling head-down during the flight had probably not helped that much.

Light spilled into the yard as Sarah emerged from the house. She ran to her husband's side and knelt in the dirt. "Let's get him inside."

Sarah took Simon's shoulders, and Petra supported him under his waist and legs. They carried him to a bed in one of the rooms. Sarah bustled around lighting lamps and gathering cloths. "Miss Petra. There is a kettle of water on the fire in the kitchen. Will you bring it to me so I can start to clean him?"

Petra brought the kettle back. Sarah cleaned the wound on Simon's head, and Petra checked the rest of his body for injuries. His knuckles were bruised, so it seemed he had fought back. Otherwise, the blow to the head was his only injury.

The sound of the door opening and footsteps made the women pause in their ministrations. Sarah poked her head through the doorway. "We're in here."

Dr. Williams entered the room, and Petra left to give him more space. Dora followed her into the hallway. Petra leaned against the wall and found her legs would no longer hold her up. She slid down the wall and tilted her head back with a sigh. "I could sleep here."

Dora sat beside her. "Me too."

The murmur of voices from the room lulled Petra into a half-slumber. Sarah's voice in the hallway jerked her awake. Sarah knelt in front of them on the wooden floor. She placed one hand on each of their knees.

"Doc says Simon should have a terrible headache for a few days but be fine after that. There are no words I can say to thank you for what you've given back to me. Please know you will always have our gratitude. If you ever need anything, all you must do is ask."

Dora covered Sarah's hand. "I'm glad he's going to be fine."

Sarah stood. "Will you both stay and have something to eat? You look done in."

Petra braced herself against the wall and stood. Her leg muscles howled in protest. "Thank you, but I think what I really need is a bed. I'm going to the depot. If his condition changes, send word, will you?"

Sarah nodded. "Of course." She stepped closer and gave Petra a swift, tight hug. Petra stiffened. "Thank you again."

Petra stepped back as soon as she was able. "You're welcome."

Petra and Dora left Sarah sitting on a chair beside her husband, and the two worn-out harpies dragged themselves over to the depot. They crept in as quietly as possible so they would not disturb Iris. Petra flopped down face first onto one of the beds in the extra bedroom. The darkness of sleep claimed her before she had taken in two deep breaths.

***

With monumental effort, Petra rolled over and sat up. She rubbed the grainy feeling from her eyes and considered flopping back down on the bed, under the covers this time. Petra rubbed a small tear in the patches of the quilt covering the bed. She wished a few more hours of sleep would unravel all the problems facing her.

Thoughts of James put an urgency in her blood. She still had the journal she had taken from James's house to give to Iris. Petra unbraided her hair and re-braided it as she left the room. The upstairs was empty, so Petra went down the back stairs to find Iris.

Iris was sorting mail into slots and humming to herself. "Afternoon, Petra. I was wondering if you were going to wake at all."

Petra poured a cup of tea from the pot on the counter and sat on a stool. "Where's Dora?"

"She left for home this morning."

"How's Simon?" The tea was room temperature but sweet on Petra's tongue.

"He woke up a couple hours ago. Doc says his mental state is fine and has ordered Sarah to keep him abed for another day to let some of the swelling go down and allow him to rest."

"And things in town? Are they the same?" Her stomach growled, and Petra looked in vain for a biscuit or scone.

"Things in town are the same. Marina and Reed have things under control." Iris stopped sorting and produced a plate from underneath the counter. It held an apple turnover, a wedge of cheese, and a chunk of fudge. "Sarah came by earlier. She knew you'd be here and dropped this off for you."

"The gods bless that woman." Petra bit into the turnover. Flakes crumbled over her shirt, but the pastry was worth the mess.

"She was sorry you were not awake when she came. She wanted to thank you again."

Petra licked her fingers clean. "She should not be thanking me. If I had taken half the interest in my territory as I should've, Atlanta and Cyrene would never have been able to take Simon in the first place. When I was young, I thought if I kept to myself, I could avoid the world and ignore what I was. The longer I live here, the more I realize that I want to be part of the world. I want to know my neighbors. I'm not sure I know how I fit into the town and all the people, but there are people here I care about."

Iris walked around the counter and stood with her face inches from Petra's. "You carry too much guilt over what you are and what you have or have not done, my bird. Like any mortal, all you can do is make the best choice you can each day and serve those you love. You think you can only be one way because you are a harpy, but you always have a choice."

Petra pressed her forehead against Iris's. "How do you always have the words I need?"

Iris laughed. "It's a gift." Iris leaned back and her eyes traveled over Petra's face. "There's something else weighing on you."

Petra sighed and pulled the journal from the pocket of her skirt. The leather had water marks on one corner and near the top there was a dark stain that looked like blood, but it was otherwise intact. "This is the family journal James had which made him think some clue to the lost Zeus would be on his land. I flipped through it, but it is in an odd mix of Latin and Greek. Do you have time to read it today?"

Iris hesitated before taking it. "Yes." She rubbed her palm over the cover. "Did you know some books retain the passion of their words, like an echo of their author? It happens more with journals and letters than with things printed on printing presses. This one feels...longing and frustration."

Petra chewed on her bottom lip. "I'm hoping it'll shed some light on what kind of Remnant James is descended from. The mine he is digging is changing him. There is something more than a passing fancy to find gold or silver. I'm afraid the mine James is digging has to do with the prophecy—the wound in Gaia could be the mine itself, and James is searching for the lost Zeus."

Iris sat on an empty stool. "But the lost Zeus is a myth. Our ancestors killed him at great cost. One of the harpy lines died that day, along with countless others. Olympus fell. There is no more Zeus."

Petra wanted to believe Iris was right, but she could no longer ignore the growing evidence that she was not. "How many times have we been wrong about the myths? So much of our history is based on hearsay and biased retellings. Isn't it possible something vital was left out?"

Iris's shoulders slumped. "Of course you could be right." She sat back up. "However, I refuse to be defeated when we do not yet know what we are facing. Give me the day to read this. You go check on James. Come back tonight or tomorrow, and we can share what we have found."

Iris's optimism was good to see, but it did not dispel her own fears. "I'll see you later then. Thank you, Iris."

***

The warm afternoon baked the last of the summer flowers and grass into a fragrance that rolled through the air with Petra while she flew to James's farm. The day was advanced enough that they should have been finishing up with the milking. Petra landed behind the milking barn and changed before walking around to the front and through the door.

The sound of arguing male voices rose over the mooing of the cows. Petra followed the sound to the back where Robert and Adam were both sitting under cows, milking and arguing. Both of them had their backs to Petra.

"It's time we went and got help." Robert said.

"I want to try one more time to bring him down and then we'll go get Miss Petra like she asked." Adam worked while he spoke.

"No need to get me. Here I am." Adam jumped, and the cow he was leaning on shuffled her feet in protest. He grabbed at the bucket and narrowly saved the floor from a milk wash.

"Thank the Lord," Robert said as he stood. Adam placed the milk bucket to the side and faced Petra. His left eye was swollen and black.

"What happened to your eye?" Petra asked.

"One of the cows we've been waiting for went into labor. I went to get Mr. Lloyd. We've not seen him since the morning you last were here."

"He's not been home to eat or sleep?" The heavy fear settled into her middle.

"No. I went to get him. He refused to leave with me, and then punched me when I would not leave. He turned around, cool as you please, and went back to work without a word." Adam picked up the pail and dumped it into the larger holding tank.

"When was this?"

"Early this morning, before dawn."

Robert spoke up. "Miss Petra, please go speak to him. If he won't listen to either of us, maybe he will listen to you."

She would get James off the mountain if she had to drag him down. "I'll see what I can do."

The walk up to the mine did not take as long as she'd remembered. The dread on her heels propelled her towards the opening of the mine. The steady thunk of the pickaxe beat a tattoo that echoed from the depths of the mine and out into the sunny day. Petra did not hesitate at the mouth of the mine, but instead stepped into the blackness.

It took a few steps for her eyes to adjust. The rocks crunched beneath her feet. The sound of the axe grew louder. Petra could see the light of a lamp in front of her, and she followed the beacon. She stopped a few feet away from the arc of the pickaxe.

"James." His rhythm did not change, so she tried again, pushing power into her voice. "James."

His swing glanced off the rock with a clatter, and he turned with eyes blazing anger. Petra gasped and closed the space between them. James's skin was pale, and there were deep circles under his eyes. His cheeks were covered in the beginnings of a short beard. His clothes were torn and dirty, and his hands were filthy. Petra did not think he had even left this hole for days.

She reached up and placed a hand on his cheek. He leaned into her touch and closed his eyes. When he opened them again, they were clear and had lost the angry haze.

"James," she repeated in a softer voice. "Oh, what have you done to yourself?"

He took her hand in his and kissed her knuckles. Her mouth opened in surprise, and he kept her hand in his. "You smell like rain. I'm glad you are here."

"Are you? I wasn't sure you would be."

James winced and gave her hand a squeeze. "I'm sorry we quarreled. The last thing I want is for you to be angry at me."

"I'm not angry." Petra reassured him. "I'm worried about you."

"Why?"

"How long have you been down here?"

James rubbed his hands over his face and paused when he felt the beard growing on his face. "I don't exactly know, to be honest."

There was little enough space between them, but Petra closed it until her body whispered against his. "I stopped at the house first. Adam said you refused to come to help with a calving and you punched him. Something is wrong here, James. This isn't like you. Will you come with me?"

"I punched Adam? Are you positive?" James's eyes acquired a wild look. "I remember him coming, but it's fuzzy after that." James took Petra's hand in his. "There's something wrong here. Why can't I remember what happened with Adam, and why have I been down here for so long?"

"Come out of the mine with me. Some fresh air will do you good. Come with me," she repeated, her eyes pleading but her tone firm.

He looked like he was about to follow her. "Let me just get my lamp to light the way." He dropped her hand and bent over.

The instant his hand lost contact with hers, his posture changed, and Petra sensed the change in him. His hand passed over the lamp and picked up the pickaxe instead.

"James, please. Look at me."

He turned back to where he was digging. The reverberations of the pickaxe striking stone shook his arms and the sound pierced her ears. Large chunks fell from the earth as he continued to swing. A glint of silver caught the lamp light. Petra reached out and the wall of power coming from the earth almost pushed her over. It tasted of greed and power.

Petra threw caution to the wind and put all of her power into words. "Stop. You have to stop. There is something evil at the bottom of this mine. We have to leave." Petra put a hand on his arm and pulled. He yanked his arm away and swung again. More rock fell, and the silver began to have a shape. It looked like the edge of something she had only seen in pictures and had hoped to never see in her lifetime.

It was the edge of a lightning bolt.

She grabbed James's arm and then his shirt when he shook her off again. Her voice was brittle with fear and certainty. "We have to leave now. I know what that is. Styx and hell. The power of thunder and lightning. Oh Styx, we are all doomed."

"You two are doomed, but I think my day is looking decidedly up. That piece of silver belongs to me."

Petra whirled and rolled to the balls of her feet in time to see Billy Royal swing a pickaxe at her head. She felt the axe graze her head and heard it thwack into the wall behind her. Rocks and dirt flew into her face. She threw a punch into Billy's face, and he staggered back, giving her enough time to pull the gun from her belt. She pulled back the hammer and pointed it at Billy's chest.

The sound of a pickaxe digging into the earth rang without interruption behind her. Petra chanced a glance over her shoulder and saw that the entire surface of the silver bolt was exposed. James had not ceased digging during the commotion. Billy took advantage of her distraction and swept his axe low, hooking the back of her legs and pulling her feet from under her. Pain shot up her spine as her tail bone connected with the rock floor of the mine.

A cry of triumph sounded behind her. It was followed by Billy's roar of rage as the large man flung himself around Petra and dove for a gleaming silver object on the floor. He was too late. James held the object firmly in his hand.

Now that it was free of the wall of the mine, Petra could see that it was indeed a lightning bolt. It did not look as if it had just been pulled from the earth. It looked newly forged, without a scratch or dent to mar its smooth surface. James's face held a look of triumph and astonishment. It vanished the moment Billy's head connected with his middle.

The silver bolt flashed in the dark of the cave. An arc of light erupted from the end of the bolt, finding its mark on Billy. Billy's body convulsed and a strangled cry came from his lips before he crumpled in a heap.

Petra knelt beside Billy and felt his neck for a heartbeat. Billy was dead. "James?"

The bolt flashed again and James dropped to his knees. His body shook, like a dog throwing off water, and his eyes closed. His body shook once more and then he lifted his head and opened his eyes. Petra saw the flash of silver in them before they returned to their normal brown shade. The thing in front of her looked like James, but it was not James. The eyes held too much knowledge. Petra sent a tingle out and the weight of the power in front of her dropped her to her hands and knees. She had thought she had felt fear before, but the sentiment curling over her spine and into her head was much worse than simple fear. It was a soul-eating feeling that threatened to leave her at the bottom of this cave.

Petra watched as not-James stood and kicked at the body of Billy Royal. "I am not surprised to find that when I finally emerge from slumber one of Bellerphon's curs is already waiting to usurp my power."

Petra stopped breathing. The voice coming from the thing in front of her was lower than James's and held no trace of a British accent. The accent more closely resembled the speech of the Grecian nobility. "Who are you?" She knew the answer, but she could not give voice to it herself.

He laughed. "Do you not know me after all this time? I know you quarreled about me with this mortal male. I am in his head and he, delightfully, is in mine. Did you know he never once suspected who he is or what you are?"

Petra stood and raised her eyes to meet those of the creature in front of her. "Who is he?"

Another laugh that sent needles down her back. "He is a fool who served my purposes. I needed someone descended from my line to touch the bolt so that I could transfer my consciousness to his. I left enough bastards in the world. I knew one of them would find my bolt eventually. He is angry to have played a part in my schemes but what amuses me more is his reaction to you."

"Why is that?"

"He cared for you, violent, thieving bird that you are, but he is repulsed by the truth of what you are. I should punish you for leading him on in this fashion, but the torment in my head from his sorrow is delicious." The man chuckled.

"I'll ask again. Who are you?"

"My wonderful harpy, have you not guessed? I am Zeus returned. Here to build a new Olympus and punish all those who betrayed me all those generations ago."

Petra did not look away from Zeus, but she took a step forward. "James, listen to me. I know you are in there somewhere. You can still leave here. Put the bolt down and let's go. We can seal the mine and no one will ever find it again. Please."

Zeus narrowed his eyes. "How dare you try to prevent me from completing my schemes? Who are you to presume to stop me? I can feel his affection for you warring with his horror at the knowledge of what you are crawling around in his head. How wearying that will be to listen to for the duration of each night and day. He is strong, but I am stronger. He will not last long."

Despair washed over her. If James were to be won back, it would not be today. She knew Zeus was too powerful for her to take on alone, and she must warn the others. If she attacked now, James could be hurt, and the others would be caught unaware when Zeus swooped down upon them. James was lost to her, for now. She balled her fists tight and vowed to do whatever she could to save him.

Zeus laughed. "This is beautiful. Did you love this human man that I have stolen from you, Celaeno? I did not create you for that tender emotion." Petra blanched as Zeus continued. "Since the day I created you three, I have had nothing but trouble from you. I rejoice to have returned the favor. Go find another man. Like mortal women, they are all the same, pleasurable for a time but then quite mundane. Go. I have work to do."

Petra turned and walked at a clipped pace down the tunnel. Each step felt like she was carrying a lodestone tied to her legs. She wanted to rip Zeus's head off his shoulders, but she could not harm him without hurting James. She tripped toward the mouth of the cave and lay there panting.

Zeus chuckled and called up the cave to her. "Celaeno, tell your sisters

I will be calling them to me. I have a New Olympus to build, and I will need all of the Remnants gathered. I know some have already heard and have come. Only the faithful will be rewarded. The rest of you will have to earn your place at my feet."

CHAPTER 17

There was dirt in the scrapes on her hands and knees, but she kept walking. Petra should have shifted right away and flown as far as she could from what she had left behind in the cave. Everything was fast and slow together. She could see each leaf with clarity but could not focus on a single tree. She was going into shock.

The Bolt of Zeus. That which had been lost in Iris's prophecy was The Bolt of Zeus and not some clue to the myth of the lost Zeus. It was Zeus himself. Somehow it had ended up in her mountain, and now James had found it. No, it had called to him. Because he was a Remnant of Zeus. And now Zeus controlled him. Zeus, a terrible and powerful god who cared for nothing but himself. Zeus, who wanted to rebuild Olympus.

A rising hysteria boiled within her. If she kept thinking about what the return of Zeus could mean for her or this world she lived in, she would start screaming and never stop. Last time Zeus had held dominion over the world, war had been the normal way of life and the harpies had been abandoned on an island to starve and die.

Her feet carried her down to the farm. Petra remembered James's face as Zeus took over. The knife of pain was immediate. She had imagined revealing her secret many times, but she had never dared to imagine that particular blend of awe and horror. The knife twisted and her breath caught. The person she'd left in the mine was not her James. While she wanted to wallow in her own pain, there was a larger problem to face. She had to stop Zeus, and she had to save James.

Adam and Robert were waiting silently on the porch of the main house. They stood as she burst from the trees.

"Did you have better luck than we did getting him to stop?" Robert asked, walking toward her with Adam on his heels.

"No. Boys, listen." At her tone, both men froze. "No matter what you see or hear in the coming days or weeks, do not go up the mountain."

"What's that got to do with the boss being crazy about minin'?" Adam asked.

"Everything. Please. Promise me you won't go up the mountain."

"Can you tell us why?" Robert asked.

Petra hesitated. She liked the brothers, but she knew all the stories and myths. She knew what happened to mortals who crossed paths with gods. She could not take the chance that they would be curious, though she knew they might be curious regardless. "I can't now. I'm sorry. When it's safe, I'll tell you. Promise me you'll stay off the mountain until someone comes and tells you it's safe." Petra threw her power into the words.

"We'll stay put," Adam said, and Robert nodded in agreement.

"I'll make sure your pay still finds you. I have some money stored by. Keep the farm going. When James comes back, he'll want everything to be running smoothly." Petra was going to do everything in her power to make sure he did return to his farm.

"Yes, ma'am," two voices chorused.

"I'll be in town. If you need me, send word through Iris. I'll check in whenever possible."

Petra turned to leave, but Adam's voice stopped her. "Miss Petra, you never said if James is all right."

"He will be." Petra prayed her words were not a lie.

Petra changed on the far side of the barn. There was little chance of Adam or Robert seeing her, and she needed speed. The cows near her scattered as she leapt into the sky in a flurry of wings and pain. In the sky, she felt free to let her anguish out. Her cries echoed off the clouds.

She could already feel it. A pull back toward Atlas's Peak where James was with the Bolt. She closed her eyes and concentrated on the steady beat of her wings. She had to stop thinking of him as James. If he was not completely Zeus now, he would be soon, and he would want his supplicants around him. Unfortunately for Zeus, his supplicants had been on their own for generations, and they liked their freedom. It was going to be a messy reunion.

Petra flew all the way to the last row of tents on the edge of town. She scared a drunk who'd passed out under a bush, but he would not remember her in a few hours and would not believe his memories if he did. Her talons were feet before they hit the ground. She ran all the way to Iris.

Iris took one look at her and drove the three men discussing a newspaper in the corner out the door. They protested loudly, but Iris told them to go occupy the benches outside the store in a voice that did not encourage arguing. They left. Men rarely argued with Iris. She was too delicate and beautiful for arguing.

"I felt something earlier. What's going on?" Iris took Petra's hands in her own and led her into one of the chairs by the window. "Petra, what happened? You look like you've seen a ghost."

"The prophecy. Styx, Iris it's worse than I thought it could ever be." Petra rubbed her face. She wanted to sleep and wake up with a new life.

Iris blew out her breath in a huff. "How bad?"

"Bad. Perhaps end of our world bad."

"Damn." Petra had never heard her cuss before.

"It's James and his mine." Petra did not know where to start. The horror of it was still beating into her soul.

Iris interrupted her. "About James and the journal. I know what kind of Remnant he is."

Petra collapsed on a stool. "Zeus. He's a Remnant of a bastard of Zeus." Petra buried her face in her hands.

"What was in the mine?" Iris's voice was steel and worry.

"The Bolt of Zeus."

Whatever Iris had prepared herself for, it was not that. She clenched the edges of her chair and squeezed until her knuckles were white. "Are you sure?"

"I saw it with my own eyes, and doubtless you feel the pull to obey and go, even now as I do."

"What happened?"

Petra told the story to Iris and managed to get through the retelling though silent tears tracked her face. Saying the words out loud gave them power, and it tore at her heart to voice them. She felt from the way Iris's hand held her hand that her sister knew what the retelling cost.

Petra stood when it was over. "The harpies have to be warned, and the other Remnants too. This is bad for all of us. Rebuilding Olympus means tearing down the world we know. There's no telling what kind of havoc Zeus will wreak. We both know he cares little for mortal life—or any life for that matter—and he is bent on revenge. It will not go well for those whose ancestors participated in the Fall of Olympus. He was very pleased that his possession of James seemed to wound me."

Iris stopped her. "Petra, I know why your hair is going grey."

"I think I do, too." Petra did, now that she considered all the possible reasons. Only one felt right, but the truth wedged the knife into her heart farther. "I love him." Her hair, like her nature, was changing because she had found someone she could take as a true mate. Someone she could love and cherish. Someone Zeus had stolen from her. It had been a ridiculous folly to let herself fall so far so fast, and now she would pay the price.

"Normally, a harpy would not age much before she died. I found one reference in a heretical text about a harpy who'd kept her mate for life. The text said she'd lived a full mortal life. I think that any break with the rules, not having a daughter or forming an attachment to a mate, speeds the aging process."

"Are you telling me I have a year to live?"

Iris gave her a sad smile. "No, the text said a mortal life. I think it means your years would be numbered the same as if you were mortal."

"I'm already seventy, more than most mortals. That still doesn't give me much time."

"I don't think it works like that. Harpies age slower and come of age slower. In human years, you are probably about twenty-five or thirty. I think you'll live another thirty or forty and then die like a mortal instead of living out your full three hundred years."

Petra rubbed her palms on her thighs, thinking. "But the myths all say if the traditions, having a daughter, removing her, not staying with a mate, are not followed, the harpy dies."

"To the gods, who were immortal, a mortal lifespan was death," Iris said.

"Styx, I hate the gods, hate Zeus, and hate this whole thing. Can we save James? I'm not giving up on him yet. God or no god. Even if at the end of all this he still hates what I am, he deserves a better fate than to be used by a cheating bastard like Zeus." There had to be a way to save James. Her ancestors had defeated Zeus once. They could do it again.

Petra did not want to live in a world without James in it, regardless of what he might think of her. He should have a normal mortal wife who could give him a house full of cooing babies with his dark eyes and hair. Petra would not let Zeus rob James of his future.

Iris took Petra's face in her hands. "I'm sorry, my bird, for what this may yet cost you. Go warn the other Remnants in town. They will not be able to refuse the call for long, but they should know what they will find at the end of their journey up the mountain. Have Dr. Williams, Daniel Vine, the sheriff, Dora, and Marina meet here at sundown. They are all strong enough to resist for now, and we'll need to pool our resources to form a plan. Zeus may have left a god, but he has returned to people who no longer wish to serve under his thumb." Petra accepted the command from Iris and left. The task gave her something to do while she kept her mind blank. A white numbness filled her, and Petra was able to keep moving and acting like her world was not crumbling.

Only Marina had pressed on the wound that had been caused by the events of the day. In response, Petra nearly tore her head off before regaining control of her ragged emotions. She left without apologizing. The others came as they were bid, though Petra had given them little explanation for the gathering beyond Zeus and trouble. Only Reed had required more explanation beyond those two horrible words.

When Marina walked through the door to the mail depot, the urge to say she was sorry for her harsh words welled up, but Petra choked them off. Guilt and misery clogged the apology before it could be voiced. Marina stalked over to Petra. Petra stared at her hands she had clenched together in her lap.

Marina leaned down and wrapped her in a hug. Petra's ribs creaked as Marina squeezed her. Tears threatened to spill over, but Petra knew that if she gave in, she would never stop, so she swallowed them past the burning in her throat. Marina's hug told her everything was understood and forgiven. She squeezed Marina back, offering her own forgiveness.

Marina stood and, with a mix of gentleness and worry in her face, kissed Petra on the forehead. The gesture was so tender and unlike Marina, Petra almost forgot her determination not to cry. Almost. Someone else came in the door and Petra leaned around Marina to see Dr. Williams. He was the last to arrive. Marina sat on the empty stool beside Petra, leaving an arm about her shoulders.

Iris waited until everyone was seated. "Thank you for coming, especially you, Sheriff. We realize all this is new to you, but what we discuss here will certainly affect the people of this town, and you are the closest thing we have to organization and order."

Dr. Williams spoke up. "Miss Petra said Zeus was back. How is that possible?"

Iris looked at Petra, but Petra did not want to say it out loud again. She could not replay again with words the nightmare running through her head.

James smiling as he kissed her. James in the mine, digging, always digging. James grabbing the bolt of silver and turning on her, seeing her, all of her, for the first time. James losing the battle to Zeus and being crushed under the power of a god. Zeus laughing at her with James's laugh as her world tumbled and she fell, face first in the dirt. She wanted to cover her ears and block out the memory of those moments from the mine. The kiss she wanted to remember until she died, centuries from now, when she was old and alone.

Iris repeated the prophecy. "Your time is coming, Petra of the line of Celaeno. A time of sacrifice and pain. A wound in Gaia will reveal that which was lost. The power of thunder and lightning will be your undoing." The words, spoken again in Iris's calm voice, not the low one which had delivered the prophecy, were a different kind of pain than her memories of James.

Petra could barely concentrate on the explanation Iris presented. She had to help James, and to do that she had to pull herself together. She would help the others get rid of Zeus, and then James would be free to be happy. Not with her, but happy. It would have to be enough. Petra shook herself and focused.

Iris was giving Reed a brief history lesson on the Fall of Olympus. He looked around the room. "So you're telling me that Zeus was defeated in an uprising led by your ancestors, but that his soul somehow survived and possessed James Lloyd, the dairy farmer up on Atlas's Peak, who now seeks to rebuild Olympus and rule the earth in the worst way possible. Did I get all the particulars?"

Daniel Vine, the one looking the least upset about the revelations spoke up. "I'd like to clarify that my ancestors were loyal to the end. I'm not sure why you're all so alarmed. It may not be as bad as you think. This bolt only held his essence, we think, so he will not be as powerful as he once was. The rule of Olympus wasn't terrible. It wasn't perfect, but people were prosperous."

Marina stalked over to Vine and jabbed his sternum with her finger. "You mean you were fine. The rest of us didn't do so well under his rule. He's a despot with little care for others. I rather like being able to go and do as I please without being ordered about. Besides, James makes damn good cheese."

Despite her black mood, Petra's lips quirked up. Iris stepped between Marina and Vine. "Though my ancestors had a fine life under Zeus's rule, I agree that if we can reverse the Bolt's effect on James, we should. The civilian population of this region will suffer if Zeus is allowed to stay here. He will see the women as fodder for his desires and the men as slaves for whatever projects he wants completed. Times have changed."

Dr. Williams scratched a hand over the stubble on his chin. "The awakening of the Bolt is likely the cause of the Remnants gathering in this area. I know I can't fully explain why I settled on this particular town to set up my practice. The harpies and Iris were here years before I arrived, but I would guess they are here for similar reasons. In the myths, Zeus was able to wield control over the other gods and creatures. We could extrapolate that the Bolt would have some ability to draw Remnants in some way."

Iris addressed the sheriff. "It makes sense. We'll have to hope the Remnants will go straight to Zeus and not spend too much time in town. Not all Remnants are as friendly as those in this room."

Reed took off his hat and ran a hand through his short hair. "If the harpies could stay in town to keep the peace and help patrol the outlying holdings, that would be useful." He jammed his hat back on his head.

Marina, for once without her usual glee at adventurous prospects, stood with her arms akimbo. "We'll stay in town as long as we can, but if the call to join him gets stronger, we'll have to go."

Worry passed over the sheriff's face, and he looked around the room before settling his eyes back on Marina. "Is he a danger to you?"

"Will Zeus harm us?" Marina shrugged. "Probably. Our ancestors led the revolt against him. He can make our lives miserable or worse, as he chooses. Dr. Williams over there, from the line of Asclepius, was not his favorite either. Even so, Zeus rarely killed any of his followers. His methods were much more creative and painful."

"Killing is too easy. Zeus prefers to teach people lessons by stealing or tainting the thing they hold most dear." The words scratched out of Petra's throat as if she had been crying. Her cheeks were dry, but her soul was drowning.

"He's not always so careful with humans," Iris warned. "The harpies will stay as long as they can. I can probably ignore the call until they are compelled, and then I'll go." Iris locked gazes with Petra. "I'll not let you face him alone." Petra did not trust herself to answer, so she nodded. A warm swell of love for her chosen family was a balm on her wounds.

"We've yet to get down to the heart of the matter. How do we stop him?" Reed asked the group. "I've the least experience, so I'm praying one of you has a plan to get my town out of this mess."

"Stop Zeus? You must be joking." Daniel pulled a pewter flask from his inside jacket pocket and took a swig.

"We can't just allow him to take over. We have to try something." Petra rubbed at the pounding that had started in her temples. "We have to save James. He's just a vessel. There must be a way to separate them and get rid of Zeus. He was defeated once. We can do so again."

"You're mad if you think you're going to go up against Zeus. Did your mother not teach you the old ways and myths? Zeus does as he pleases and we go along. I'll not be a part of your rebellion. I know my place, and I'm contented with it. I like my skin the way it is." Daniel screwed the top back on his flask and walked out of the door.

"Bastard," Marina said as she plopped down on her stool.

Dora patted her arm. "You had to have known he wasn't going to help. He only cares about his own interests, and Zeus being here is likely to help him more than any of us."

"So what now?" The sheriff prompted. "There's been a lot of talk but nothing about how to get rid of our problem. How do you go about getting a god to leave town?"

Dr. Williams snapped his fingers together. "If our theories are correct, it was the Bolt that called us all to this place and the Bolt that put the current events in motion when James touched it. Clearly, it is the key to solving our problem."

Dora turned to Iris. "Was the Bolt of Zeus found in the ruins after Olympus fell?"

Iris tapped a finger on the counter. "I don't recall for sure, but I think the doctor is right. The Bolt is the key. We have to figure out a way to get it away from James." Iris walked around the counter and started pulling books from beneath it. "Here are a few books to get us started. I have more upstairs. Dora, you can help me bring them down. Doc and Petra can get started with the research. Reed, you go back out and keep the peace. Marina can go with you if you'd like, or she can stay here."

Reed nodded. "Marina can stay if she'd be of better use to you here."

Iris pointed at Marina. "Will you be of use here, or are you likely to be pacing the room in ten minutes?"

Marina smiled. "I'll go help the sheriff keep order. I'm better with my fists than flipping through books."

Petra puffed a breath out. "I suggest we do what research we can tonight and tomorrow, but after that, I suggest we go on up the mountain. We can't do anything useful hiding here, and we need to find out what's going on up there." Petra hated the edge of pleading in her voice.

"I hate to say this, but Miss Petra's right." Dr. Williams tapped a finger on the book in front of him.

"Thanks, Doc. You're all right."

"I said you were right. I didn't say it was a good idea."

"If one of us goes, all of us should," Petra said.

They all agreed. Desperation and despair were present in equal parts for Petra. She knew finding what information they could over the next day might very well prove useful, but it felt more like needlessly waiting. Wait and see was not an action plan. Killing something was a plan. Still, she knew that nothing would make the coming days easier. They had only each other for courage and comfort, and Petra was glad to not be alone. It was a small thing, but it was something.

CHAPTER 18

The following morning bloomed like any other. The pain of waiting was like a cut, small at first, but made larger and more painful through worry until it was a large and bleeding wound. The pull toward Atlas's Peak was an incessant buzzing of a fly, easily ignorable, but grating on the nerves. The waiting and the pull wore down Petra until she snapped and barked at everyone. Iris sent her out of the depot to get some air and calm down.

The street was quiet. A light morning frost touched the buildings and covered the courageous weeds growing on the sides of the boardwalk. The frost would be gone in an hour, but it shone in the sun and gave everything the appearance of diamonds. At this hour, the street should have some traffic, but only Simon was out, sweeping the boards in front of the mercantile and putting out some boxes of fruit. The mortals must sense something different, something dangerous in the air. Approaching riders broke through the rasp of Simon's broom.

Petra held a hand over her eyes to shield the morning sun. Four riders were coming into town. The closer the group got, the more apparent it was that they were not typical travelers. They had no heavy packs of gear or a wagon with mining supplies or house goods. Petra straightened and put all her weight on the balls of her feet. When the group came close enough for her to see, it was apparent that each rider was armed to the teeth. There was even a sword handle visible from between the shoulder blades of the largest rider, a man with black hair and eyes with no mercy.

The other three riders were peculiar. A lean woman with hard features carried not only two pistols, a rifle, and two knives, one in each boot, but also a crossbow. A brown-haired man with deep circles under his eyes carried only one gun, but he had enough knives attached to his person that he could have armed four more people. Time had turned the face of the last rider, another woman, into a mask that clung to its humanity but was on its way to something much more horrific. Her hair was pure white. A chill danced down Petra's spine. There was no way in Hades these riders were mortal, and no one arrived this heavily armed for a social call.

Petra pulled on her harpy strength and felt out the newcomers. A wall of power bashed into her, and Petra had to force herself not to sway on her feet. This was bad. She stared down the man with the sword. If they meant to cause trouble, she could hold her own for a short period while praying someone would hear the commotion and come to help. She counted up the arsenal she could see again, but her number did not include all the things they would have hidden. She would not last long. Out of the corner of her eye, she saw Reed and Marina walk out behind the riders.

"We're looking for someone." The man with the sword spoke in a voice low enough to make Petra's ears rumble.

"This is a peaceful place. We don't want trouble." Petra put all the power she had into the words.

The man's bushy eyebrows rose a fraction. "Those tricks don't work on us, harpy."

"I'll repeat. We don't want trouble."

"Oh, but we want as much trouble as possible." The man with the dark circles under his eyes turned his lips up in a caricature of a smile.

Reed and Marina moved into position behind the four. Petra dared not look in their direction and give them away. The click of a gun hammer sounded and the riders turned.

"You heard the lady. This is a peaceful place. You four best be moving on." Reed was steady, pointing his gun at the sword man.

The old woman's face wrinkled even further as she squeezed out a wheeze that Petra assumed must be laughter. The sound made her want to lose her breakfast. The riders were powerful. They needed to get them to leave with as little bloodshed as possible. If this was the type of Remnant Zeus would be collecting, things were going to get bad quick.

The wheezing stopped and the woman spoke in a voice reserved for dark corners filled with cobwebs. "If she's a lady, than I'm Athena herself." The woman's gaze was a chill Petra could not shake. When she redirected it toward Marina, the chill dissipated but did not leave entirely. Styx. This was more trouble than they could handle. "Don't you know a pair of harpies when you see'm boy? Not too bright for a sheriff, are ya?"

"You seem to have us at an advantage. You know us, but we don't know you. Care to make introductions?" Marina's voice was hard, and lesser mortals would have dropped crying at her feet. These were not mortals.

The silence stretched. Petra clenched her fists in an anticipation of the coming fight. She would go for the man with the deep circles under his eyes. Reed had the sword man in his sights, and Marina would probably choose the old woman who was closest to her. If they were lucky, they could dispatch one or two quick enough to get to the other two without one of their own dying. Petra shifted her weight and held her breath.

"We felt the call and have come to join Zeus's guard. We have kept the tradition and training for generations in anticipation of this day. I am Alke," the sword man pointed a large thumb at his own chest, "the man with the knives is Eris, the churlish young beauty," Alke indicated the wrinkled woman, "is Phobos, and the last is Ioke."

Petra let out her breath in a huff. Of all the things she had imagined, this was much, much worse. Alke, Eris, Phobos, and Ioke of the myths were the personification of warrior attributes who made up the protective shield of Zeus. Each had their own power. Alke was strength, Eris strife, Phobos was terror, and Ioke was pursuit and onslaught. Styx and fire. They would be lucky to make it out alive.

"I don't care who or what you are." If Reed gave any indication he knew what the introductions meant, he did not so much as bat an eye. The man had courage, however foolish. "Turning Creek is a peaceful place. Anyone disturbing the peace will pay the very real consequences. I expect you'll bleed as red as the next. I ask that you conduct your business in town in a quick manner and then leave just as quick."

Alke put his hands palm up in a gesture Petra doubted was sincere. She kept herself ready. "We're just passing through. We're looking for the man himself, not some minor players."

"This minor player's bullet will rip through your head as well as anyone else's. Move along." Reed's hand remained steady as he aimed at Alke's forehead.

"We can see Zeus is not here. We'll move on. Later, Sheriff. Harpies." Alke turned his horse and the three others followed.

Phobos twisted around in the saddle and threw her cobweb voice back at them. "We'll see you soon, harpies. Don't wait too long. You know he's not the most patient of gods."

When the four were out of sight, Marina shivered. "I'm not sorry to see them go, but that they are here at all means more trouble than we bargained for."

"They said their names like we should know who they were." Reed put his gun away.

"They are the living manifestations of the shield of Zeus. They were his personal guard and carried out whatever orders he gave," Marina said.

Reed frowned. "That does not bode well. Let's just hope it doesn't get much worse."

Petra could still feel the sticky darkness of Phobos's voice. "It's not going to get better." She walked back to the depot and thought about their options.

Iris, Dora, and Dr. Williams looked up from their books, blinking like startled owls when Petra walked through the door of the depot. "We have to find out what's going on. I'm going up there now," she said without preamble.

Dora put her finger on the page she was reading before looking up at Petra. "We agreed to go tomorrow."

All the anxiety and pent up rage boiled over. "I know what we decided, but James is up there, and I have to know what is happening to him. I have to find a way to help him. I can't let Zeus win."

Iris came around the corner and placed a hand on her arm. "None of us can. If there is some weakness, anything, to get rid of Zeus and get James back, we'll find it."

"What do we know?" Petra asked.

Dora ran her fingers over the words on the page in front of her. "His main weakness seems to be beautiful, though not always willing, women."

Marina laughed. "Wonderful. If we could find a plethora of beautiful prostitutes, we'd have the perfect distraction."

"We also know," Dr. Williams said, "that, like many other weapons of the gods, the original Bolt was forged on Olympus by Hephaestus."

"I'll go visit Henry and see if he knows anything that could be of use." Petra started towards the door.

"Wait." Marina called. "I saw Henry leaving town yesterday morning. Likely, he's up on the mountain already."

"So we basically don't know much else than when we started yesterday." Petra crossed her arms and squeezed herself as the frustration coiled within her. "I should have dragged him from the mine. I'm stronger than he is. I could've done it."

"It was his decision, and you cared about him enough to respect his choice. You couldn't have known what would happen," Iris said.

Petra wiped a hand over her face. "That's just it. That damned prophecy. I was warned. I should've put the pieces together sooner than I did. 'A time of sacrifice and pain. A wound in Gaia will reveal that which was lost. The power of thunder and lightning will be your undoing.' "

"The answers are always easier to see when you are looking at things that've already been. It's not your fault." Marina pulled a knife from her belt and flipped it in her hand.

Petra wanted to believe Marina was right and absolve herself. There was nothing she could have done to prevent their current situation. It warmed her that Marina loved and trusted her enough to not only think it but to tell her out loud. "When did you get to be a sage who gives good advice?"

"I have many hidden talents." Marina winked.

Petra stood. "He's not going to win. I'm a violent, dark-souled harpy, and I will be damned if I let that bastard win. I'm still alive, so we're not giving up."

"Thank the gods. I thought you were going to be emotional and ridiculous. This is our town. It's about time we took it back." Marina flipped her knife.

"By the Styx, yes." Dora swore.

The three women grinned, their faces full of malice. Reed shrank back in his chair as their teeth sharpened and their smiles turned predatory.

"Don't worry, Reed." Petra patted his knee and spoke around her pointed teeth. "You aren't in any danger from us."

Marina, her teeth still on the pointy side, added, "We're saving our violence for much larger game."

***

Petra went over the contents of her pack one more time: one set of extra clothes, a blanket, some dried meat, apples and dried peaches, and an array of weapons. Marina argued that they should go in as armed as possible. Petra felt most of their weapons would be confiscated. They compromised. They would each carry three or four well-concealed weapons and two obvious ones, then hope at least one or two of the better concealed ones made it past the aegis.

When they left the mail depot, Iris tacked a sheet of paper on the door which read: "Mail depot closed until further notice. Please leave any parcels with Sheriff Brant." The note had been Marina's idea. She had chuckled as she had written out the note. Petra guessed Reed had not been warned about the redirection of mail through his office.

Reed was in his office when they stopped to say goodbye. "I don't like this part of the plan. You don't even know what you're up against."

Marina took a step towards him. "We do know. We're going up the mountain to see if we can overthrow a god."

"If I didn't know any better, I'd say you were excited about the prospect." Reed ran a hand through his hair.

"Looks like you know more than I thought then." Marina flashed a smile.

"You're trouble. If you make it out of this alive and if the town is still here, you can come work for me anytime. You're one scary, crazy woman."

Marina executed a small bow, which made him laugh. "I think I'll take you up on that."

"Good. Don't get killed." Reed called to them as they left.

Next stop was Dr. Williams' office. He was packing things into a leather satchel when they found him. They had decided to travel together up the mountain, but the doctor would split off from them before they arrived. The harpies did not want Dr. Williams to be associated with them.

Given her last encounter with Zeus, Petra was certain he had some animosity for the harpies, and they did not want any of that spilling over onto the doctor. Iris was already known to be closely associated with the harpies, so the four of them would go in together.

"Ready to go, Doc?" Petra asked.

Dr. Williams put one more bottle of something green into his bag and strapped it shut. "Almost. Let me retrieve my regular pack. This black bag is just for medical supplies." He left the room and returned quickly with a brown leather backpack. He strapped the black bag onto the backpack and hefted the entire thing on his back.

They left the doctor's office in a quiet line. Henry's forge, no longer on the very edge of town, was cold and dark. The gnaw of worry in Petra kicked up a notch. There were tools missing from the wall of the forge. Petra turned back towards the mountain and prayed to the gods that Henry was safe.

CHAPTER 19

Pine needles crunched under their feet and the air smelled crisp. The sun lit the path ahead of them and birds twittered. If they had been walking for any other purpose, it would have been a perfect day. The sky above the peak was brilliant blue. The peak itself was covered in white snow and grey stone. Petra's resolve hardened. Zeus would not make Atlas's Peak his home. It belonged to her and the other Remnants. It belonged to James.

Petra had briefly wondered if she might see her mother on the mountain, but the Bolt's call had only strengthened recently. Her mother, and Dora and Marina's for that matter, would not have had enough time to travel to this side of the world. If they did not find a way to stop Zeus soon though, Turning Creek would be bursting with Remnants of all shapes and sizes, Petra's mother included. She had no desire for that reunion, and her resolve hardened.

They gave James's farm a wide berth, not wanting to explain to Adam and Robert the purpose of their journey, and they did not stop at Petra's cabin. There was nothing there she needed and they wanted to reach their destination before the sun started to dip behind the mountains. Petra said a silent prayer that she would be alive at the end of this to sit by her fire and enjoy the moods of Atlas's Peak once again.

About an hour past her cabin, Ioke stepped out from behind a shield of trees. She sneered at Petra. "Not such big talk from you today, I see. Zeus has been expecting you. You lot are one of the last to arrive. I'll escort you to him." Petra desperately wanted to punch her in the face, but she followed without arguing.

Ioke led them into a clearing where a small village of sorts was being constructed. There were log cabins, an open eating area, and people bustling everywhere, carrying boughs of evergreens, dried flowers, and platters of food. The entire area was free of snow, and there were blue columbines growing everywhere. The happy faces of the flowers stretched towards the late fall sun. Normally, they bloomed in late spring or early summer, but Zeus must have found a Remnant who could control the seasons. Demeter or Rhea were the most likely candidates.

All the buildings were turned to face a stone dais. It was rough and the color of the mountain, as if it had been pulled from the earth itself and fashioned into a seat for a god. Ampiaraus, who had been swallowed by the earth in the old myths, would have been able to make a throne like this. There were a handful of people standing near the dais. The three other aegis, Alke, Eris, and Phobos, were there.

Petra had thus far avoided looking at the figure on top of the stone chair. She braced herself, but it did nothing to lessen the shock of seeing James, who was now Zeus, staring at them with proprietary malice in his eyes.

James, polite and courteous to a fault, would never have looked at anyone in that fashion. Petra could see nothing of James in the posture of the man sitting before her. If Zeus had taken over, was there anything left of the man she loved behind those cruel eyes? Those eyes fed her anger over what Zeus had done. He would not win.

Zeus smiled but the movement did not reach his eyes. "At last, my harpies and The Messenger have come to me. Dear Messenger, I am glad you have come." His face hardened as he pointed at the harpies. "Your tardiness displeases me. There have been some uprisings you could have solved, but I was forced to take care of them myself." It was strange to hear James's voice without his accent.

Zeus waved his silver bolt to his left, and Petra caught her breath. There were two bodies hanging from a tree on the side of the clearing. Their entrails were a mess of blood and offal on the ground. Crows, oblivious to the people, hopped happily in gore, eating and squawking over an eyeball. Petra's shoulders sagged with relief. She did not know them.

Petra turned her pity into malice for the thing in James's body. She pulled on the violence in her soul, the black part of her that was harpy and terror, and let it seep from her pores. Throwing caution to the wind she gathered it and pushed it out from herself and towards Zeus.

"What are you doing?" Dora hissed.

Marina smiled and Petra saw the harpy shift in Marina's eyes. Being this close to Zeus and the power emanating from him and the Bolt made it hard to control their harpies. Petra reveled in the energy flowing between the three of them and continued to push it towards the stone dais. She had been angry for days, and it felt good to have an actual target for her gall in front of her.

Zeus threw back his head and laughed. It was a deeper sound than James had ever made. "My wonderful harpies. How I have missed your displays of impertinence." His gaze sharpened on Petra. "You are amusing to me now, but do not think I will hesitate to banish you as I once did." He smiled without warmth. "Do you like the preparations we are making? Dionysus is throwing a feast in my honor to celebrate the beginning of my new reign."

Daniel Vine looked up at the use of his Remnant name. Barrels of ale and wine were stacked in piles around the open eating area. He ignored the harpies and bowed low to Zeus. Crafty man. He was not one to take sides unless he was sure of victory. Petra would not forget his abandonment.

Zeus directed his attention back to the harpies. "Everyone is to return here an hour before sundown. You three will patrol the area. No mortals are to get anywhere near my New Olympus. I am not ready to reveal myself to them. This body is still weak," he flexed the arm holding the Bolt, "and I want them to see me in all my glory. Messenger, you will stay here. After the feasting tonight, I plan on sending messages out to those who are not yet here."

Iris inclined her head in acknowledgment. "I will need some help to accomplish this task."

"Of course. Young Thomas, where are you?"

A scrawny, tawny-haired boy stepped out from behind a tree. He juggled himself from foot to foot. "Here, sir."

"Messenger, this is your apprentice. His mother informed me he is a Remnant of Achilles. Is this sufficient help?" Zeus asked in a pleasant tone, reminding Petra that those in his favor were not in danger for the moment. In the myths, Zeus's favor was not always long-lasting, but Iris was safe for now.

"Yes, thank you." Iris gathered the boy to her and led him to a table on the opposite end of the clearing.

There were footsteps behind them, and Zeus shifted his gaze. "Asclepius, I am pleased you are here. Stay out of the way and do not make trouble. Go." Zeus waved his hand and leaned over to whisper in Phobos's ear. The rasping sound of her laughter followed them as they obeyed.

It would have been easier to complete the job of sentry in her harpy form, but Petra did not want to make the job easy. Marina and Dora changed and flew off in opposite directions. Petra caught sight of them circling every few minutes. She circled the clearing in ever widening circles as the sun traveled overhead. There were small groups of Remnants building shelters and gathering food, but they ignored her and she them. When Petra estimated that she had less than two hours until sundown, she headed back to the clearing.

The crunch of snow came from the path in front of Petra. The magic of the clearing did not extend this far. No flowers smiled in the sun. Petra waited, tense. If it was one of the aegis, she was going to put her fist in their face and damn the consequences. Those four rubbed her in all the wrong places. She clenched and unclenched her fists.

Iris came around the corner, and Petra dropped her readiness stance. "I was hoping you were Ioke so I could break your nose."

Iris enveloped her in a hug. "My bird. I love you, but you must try to reign in your violence. I don't want to see you on the end of a rope or banished."

Petra shuddered. "I'd prefer to keep my innards where they belong." Petra hugged Iris back as hard as she could. "I love you too."

Iris pulled back enough to look at Petra, surprise plain on her face. "You've never said that to me before."

"Consider this a new, more in touch with my emotions, me. Unfortunately, I am also a lot more in touch with my rage."

Iris's brows drew together. "I think the power leaking off Zeus makes Remnants more likely to revert to their original state of being. We don't have much time, and I need to tell you a few things I've learned. First, watch yourself tonight. I don't think this feast is going to be a genteel affair. Second, I think we were right about the Bolt being both the source of his power and the way we can defeat him. It never leaves his hand."

"We have two problems, then. One, how do we get the bolt from Zeus? Two, how do we destroy it?" Petra chewed her bottom lip.

"I think one of us needs to have a visit with Henry."

If there were anyone who might know the secret of the Bolt, it would be Henry. "I'll do it when I can get away." A chill settled over Petra. She could feel snow sliding down her neck, but it was not as cold as the conclusion she had reached during her sentry duty. "I thought the prophecy meant I would have to sacrifice you, or Dora, or Marina, but it's me. I'm not going to get out of this alive."

"What? Why would you think that?" Iris was angry, but Petra saw the fear in her eyes. Iris knew it was true. They would not all live through this.

"The prophecy was for me. Not you or any of the others. Me. ' The power of thunder and lightning will be your undoing.' Those were the words. My death is what ends this. I've been thinking about it, and I'm glad the only one this will hurt is me."

"We can't know that."

"What else could it mean?"

"Prophecies do not often end the way we think they will. I'm not letting you give in that easy."

"Who said I'm giving in? If I die, I'm taking that bastard down with me. I'll drown him in the River Styx myself if I have to. Let's get back to the clearing. We have a celebration to attend."

Torches lined the clearing and tables groaned under the weight of the food and drink laid out. Petra had tried to catch Henry alone, but there were too many people around. She settled for giving his arm a squeeze as she walked past. He remained silent but nodded in acknowledgement.

There were over a hundred people in the clearing once they were all assembled. The number took Petra's breath away. Many of the faces around her freely expressed uncertainty and fear. Some, like Iris, who was again up towards the front, were stoic. There were a minority who were obviously happy at the turn of events, the four aegis being chief among them. They had much to gain from the ascension of Zeus and a New Olympus.

The top of Atlas's Peak glowed red. It looked like the shadow of blood. Petra shivered. Zeus stood and raised his hand for quiet in the red light of the sunset. "I give thanks to all of you who heard my call and came to me. I am your god and Father, Zeus, the most powerful in all of Greece and all the world. I have returned to you, at this time, to rebuild our sacred Mount Olympus. I will return all of us to our former glory. Mortals will again bow before us with fear and supplication. We will again be gods.

"Just as I rose civilization out of its darkness in the age long past, so I will do again for this age. They will see great wonders and they will worship me." There was a smattering of applause. "Before we start the feasting, I think it is time you were returned to your original forms. I grow tired of looking at your mortal bodies."

Fear, hot and tight, washed over Petra. She stepped closer to Dora and felt Marina at her back. Whatever Zeus had planned, they would stay together. The harpies were in the middle of the crowd and a commotion started in the rows closest to Zeus.

Iris, who had been standing near the dais, cried out and dropped to all fours on the hard ground. Petra tried to move towards the front, but the swell of people pulled away in panic from the front and she made no progress. Petra pushed her power into the crowd to get them to move, but Zeus's hold was too strong, and their fear was too great. Petra and the others could only watch in horror.

Iris, her face red with pain, ripped the buttons of her shirtwaist, pulling it from her shoulders until she was only covered in her skirt and camisole. Petra could see the golden wings on Iris's back glinting in the torchlight. Iris dropped to all fours again and screamed in pain. The wings on her back burst from her skin, dripping blood and shining gold. Iris's shoulders were shaking with sobs, but Petra could not hear them over the cries of other people in the crowd.

All around her, people were changing and crying out, but Petra could not take her eyes off Iris. Iris was hidden underneath huge wings of pure gold. Blood dripped steadily from below her shoulder blades, where the wings had pushed their way out of her skin. It was the most beautiful and grotesque thing Petra had ever seen.

Petra felt the power roll over her, and her harpy burst painfully from her. Even when she changed in anger, it did not hurt the way it did this time, as if each feather were a knife coming out of her human skin. After the change was complete, Petra crouched, panting as the pain subsided.

Zeus stood on the dais, smiling. He had made them transform as painfully as he could for the purpose of his entertainment. Hatred boiled in her blood, and her claws clenched as she imagined his head under her talons. She wondered if his head would pop as easily as the rabbits she sometimes hunted.

Petra shook her head, clearing the rage. She could not let Zeus's influence make her forget why she was here. She needed to separate James from Zeus without harming James. Her anger boiled anew. Zeus would pay for this.

The crowd now standing before Zeus was filled with people who no longer looked like people at all. Many had bodies that were part or all animal. Others were achingly beautiful or so ugly Petra could not look directly at them.

Zeus raised his hand for silence again, but there was still quiet sobbing coming from different parts of the crowd. "Now, you are all back in your original forms, in the forms you were given at the beginning. Tonight, we celebrate the dawn of this new age with feasting as we have so many times before. Dionysus, the floor is yours."

Daniel Vine stepped in front of the dais. He had gained a good seventy pounds and a crown of vines circled his brow. He was calm as he announced the next event of the evening. "Citizens of the New Olympus, let the feasting begin."

CHAPTER 20

At Vine's announcement, satyrs weaved in and out of the crowd, carrying large platters filled with sloshing mugs. Petra was unsure she could walk on two hoofed legs, let alone pass out platters of wine and beer with the grace they displayed. A mug was shoved into her clawed hand, and she hissed at the satyr who had snuck up on her. He shrugged at her display and moved on to the next person. Vine's sisters and other women, maenads by the look of them, were handing out food.

Petra stifled the urge to run to Iris. This was a complicated political play they were caught in, and Petra knew they could not act too rashly. While Iris was in distress, she was not in any danger. Zeus would already know Iris was affiliated with the harpies, but it would not be prudent to let him know how close the four of them were.

Petra took a careful sip of the golden liquid to buy some time. It tasted like honey mead and the sweetness of it caused the back of her mouth to pinch in pain. It was heady stuff. She would have to watch her intake of it to keep her wits about her. Dora and Marina sipped their own cups of mead, flicking their eyes back to where Iris was, towards the front.

The crowd opened up as people mingled in groups, eating and drinking. A tension hung over the low conversations, but most seemed resigned to being a part of the forced celebration. No one in between them and Iris seemed interested in the harpies or the winged messenger. Petra took another sip of mead.

Zeus sat, looking pleased, on his throne. The sight of James's face with that smug expression on it was a blow. Petra closed her eyes and rolled another sip of mead in her mouth. She could not let Zeus distract her from her purpose to rid them of the god's presence.

Petra walked as carefully as she was able in her harpy form towards the front of the clearing with Dora and Marina on her heels. She made a show of looking directly at Iris, but kept Zeus in the corner of her vision. It was not smart to ignore the largest monster in the room. People moved aside for them, making sure there was enough space that they would not brush against the harpies. Even some of the strangest ones, a man with an eagle head and snakes for arms, avoided touching them. Harpies were feared, not because of their appearance, which was hideous enough, but because of the violence that followed in their wake in the myths.

For once, Petra pulled her dark heritage around her and used it as a shield. Violence was a weapon she could wield if it was for a just purpose. Petra had spent her long life running from what she was, but tonight, she would use it to her advantage. She would do anything to save them all from Zeus, even if it meant giving in to the side of herself she loathed.

Petra swiped a glass of mead from a passing maenad and knelt beside Iris, who was still crouched on the ground. "Drink some of this. It's strong, so go slow." Iris took the mug, spilling some of the gold liquid and avoiding looking at the three of them. "Can you stand?" Iris nodded.

Petra grabbed Iris's left arm and Dora grabbed her right. Marina stood guard over them. Petra held on to Iris for a span of moments, waiting to make sure she could stand on her own. Iris's hand dug into Petra's arm, but Petra remained still.

This close, the golden wings on Iris's back were breathtaking. They shone with their own light. Iris released Petra's arm, and Petra reached back to touch the feathers closest to her. She suppressed a sigh when her hands met feathers softer than any duckling's. Here and there blood marred their shining surface, but it did not detract from their beauty. Petra noticed Iris watching her and she snatched her hand back.

"It's all right. It doesn't hurt anymore. They're beautiful. I could never really see them before, and now that they are real...they're heavy." A reflection of the horror Iris had endured floated in her blue eyes.

Dora put her arm around Iris. "I'm sorry."

Iris leaned into Dora's embrace. "None of this is your fault or anyone else's." Iris glared at Petra. "There is no blame to place. Now that we're all here, we can formulate a plan." The volume of the crowd had grown since the harpies had joined Iris. A small musical ensemble was playing a folk tune on a guitar and fiddle. They could talk without being overheard.

Marina guided them to the side of the clearing where there was some empty space. "We should gather information tonight, see if there is a routine to the aegis's movements. They're going to be the biggest obstacle in getting to Zeus."

"If we can take the Bolt away from Zeus and destroy it, he will probably lose his hold on James." Iris's eyes looked over the crowd but returned continually to Zeus, who lounged at ease, drinking.

"There's a lot of room for mistakes. How do we know for certain if the Bolt is the key? How do we get it away from him? How do we destroy it?" Dora's list of uncertainties should have built up the worry within her, but Petra glared daggers at Zeus. He would not win this battle.

"We could ask him for it, polite like." Marina raised her mug in Zeus's direction when she caught him looking their way. He raised his mug in response, but his facial expression did not change.

"Excuse me?" Petra pitched her voice to sound airy, no small feat in her harpy form. "Could we borrow that wee trinket there? It's ever so shiny, and I'm tired of you using my beau in such a beastly manner." Petra batted her eyelashes at Marina, who burst out laughing. Petra's laughter shook her mug so violently that the mead sloshed to the ground. Dora laughed but covered her mouth.

Iris rolled her eyes. "Don't the three of you take anything seriously?"

"Where'd the fun be in that?" Marina tapped her mug against Petra's. Petra drank. The laughter had eased the weight in her gut, and the mead had loosened the vice in her head. However Zeus was to be defeated, she would not do it alone.

The laughter was fleeting. "I'm not sure what the rest of you remember, but celebrations involving Dionysus, the satyrs, and the maenads never end well. They tended to end up with the women being attacked by the satyrs and the men being eaten by the maenads," Iris said.

"What a wonderful evening we have to look forward to," Marina snickered. It was enough to send them all into gales of laughter again.

"Really. We shouldn't be laughing. This is a bad state of affairs," Petra said. She would be able to defend herself against the satyrs, but others, like Iris, would not.

"I am grateful for once that we are so ugly in this form. Not even the satyrs would look twice on the three of us." Dora smoothed the feathers on her chest with clawed hands.

"I wish I could carry more weapons in this form." Marina rubbed her empty, clawed hand over her feathered breast.

"Iris will not be safe tonight," Petra said.

Iris, instead of being alarmed, said, "Satyrs can't fly, and I'm almost certain I can." She spread her wings, which were impressive, and beat them a few times until her feet rose off the ground a few inches. A few of the Remnants around them paused to watch.

Petra looked around the clearing. "Many of the Remnants will have their own defenses, but not all."

A young girl and her mother sat at the end of a table. Their heads were down as they tried to remain unnoticed by the crowd. They could be mistaken for any mother and daughter pair in Turning Creek. They could have walked into the mercantile with lists for their farm. The pair were not the only ones seeking to go unnoticed. There was a family occupying one table in the very back of the clearing and a small circle of boys behind the harpies. If things went downhill, these small groups would be the first casualties.

"We can't let the satyrs and maenads get out of hand." Petra eyed the group of boys who were whispering to each other.

"Think we could appeal to his sense of justice?" Dora gestured towards Daniel Vine. "He should have some control over them."

Marina curled her lip. "I doubt it he'd make the effort. He only seems to care for his own affairs. That course would be a brick wall. Forget it."

"We're harpies. We're made to influence people and herd them. Remnants are mentally stronger than mortals, but together we might have enough power to keep things from getting messy." Other than the crowd at the hearing for Dr. Williams, Petra had never tried to influence a large group. This crowd would be drunk on mead. It was a dangerous combination of circumstances.

"Do you think Zeus knows this celebration could get out of control?" Dora asked, ever the optimist.

"He's betting on it." Petra narrowed her eyes at him but then looked away when he caught her.

"What will he do if we interfere?" Marina wondered.

"I don't give a damn what he does. I'll not stand by and let it happen." Petra ground her teeth.

"Birds, settle down." Iris laid a calming hand on Petra. "We won't stand by and let people get hurt, but we will need to be as inconspicuous as possible. We don't want to draw too much attention to ourselves."

Marina snickered. "And being a big bird with an ugly hag's face is something we can hide in a crowd?"

"Under normal circumstances, I'd say no, but," Iris pointed to a woman with two heads, "tonight I think will be the exception."

"Point taken." Marina agreed.

"The evening may not progress as we fear. Let's take one step at a time. If we have to interfere, let's do so without causing a scene. You three keep an eye on things. I'm going to talk to Henry about the Bolt." Petra gulped the last few swallows of mead and set her mug on the table. She put a hand on the table to steady herself. "Damned magic mead."

The horizon dipped and Petra closed her eyes and breathed through her mouth. When she opened her eyes again, the other three were looking at her. "Shut up." They burst out laughing. "Lot of good we're going to be at this rate." Petra muttered.

Iris was the first one to gather her wits. "Look, Petra. I know you want to get on with getting the Bolt, but we can't do it without talking to Henry and without some kind of plan. It won't be tonight. We need to handle one problem at a time, and right now, that problem is keeping this celebration in hand."

Petra wanted her to be wrong. If they fixed the Zeus problem, all the other ones would cease to exist. She caught herself grinding her teeth again and stopped. She clenched them instead. Iris was right. While the party was a natural distraction for stealing a bolt of silver, they needed to know what to do with it once they had it. Having a conversation with Henry in the midst of what was becoming a wild celebration was unwise. One more day would matter little to James, she hoped.

"Tonight, we keep the peace. Tomorrow, I'll find Henry first thing. Then we'll think of some brilliant plan." Petra sat back down.

The celebration proceeded downhill and into Hades in the manner that Petra had predicted, with the satyrs getting ever freer with their affections and the maenads getting meaner. Petra almost suggested Iris fly away or find a tree in which to take shelter, but away from the fires of the clearing it was cold, and Iris was clad only in her camisole and a skirt. None of the trees at this altitude would have supported the weight of a grown woman with large wings.

The three harpies took different areas of the clearing to patrol. Iris moved between them, talking to people and never straying too far from one of the harpies. A satyr sitting next to a woman with flaming red hair leaned over to kiss her not far from where Petra stood. Petra positioned herself to move if needed. The satyr jumped back in a howl of rage, his chest hair and eyebrows on fire. The woman had spit real fire on him. Petra chuckled. That one did not need her assistance. The woman noticed Petra and raised her mug. Petra returned the salute.

Petra, making a circuit of the clearing, found Daniel Vine drinking alone. He had refused to help them before, but maybe in the intervening time he had developed a functioning conscience. "Things are going to get ugly unless you reign in your minions."

Vine sipped his mead and shrugged. "They are only acting on their true natures. Who am I to stop them?"

Petra seethed and clenched her hand to keep from bashing it into Vine's nose. "You're a weasel." She left him before he could say anything in response.

The moon moved over the sky and still the celebration continued. The mother and daughter who had been sitting alone earlier in the evening were now surrounded by four satyrs. Petra made her way towards them and saw Dora moving in her direction too. Petra cracked her knuckles. She was ready for a fight now.

"We just want to have a drink with you. No need to act like you're too good for us." A satyr with fawn-colored goat legs loomed over the young woman and wound her hair around his finger. He grabbed a fistful of it and yanked her head back. "I think I'll teach you a lesson in what the proper response should be when a man offers to buy you a drink."

Petra stopped six inches shy of crashing into the satyr. "That's the problem. You're not a man at all." Petra wound back and smashed her first into the satyr's temple. Her knuckles protested but it paled in comparison to the indignant yelling of the satyr.

He whirled, but when he saw his attacker, his response fizzled. Petra towered over him. The mantle of violent intention she pulled around her caused the little goat-man to pale. Dora stepped beside her, and his companions melted into the crowd.

"The woman said no. If you want some female companionship so badly, you can have a drink with me." Petra smiled, making sure to show all of her pointy teeth.

"My mistake. Won't happen again," the satyr muttered.

"Too bad. I wanted to beat you to a pulp. Go find a hole to stay in until morning. If I catch you harassing anyone else tonight, I'll rip your throat out."

Dora leaned over until her face was inches from the satyr's. "Go." He did not have to be told again. Dora turned toward the girl. "There are some empty cabins on the east side of the clearing. Find one, get inside, and bolt the door. Things aren't going to get better."

Petra looked at Zeus, sitting on the dais. He watched her with blue eyes. Petra could not see them in the darkness, but she knew exactly what color they were. He was smirking as if their paltry efforts were amusing to him. He would be smirking less if she shoved his Bolt down his throat.

Petra shook herself. All the power in the clearing—and the mead—made it harder than normal to keep her violence under control. She would not be surprised if Zeus wanted them all to lose control. He was not the god of peace and rainbows. She checked the progress of the moon. There were still four hours until sunrise. A lot of bad could happen in four hours.

A scuffle at the next table sharpened Petra back into focus. Cyrene and Atlanta had the upper hand in a fight with two men. One of them had baby face and the other sported a full beard. Cyrene slammed her fist into Baby Face's nose. A sickening crack sounded before his nose started bleeding.

"Eros, a woman broke your nose." The bearded man opened his mouth to laugh but Atlanta's punch took his wind from him. He emitted a low pitched whine and fell to the ground.

"Next time you want to harass a woman, make sure she's willing." Cyrene leaned into Eros, and he stepped back to get away from her.

"Women never turn me down." The prideful words were made less believable when spoken through dripping blood.

Petra stepped beside Atlanta. "Didn't your momma teach you to leave huntresses and harpies alone? Go shoot your love arrows somewhere else."

Eros put his still-wheezing companion's arms around his shoulders and the two stumbled away. Petra rounded on Atlanta. "I told you to stay out of our territory."

Atlanta stood her ground. Good. Petra wanted another fight. "Things are different now, and you know why. Zeus called us and we came. I'm not here of my own free will, and I don't think this territory belongs to you anymore. Someone higher up has come to claim it."

"Not if I can help it." Petra narrowed her eyes.

Atlanta laughed hard, doubled over, until tears leaked from her eyes. "What're you gonna do? Go ask Zeus to leave? You of all creatures should know the pain of his wrath. We do as we're told, or we and all our progeny face the consequences."

"I don't need a history lesson." Petra did not require any reminders of what disobedience earned a harpy. Exile. Loneliness. Violence.

"I like you, so don't get dead over this. I'm still hoping to best you in a fight someday." Atlanta put her hat back on her head and went to grab another mug of mead.

Huntresses were a strange bunch. Petra supposed harpies were not much better. She surveyed the damage. Broken glassware and an overturned table were the worst of it. Petra flipped the table back onto its legs, moving to the side to avoid the mead and other liquids dripping from its surface. It could not be morning soon enough.

"Let me go, you crazy hags." The demand broke through Petra's longing for the dawn. Three maenads were dragging a man out of the clearing and into the trees. His movements were jerky and slow. He had indulged in too much mead to effectively fight back.

There was too much crowd to get there fast enough on foot. Petra opened her wings and flew over the heads of the people celebrating. She pumped her wings once, twice, gaining speed before crashing into one of the maenads, talon first. Petra dug into the maenad's shoulder until she could feel wetness dripping from between her talons. The scream of the maenad hit her at the same time as the copper smell of her blood.

Maenads were not courageous creatures, and once the three women saw the harpy and the blood, they scattered. The one under Petra tried to run, but Petra held on. It was the large-nosed woman from Vine's. Petra dug her talons in farther, and the woman dropped to her knees and leaned over. Petra lost her balance and released the woman.

The woman curled into the fetal position. Petra put her mouth to the woman's ear. "You and your sisters have had enough fun for one evening. Go find a bed and sleep it off." The woman did not even look up before obeying.

Petra kept her eyes on the maenad until she was well beyond the clearing. She bent down to examine her taloned foot and stopped with it halfway to her mouth. Petra shivered. She had been about to lick the blood off her talons. She shook herself. Being close to Zeus's power was making her more primal. This business needed to be concluded so they could all go back to their peaceful, lonely, boring lives.

With only a couple of extremely drunk satyrs left to cause trouble, the harpies had no problem keeping peace the rest of the night. A small fight broke out, but the harpies let the men, one with a snake face and one with the body of a lion, work it out themselves. People drifted away from the clearing to find a bed or a place to hide until daylight.

Weariness settled over Petra, and she longed to find a place to sleep. The other harpies and Iris were the only ones left besides Zeus. He sat, moving so little he seemed a part of the stone, and tracked their movements with his eyes alone. The hair on Petra's neck stood. She did not like being hunted.

"Bravo, harpies. I see you have not lost your touch with others, though I do find it wearisome that you spent your time preventing violence and mayhem instead of creating it. You are not the same harpies I created generations ago."

Petra's rage was fierce, and though she knew she should try, she did not contain it. She instead let it burn in her eyes and in her voice. "No. We're not the same creatures you created. We're not yours at all."

"Petra," Iris pleaded, "be quiet."

Petra shook her off. "You created our ancestors and then cursed them for being the very thing that you created. You're an unjust bastard." Marina grabbed Iris and shoved her behind the three of them.

Zeus laughed, but there was no humor in the sound. "Celaeno, you always were an emotional one. I am pleased to see you have not lost your penchant for violence and destruction."

Zeus rose and stepped down from the dais. His movements held the ghost of James and the anger in Petra fled. She had allowed this to happen to him. She should have tried harder in the mine. She could have been honest with him earlier and told him the truth about herself. She had to fix this.

Zeus walked in measured steps towards them. Petra moved in closer to her sisters and felt them do the same. They always faced things together, and this would be no different. Petra gathered her power to her and she felt the ripple of her sisters' power at her back.

He paused five feet from them. "I see you still act together. Even you, Messenger, align with them still." He chuckled but it was an unpleasant sound. "Do not worry. I only have prosperous plans for each of you. This will be a new opportunity for us all to build a better world and rule as we should. I have need for you in my New Olympus, and so I will forgive tonight's impertinence. Do not, however, make a habit of it. Gods always have need for creatures of violence. So many people need punishing." He gave a mock bow that mirrored the movements James had made the first time Petra had shown up at his farm. She turned away, unable to look. "Goodnight. Rest, my harpies. We have much work once we all awake." Zeus walked past them and disappeared into the lightening shadows of the trees.

Petra followed the glow of Iris's wings as she led them away from the clearing. It was awkward, walking on bird legs made for perching and grabbing prey. The harpies managed with small hops. Any other time, Petra would have laughed. Iris led them to a thatched shelter made with newly hewn logs, topped with a roof of pine boughs. It would not keep out even a moderate rain or heavy snow, but it was shelter enough for one night. Petra prayed it would only be one night.

Watching Zeus walk around in James's body set her on edge. She vacillated between being infuriated and feeling hopeless. The swinging back and forth was making her sick. Her stomach felt like it was filled with acid.

Their packs were waiting in the shelter. Petra took out her blanket and wadded it up like a pillow. Her feathers would keep her warmth enough. Her sisters all lay down close together with Iris among them and Petra fell asleep with the smell of dirt, harpy, and fresh-cut pine filling her nose.

CHAPTER 21

Petra woke before the others and lay there in the dirt, staring at the still green pine of the roof. Warmed from the heat of their collective bodies, Petra loathed leaving to start the day. Once she got up from her crude bed, the day ahead was filled with uncertainties. Only one thing was certain. There would be trials, and sorrow. The prophecy was not done with her, Petra knew.

With small movements and pauses, Petra extracted herself from the pile of feathers and limbs. The muscles of her back stretched and popped when she pulled her wings as far over her head as she could. Petra concentrated and tried to revert back to her human form. Being human would make walking easier, but her efforts yielded no results. She left the shelter behind and half-flew, half-walked towards the smell of burning wood and metal.

In the middle of a circle of trees, Henry had set up his portable forge. It was a small version of the one he kept in town, intended for the times when farmers had large jobs for him that he needed to complete on site. It could be disassembled and carried on burros through the mountains. It was glowing brightly when Petra stepped from the trees into the circle.

Henry worked the bellows and did not look up when she approached. He was the same Henry Petra had known before, but there were slight differences. He had always been good looking, but now his features were adjusted slightly, and he was beautiful. His glossy brown hair shown in the early light. He filled the small clearing with impossibly broad shoulders, and when he moved, his movements were liquid grace. His limp was gone.

Petra racked her tired brain for what she knew about Hephaestus. He had been the blacksmith and weapons master for Mount Olympus. There were different accounts in the myths. Like many others, Hephaestus had been thrown from Olympus by Zeus for some infraction. He was the only

Olympian to be exiled and then allowed to return at a later date. Hephaestus had created most of the weapons of the gods and an army of automatons on his forge. She took her eyes from his enhanced form and concentrated on her purpose.

Henry caught her staring and Petra met his eyes head on. "Figured you'd come soon enough."

Petra perched on a log far enough away from the forge that the heat was a pleasant caress. "You're positively beautiful in this form."

"Well, can't have all the ladies distracted by my face every day, now can we. Nothin' would ever get done." He winked at her.

Petra chuckled. "I'm not sure your face is the only distracting part of you." Petra winked back. It was nice to joke for a few moments and avoid the hard conversation ahead.

A red tinge crawled up Henry's neck. "That's enough from you. I will admit, it is nice to have the limp gone, but I know it's short-lived. I have no power to change my own form. You plan on fighting him again. I know you came here to ask me some questions about the Bolt."

"Is it safe to talk here?" They could not risk this conversation being overheard.

"Yes. All the others are still sleeping, and this small clearing is spelled to be hidden unless you are looking for me. No one passing by can hear or see us. If someone does come this way looking for me, I will know before they get here."

"How?"

"I made the wards. I can feel them vibrate when anyone approaches."

"Nice trick."

Henry sat beside Petra on the log. "I've a few stored by. Ask your questions."

Petra licked her lips and plunged ahead. "The Bolt. Is it the original one from the myths?"

"Yes."

It was the answer she expected, but Petra had so hoped it would not be true. "The original Hephaestus made it, but how did it get here after the Fall? And how did James become possessed by Zeus after he found it? It happened almost as soon as he picked it up, and it somehow compelled James to dig and called the rest of us here before that."

Henry ran a hand through his hair. "I've been considering that. I think Zeus sent the Bolt as far away as he could imagine and placed a piece of his soul in the Bolt itself. It was that sliver of soul that called to James and drew us all to this place. Why James though?"

Petra sighed. "I found an old journal, a family heirloom, of James's. He was a Remnant of one of the by-blows of Zeus. He did not know it, though. The journal did not state it directly, but Iris knew what she was looking for."

"I always figured he was a Remnant of some minor nymph or sprite. His power was so slight." Henry shrugged. "Once there were people in the region where the Bolt was hid, Zeus figured he could compel some Remnant descended from himself to find the Bolt, and then he'd possess them and rebuild Olympus and become a worshiped god again. Looks like his plan was sound."

"Is there a way to destroy the Bolt?'

"Yes. The Bolt can be unmade in the fire from which it was forged. "

Hope surged through her. The Bolt could be unmade. She could release James from its hold. The hope drained away, and Petra looked at Henry. "The bolt was made in Olympus, but Olympus was lost generations ago. My ancestor helped tear down the cornerstone."

"The temple, yes, but, the last fire of Olympus burns before you." Henry pointed towards the forge.

"Your family has kept the fire burning from the original all this time?" Petra could not hide her astonishment. She rose and hopped over to the fire. The heat on her clawed hand felt like all the other times she had been to Henry's forge in town.

"We've protected a part of the original fire all these years. We knew a time might come when it would be needed."

Petra turned and stood in front of Henry. "But this is wonderful news. If you have the fire here and if we can get the bolt, we can destroy it. Zeus will lose his hold on James, and we can keep Zeus from destroying our homes." The hope buffeted up again, bright and shiny.

Henry looked up into her face with sad grey eyes. "It's not that simple."

"I know getting the Bolt won't be easy, but harpies are thieves. We're just out of practice." Petra's smile faltered when Henry's expression of concern did not change. "There's something else." It was not a question.

"If you can get the Bolt and put it into the forge before you're caught, then Zeus will be destroyed." Petra opened her mouth to speak but Henry held up his hand and continued. "But Zeus and Mr. Lloyd are entwined now. Zeus's essence has entangled itself with Mr. Lloyd's, and the change is too complete. If you destroy Zeus, the body he inhabits will likely die also."

Black spots wavered on the edge of her vision. "No. I won't accept that. No." Petra closed her eyes and covered her face with her wings.

"I'm sorry. Mr. Lloyd stopped existing when he tore the bolt from the earth. He was dead days ago."

"No." Petra shook her head. Sacrifice and pain, the prophecy had said. Petra could choose to attempt to save the man she loved or protect the world from Zeus. Her insides were being shredded. She had come to a place in her life where she found love and now it was all ashes in her mouth. "There's no choice, is there?"

"There's always a choice, Miss Petra."

"I couldn't live with myself if I didn't try everything to destroy Zeus. James wouldn't have wanted to become what he has, but maybe I can still save him. You said it was unlikely, not impossible. I'm a harpy. I was never meant for anything but ugliness and violence, and yet I have learned what it is to love."

"You're wrong. You're beautiful in many ways. You just don't see it clearly. But I do not think James will survive."

Tenderness for Henry welled inside of her briefly before being overwhelmed by the growing grief in her soul. She laid a clawed hand on his cheek, careful to keep her nails from his skin. "You are a better friend than I deserve." Henry placed his callused hand over hers. "It'll be sometime today. Keep the fire high, and be ready for anything."

Henry squeezed her hand before letting it go. "Remember, you can only find the clearing if you are looking for me, not the forge or the fire, me. Tell the others. As long as they think of me, they will find their way here."

Petra nodded and understood what he did not say. If she was successful in stealing the Bolt, whoever chased her would be looking for the Bolt, not Henry. Once she made it to the clearing, she would be hidden and safe. "Thank you."

Petra moved far enough away from Henry and then launched herself into the air. She would need to face her sisters soon, but the knowledge Henry had given her was too raw to share. She could not put to voice the words stampeding through her mind and trampling her heart. If she said them out loud, she would lose what small hold she had on her emotions.

The mountain air was frigid this high up. Small particles of ice stung her eyes and clung to her feathers as she flew. Petra went through a cloud and the damp chill of the air caused her to shake. Her wing beats faltered, and she plummeted a few feet. If she just kept falling, the impact might kill her. She wished she were coward enough to try it.

Petra flapped her wings, warming her muscles, and regaining her altitude. She remembered going to James's farm the first time. He had surprised her with his manners and polish. She had been pleased that his polish wore off with time. She enjoyed his company and loved making him laugh. She still felt the bold elation that had flashed through her body when she'd kissed him the first time. That memory made her chuckle.

James cared for her. She wondered if he could have looked past what she was to care for her with the truth between them. Petra loved him enough to have taken the chance, eventually, but that opportunity was gone now. She gathered each memory she had of James and tucked them away. One day, she would be strong enough to take them out, but now they would only keep her from her purpose.

It was unlikely James would survive if she destroyed the Bolt, but she had no other choice. Petra knew she might not survive stealing and destroying the Bolt either, but, without James, she cared little about what happened to her after this day. She stuffed all her tender emotions away and replaced them with what she was meant to feel, violence and darkness. If there was a kernel of hope for James, she hid it deep.

Petra returned to her sisters as they were finishing breakfast. Her stomach reminded her she had not eaten since sometime early yesterday, but she ignored it. Her hunger pain was a small prick compared to the blackness overwhelming her now.

Iris took one look at her and stopped what she was doing. "What happened?"

"Everything and nothing. I spoke to Henry this morning."

"What did he say?" Marina joined them, with Dora close on her heels.

"If we can steal the Bolt, we can destroy it in his forge. It's a few minutes beyond the main clearing to the northeast. It's warded and can only be found if you are looking for Henry. Not the forge or his fire."

Marina's grin was feral. "Finally, some good news."

"There's more," Iris said.

"Yes." Petra could not say the rest. The prophecy was crashing around her and beating her to a pulp. She swallowed past the burning in her throat. "James and Zeus are too closely connected. He will not survive if Zeus does not." Petra closed her eyes. She felt the pain of her soul burning out of them, and she did not want the others to see.

She felt Iris's hands on her face. "Oh, my poor bird. I'm so very sorry." Petra was unable to say anything else, but there was nothing else to say. The worst was out. The others crowded around her. The golden glow of Iris's wings wrapped around her.

When Petra had again tucked all the emotions away, she opened her eyes. "We have plans to make, and a piece of silver to steal."

CHAPTER 22

The area Zeus had designated for his New Olympus came to life slowly over the course of the morning. The celebration had hit some harder than others, and many faces were green around the gills. Sounds of hammers, saws, and industry filled the clearing when Petra and the others entered it. For a moment, Petra was taken back to the day she had walked the streets of Turning Creek when Vine's was being constructed. The smell of fresh-cut wood permeated the air.

Zeus sat, as he had the previous night, on his stone dais, surrounded by the four aegis. The four guards watched the harpies approach. They looked at ease, but Petra knew they were ready to move in defense of their god at the slightest provocation. "Good morning, my harpies and Messenger."

Petra ground her teeth. She did not belong to him. Iris took her place to the side of the dais and the harpies stood waiting for orders. If fate was with them, Zeus would send at least one of the aegis out on patrol. One of the harpies would likely have to go, though they were going to try to make sure Petra was not one of them.

"Aello, go with Alke and Eris on patrol today. You can cover the skies while they are on the ground. If you encounter any mortals, I care not how you get rid of them."

At that, Eris gave his rendition of a smile. Petra fervently hoped they did not find anyone on the mountain. Adam and Robert had better be safe at the farm, caring for the cattle. Dora stepped away from Petra's side and joined Alke and Eris.

It rubbed her feathers the wrong way when Zeus used their myth names as if they were defined only by what they were. It had taken her years to hope she could be anything else other than a monster, and she had only recently begun to believe the sentiment. Her experience with James had taught her to believe she was something else, a woman who could be loved. Petra looked at Zeus in James's body, and the vise around her chest was tight enough to bind her in place. She shifted her gaze to the Bolt and concentrated on her part of the job. Steal the Bolt. Put it in the fire.

"Send the harpy back here at noon with a report." Alke bowed as Zeus gave him the last order.

Dora gave Petra a meaningful look before taking to the air. Petra followed her progress until Dora disappeared behind some clouds. Two aegis down. That left only the two female aegis to distract. Petra would rather have dealt with the men. Ioke and Phobos were creepy. Alke and Eris were formidable, but Petra could combat strength with strength. Ioke and Phobos made her skin crawl.

"You two," Zeus pointed to Marina and Petra, "visit all the work groups and make sure they are all putting forth their best effort for the cause. If anyone is shirking their assignments, remind them there are consequences to disobedience."

"As it pleases you." Petra answered for them in her harsh voice. Marina followed her out of the audience area.

When they were alone, Marina said, "I'll not be his hired thug, especially against people who are not here of their own free will."

"It's only the appearance of it we need to maintain for a couple more hours. When Dora checks in, we grab the Bolt and destroy it."

The first group they came upon was laying down the foundation for a judgment hall. Three satyrs carried rocks from a pile and laid them within the confines of the marked off space. There were a dozen others working, but all conversation hushed to whispers when the harpies appeared. The men darted glances at them, but one woman smiled. It seemed their help the night before was remembered.

The sound of sobbing drifted to Petra's sharp ears. She followed the sound away from the workers and around some pines. Marina's footsteps followed her, but Petra concentrated on the sound of distress in front of her. She rounded a large rock and nearly stumbled over a small child. Lines of tears tracked lines down dirty cheeks.

Petra crouched down, but she was unable to make herself much smaller. She gathered her power and tried to shift, but her harpy form stayed. Zeus's influence over her power rankled. Petra did not want to be in her harpy skin forever. It was not a form comforting to a child, or many other people for that matter.

Petra sighed. The sound came out with a rattle in her harpy throat, and she had to suppress another sigh. Using only the pads of her fingers and keeping her movements slow, she wiped the tears from the little girl's face. "What's your name?"

"Annika. Ann for short."

"Ann for short, why are you crying here by yourself?"

Ann's lip trembled. Petra longed for real arms and not wings so she could scoop up the girl and hug her. "I want to go home, but my mam said we have to make the best of it. She told me to go cry somewhere else 'cuz if I was caught cryin' I'd be punished. I don't want to be punished." Ann chewed her bottom lip. Liquid brown eyes looked over every inch of her, and Petra held herself still. "Are you here to punish me? Mam said to stay well away from anything looking odd. You look odd but you don't look mean."

Petra's heart, so full of pain over James, filled with warmth at the girl's proclamation. Petra could crush the small child easily, but Ann bestowed trust with the innocence of the young. Petra placed a soft kiss on the girl's head. "I look ugly, it's true, but I wouldn't ever hurt you."

Ann smiled. "You and you," she pointed to Marina, "aren't ugly, just different."

Petra patted the child's head. "Thank you for that reminder." Ann picked at the hem of her dress and chewed her lip. "Is something else bothering you?" Petra asked.

"Are we gonna hafta live here forever? I don't like Zeus. He's not nice. He took my mam away, and she came back cryin'." Anne whispered.

Petra throat constricted. "No, child, he's not nice, but don't worry. I'll tell you a secret." Petra leaned as far as she could and whispered in Ann's ear. "He won't be around long, and afterwards, you can go home, but don't tell anyone, all right?"

Ann's eyes glittered. "Cross my heart."

Petra ruffled the girl's hair. "Run along and steer clear of all the odd ones. Your mam is right. Most of them are dangerous."

Ann darted through the trees in the direction of the group working on the hall. Marina shook her head. "You're becoming a ball of fluff. Who would've thought a big, mean harpy would have such a soft spot for children?"

Petra shot her a look. "You have soft spots too, somewhere very deep inside your heart. One day, you'll find 'em, and then I'll laugh at you."

"Not gonna happen."

Petra made a non-committal sound. They walked through the other work areas. More living spaces were being constructed as well as a large scale dining area and, most disturbingly, a jail. The jail, which was more like a dungeon, was sunk into the side of the mountain. A man with arms as big as most men's legs was stripped to the waist and hammering hooks for chains into the rock wall of the chamber. It was an unneeded reminder. Failing to get the Bolt from Zeus was not an option.

"It's almost noon. We need to get back to the clearing." Marina brought Petra out of her own thoughts. Marina led the way.

Petra used the time to empty her mind of everything but the task ahead. Her feelings for James could not interfere. Ann's tear stained face gave her strength. There were other children here, other families, and they all should have the opportunity to go home and live their lives in peace. With certainty, Petra knew she would get no such chance. Whether she managed to live through this or whether James lived through it or not did not matter. A time of sacrifice and pain would be her undoing, the prophecy said. She would be undone, but if she could do something to allow others to continue, it would be enough.

Ioke and Phobos stood on either side of Zeus when Petra and Marina entered the clearing. Iris stood away from the dais with her eyes trained on the sky, looking for signs of Dora. Once Dora returned, the wheels would be in motion. The harpies would then do what they did best, create violence and steal things. A perverse feeling of anticipation filled Petra. She was going to win this.

Marina walked to the dais and inclined her head towards Zeus. "All the groups are working as you have ordered. There are no problems to report." Petra suppressed the urge to snort at Marina's deferential tone. She could lay it on thick when she wanted. Marina did not have a submissive bone in her body.

"Your services are appreciated, harpies." Zeus dismissed them, and Petra and Marina joined Iris.

The sound of something being dragged along the forest floor was muffled by footsteps as a group approached the clearing. Dora came first. Her face was blank, but when her eyes met Petra's a flash went through them. Dread, heavy and acidic, landed in Petra's stomach.

Ioke and Eris walked behind Dora. Each had the arm of a man around their shoulders. Petra smelled the blood before she saw it on the man's clothes. His head swung low between his shoulders, obstructing his face, but his tousled hair looked familiar. The dread crawled up her throat.

Ioke and Eris dropped their burden at Zeus's feet. The man's dead weight fell with a thud into the dirt. His neck twisted badly, so his face was visible from where Petra stood. Petra cried out. One eye and the side of his face was swollen, but it was Robert on the ground before Zeus. Iris's hand was hard on her wing, keeping her in place.

"A present?" Zeus asked.

"We caught him snooping around the mountain, sire. We taught him the mistake of his trespassing." Ioke kicked Robert in the ribs. Petra heard bone crack, and a moan escaped through Robert's lips. Sharp relief cut Petra. He was not dead, yet, but he would be soon if they let him stay in the hands of the aegis and Zeus. Petra clenched her claws and waited.

"Good. The local mortals need to know they are no longer in charge of this mountain. It is mine, and I will crush every one of them that defies my right to it." Zeus's hand clenched on the silver in his hand. "Take him to the dungeon. The chains should be in place by now. When he can walk, we will send him down to the town with a message." Ioke and Eris lifted Robert up and dragged him off in the direction of the newly constructed dungeon.

They would not get another chance today to steal the bolt. Petra pitched her voice low for her sisters' ears alone. "Ioke and Eris will return soon. We must do it now while they are gone. It may be our only chance today."

Marina nodded. Dora shifted her weight.

Petra took a steadying breath. "Steady." The sound of Robert being dragged away faded to nothing and they were alone with Zeus, Alke, and Phobos. "Now."

At her whispered word, the harpies launched themselves into the air. Petra called her power to her and the sun disappeared behind a cloud. Darkness dropped like a shroud. Dora's power rolled over her as a wind smelling of power whipped around them. Marina, whose power was swiftness, barreled into Phobos before Petra was halfway to Zeus.

The rasping cry of the hag aegis was lost in the wind. Petra trusted Dora to reach her target as she concentrated on Zeus, who had risen with anger contorting his features. Petra's momentum as she crashed into Zeus sent them flying off the dais and into the rocky ground. She landed on top of him and the air whooshed out of his body. The horrible sounds of battling harpies caused the blood lust to rise within Petra. Her sisters were doing their jobs well. She had to get the bolt from Zeus without harming James more than necessary.

Zeus was strong, and Petra had to dig her talons into his side and use all of her weight to keep him pinned to the ground. The clouds dropped lower and the storm pressed on her back. She smelled the tang of electricity moments before lightning struck the ground, inches from her head. Zeus used the distraction to hit her with the end of the Bolt clutched in his hand.

Petra felt her skin split and warmth spread over her cheek. Blood dripped down her chin and splashed onto Zeus's face. His grin was full of malice. It was not a look James would have ever directed her way. Zeus hit her again, and Petra cursed herself for losing focus.

The smell of lightning filled her nose again, and this time it did not miss. The bolt grazed her shoulder, and her senses went dark as it hit. Petra came to with her back pressed into the ground and Zeus on top of her. Something cold was pressed into her neck, and she could not breathe.

Black pin points swam in her vision, and Zeus pressed the Bolt harder, sensing victory. She was going to die at the hands of the man she wanted to save. She had failed. She pushed on the side of the Bolt, trying to relieve the pressure enough to draw some air into her lungs, but she could feel her strength weakening as her body cried for air. Zeus was sitting too high on her chest for her to get her talons on him and shove him off.

Dora, in a blur of brown and white, hit Zeus from the side. He flew off Petra, tangling with Dora in a heap. The bolt skittered along the ground and stopped a few feet from where Dora and Zeus fought for purchase on each other. Petra pulled air past her battered throat. Each breath tore at her, but the pin pricks receded.

Petra flapped her wings and landed on the Bolt. She wrapped her talons around it and launched herself into the air. She did not look back. Zeus's roar of rage filled the clearing, and the sounds of struggling increased. Petra pumped her wings hard and fast, the ground a blur beneath her.

She cleared her mind of the battle raging behind her. She emptied her worries about whether her sisters were hurt or if James would survive the next step. Petra thought of only one thing. Henry. Henry. She needed to find Henry. Please gods, let this work. Henry.

It was as if a curtain lifted, and she was suddenly in Henry's small clearing. The fire of the forge was twice the height it had been that morning. Petra dove into the ground in a graceless heap. She managed to miss crashing into the forge by inches. She stood on shaking legs and pushed the end of the Bolt into the fire. It sizzled and popped in a way no ordinary Bolt would.

A bellow of rage shook the trees, and Petra pushed more of the Bolt into the fire. The forge was hot, and Petra smelled burning feathers. Henry stood facing the direction of the clearing, holding a long metal spear in his hand. He would stop anything coming for her and the Bolt for a few moments. It might be enough time.

Only a small portion of the silver was left. The heat cracked her skin, and Petra released the last few inches into the fire. She reached over and pumped the bellows to give the forge one last burst of heat. The Bolt was a puddle of silver among the glowing coals.

Henry was at her shoulder. "Go. I will take care of the rest. It is destroyed, but I will corrupt the silver and grind it to dust so it can never be refined again. " He picked up a bucket sitting by the bellows.

Petra did not wait to see what Henry intended to do. If the Bolt was destroyed, then James was free of Zeus at last. The band tightened around her chest as she flew, praying and pleading to the gods. *Please let him live.* She would make any exchange they required, if he could just live his normal human life. She could not get back to the clearing fast enough.

It was chaos in the clearing. Blood and bodies were scattered like forgotten trinkets on the ground. There were others standing around, but Petra's focus was pinpointed to the spot where two harpies and one golden-winged messenger huddled around something on the ground.

James.

Petra landed behind Marina, and the harpies parted for her. There was blood on his shirt where her talons had pierced him, and one of his arms had a gash along the length of it. There was so much blood. She did not know if it was his, hers, or someone else's. Petra leaned over his chest, but there was no thumping of his heart. She placed her face next to his, but no air came and went from his lungs.

He could not be dead. Petra slid one wing under his head and cradled his lifeless body to her feathered chest. She had succeeded, and she had failed. James was gone and yet she was still alive. Hot tears spilled from her eyes. They mixed with the blood and dripped pink rivulets on James's face. Petra clung to him.

This was her fault. She never should have wished for more. She was a harpy, a creature of violence and pain. She was meant to be alone and to live in darkness. This was what came of her wanting beyond her fate of death and destruction. Her wayward desires had cost this beautiful man his life.

Petra laid James back down onto the ground. Her hands trembled when she placed them on either side of his face. She pressed her lips to his and then kissed his forehead. James's skin was already starting to chill in the mountain air.

Petra put her forehead to his. "I loved you. I'm so sorry," she whispered in a broken voice with her broken throat. Her whole being was shattered.

The tears continued to fall, and Petra stayed with her face low. There was nothing for her here and she knew now it was folly to want anything good in her dark life.

Petra stood and spoke with her eyes fixed on the pale figure on the ground. "Are you three all right?"

"Yes." The answer came from behind her. Iris, she thought, but everything was muffled and she could not be sure.

She had to leave before she lost herself in the crushing grief and shock bearing down upon her. "Please give him a proper burial. Ask Robert and Adam to look after the farm. If they want it, I'm sure James would have wanted them to have it. He was estranged from his family."

"Why are you telling us this? You'll be here to do those things." Iris's voice was firm, and Petra felt a hand on her shoulder.

Petra shrugged off the hand. "No. I have to leave." Before they could stop her, Petra launched herself into the air and flew north. She flew hard and did not look behind to see if she was pursued. She flew until the ground beneath her was white tundra and her wings gave out. She crashed into the ground and lay in a heap in the hardened snow. Even if she flew for the rest of her life, she would never go far enough to escape the hole in her soul left by a dairy farmer from England.

CHAPTER 23

Petra wandered for days, weeks, or months. She'd lost track. She stayed on the snow-covered tundra, alone with her grief. She'd built a crude shelter made of snow. It was very crude, since she'd made it with her clawed harpy hands. Her mortal form was not clothed well enough for this cold. Even with her feathers, the chill was bone deep. She ate what game she could find and watched the moon grow and wane from her snow shelter. Her grief ruled her.

She was not alone. She had the ghost of James keeping her company, and the voices of her sisters and Iris in her head. Some days they were a comfort and some days they clawed at the raw wounds of her heart.

One day, she saw a tuft of grass poking through the snow, and she knew it was time to go. She planned to collect what few things she needed from her small cabin on Atlas's Peak, leave a note for her sisters and Iris, and disappear. She did not know if she had a mortal lifespan to live out, or the life of a harpy, now that James was gone, but she would live her years alone, away from all the things she did not want to face. In the end, she thought, she had become a coward, but she no longer thought it mattered. Nothing really did.

Petra was careful to fly from the north and go straight to her cabin. She did not want to be tempted to go farther south. She did not want to see anyone who might convince her to stay, as her sisters and Iris surely would.

The first flowers of spring and the smell of new grass was stronger here than it had been on the tundra. Petra drew the smell of new life deep within her, and she felt a comfort she had not encountered since before James had started digging. Her cabin perched like a memory on the side of the mountain, and Petra's heart beat in recognition. She landed and changed into her mortal form. She lifted a hand to the door pull and was shocked to see her own skin again. She had not changed forms for months.

She left the door open. No one would be looking for her, and she did not fear interruption. Everything was the same as when she had left it, but it looked tidier than she remembered. There was no dust on the shelves or table. Someone had been keeping things for her until her return. Petra ran her fingers over the top of the table and walked to the bookshelf. She knelt and considered which volumes to bring. She could not take all of them, as much as she wanted to. Petra pulled two volumes from the shelf, both poetry. She would leave instructions for Iris to ship the rest to her once she got settled wherever she was going.

The sound of footsteps on the gravel outside alerted her that she would not be alone for long. Petra made herself as small as possible and closed her eyes. She looked up from the books in her hands, and her heart faltered. She should not have come back here, where her ghosts could find her so easily.

Petra looked at him for a long moment. Her hands shook and her lips trembled. She pulled herself together and went back to pulling books from the shelf and placing them in a bag.

Her voice was quiet and scratched. She had not used it in a long time. "I suppose it serves me right for coming back here. As if my own memory was not enough, now I have a ghost on my heels. You're too late to do any more damage. I've nothing left. Go haunt someone else."

James stood rooted to the spot, watching Petra fill her bag with books. He put the gun in his hand away and knelt on the floor beside her. Her hands trembled again, and he covered them with his own. The hands on hers were warm and full of life. She sucked in a breath, and her wide eyes met his.

"I am not a ghost," he said. "You look like you might be one, though. You are too thin and pale."

Petra continued to stare at him. Afraid to move lest he disappear. She took one of her small hands from his and laid it on his cheek. James turned his face and kissed the palm of her hand. "Are you real? I see you all the time, but you're never real. Is this what going mad feels like?"

"You're not going crazy. I'm as real as you are," he said.

"How?" The question was a whisper.

James took her hands in his and kissed them both. "You, Petra. You saved me."

"You were dead. I saw your body." Her voice broke on the last word, and James gathered her into his arms.

She burrowed into his lap and he spoke. "Dr. Williams said it was your tears. The tears of a harpy with a broken heart held a magic more potent than his. To make a creature of violence cry over lost love was something the world had never known. They brought me back. I was in a deep sleep for a month, and it was a long time before I felt the same again, but I'm recovered."

Petra scooted off his lap and sat so she was facing him. "Why are you here?"

He jerked with surprise. "Why would I not be? Iris said you might come back. I come every day. I make tea, eat biscuits, and clean up a bit. I try to stay for a time. I was afraid that if you did come back, you would pack quickly and be gone before anyone knew you were here."

"That was my intention. I didn't want the others to try to keep me here." Petra's hand came up to touch him again, but she snatched her hand back. "You saw me, my harpy." She paused and licked her lips. "You know what I am. Why are you here?"

"Petra. Look at me." She did and he continued, "You are amazing and beautiful. You are the most courageous woman I have ever met. You're loyal, and you make me laugh. You made me long for things I never thought to have again, a family and a place to belong. I love you, Petra. I love all of you. That wasn't me before who said those hurtful things to you. I would rather cut off my own arms than ever hurt one feather on your body. I love you."

Petra covered her face with her hands. Her shoulders shook with sobs. "I don't deserve you."

"It doesn't matter what you think you deserve. You have me, all of me, just the same."

"I'm not sure I'll make a good dairy farmer's wife."

He tucked a lock of hair behind her ear. "I don't care if you're terrible at it. I still want you to be my wife."

Her whole world exploded in light, and the past months fell from her. "I love you. If you'll have me, then yes, I will be your wife."

He kissed her then, with all the months of longing and endless nights in his touch. He burned himself into her. She was never going to let him go.

When he broke the kiss, her eyes danced and she laughed. "James, I have a confession to make about your stampeded cows."

THANK YOU

Thank you for reading the first book in the Turning Creek series.

Would you like to know when the next book is available? You can sign up for my newsletter at www.wanderingeyre.com. On my blog, you will find all kinds of fun information and general shenanigans. Follow me on Twitter @wanderingeyre, or like me on Facebook at https://www.facebook.com/MichelleBouleAuthor.

I appreciate all reviews. They help readers find books and mean the world to authors.

Turning Creek Reading Order
Lightning in the Dark
Storm in the Mountains
Letters in the Snow
Plagues of the Heart
Journey of the Lost

MYTHOLOGY CODEX

This is a list of mythology characters and mythological locations mentioned in the Turning Creek series and a brief description of each. The information in this codex is for the mythology as it relates to this fictional series. As an author, I have taken some liberty with the original myths.

***

Achilles - The original Achilles was fatally wounded by a shot to his heel because this was the source of his power, speed, and strength. Thomas, the Remnant of Achilles, has the gift of speed and delivers mail in Turning Creek.

Aegis - The aegis is the name for the four warriors who make up the Shield of Zeus which is the title for his bodyguards and henchmen. They are Ioke, Alke, Eris, and Phobos.

Alke - Alke is the personification of strength. He is part of the Shield of Zeus and his main weapon is a sword.

Aphrodite - The Greek goddess of love.

Asclepius - A Greek physician who was granted the power over life and death by the gods. Lee Williams is a Remnant of Asclepius and the doctor in Turning Creek.

Atlanta - Atlanta was a famous huntress who made an oath of virginity to the goddess Artemis, but was later tricked into marriage by Aphrodite. Atlanta, named for the first of her name, travels with her companion and partner, Cyrene, in a quest for the next adventure and hunt. (also known as Atalanta in the Greek myths)

Bellerophon - Bellerophon was one of the hundreds of bastard sons of Zeus who spent his life trying to attain acknowledgement and vindication from the gods.

Charon - Charon is the ferryman who took souls across the River Styx on their way to the god Hades in the underworld, sometimes also referred to as Tartarus.

Cerberus - A three headed dog, the son of Echidna and Typhon, who guarded the door to the underworld for Hades.

Chimera - A monster, sired by Echidna and Typhon, whose front and torso is that of a lion and whose bottom half is that of a snake.

Cyrene - Cyrene was a princess and huntress who once wrestled a lion with her bare hands. The current Remnant of Cyrene travels the world with Atlanta in search of the next greatest hunt.

Dionysus - Dionysus, god of the vine, stayed neutral during the battle and Fall of Olympus, making him unpopular with those on both sides. The Remnant of Dionysus, Daniel Vine, owns the saloon in Turning Creek.

Dryad - Similar to a nymph, a dryad is a spirit of the forest, the trees, or other natural phenomenon. This affinity to nature can give them the power to communicate with nature or similar abilities.

Echidna - The original Echidna was called the Mother of All Monsters in the time of the old myths because her children became the nightmares of the Greek era.

Eris - Eris is the personification of strife. He is part of the Shield of Zeus.

Hades - The god and ruler of the underworld.

Harpy - A harpy has the body of a bird of prey and the head of a woman, though their face is more angular in this natural form. They have the ability many Remnants have of taking the form of a mortal when needed. There were four harpies who stood against Zeus in the uprising; Aello, Celaeno, Ocypete, and Podarge. The Remnants of the three surviving harpies lived in isolation from each other, and most of the world, until the current generation.

Hephaestus - Blacksmith to gods, he had the ability to craft weapons of magic and power in his forge, lit by the fires of Olympus. The Remnants of Hephaestus carry some of this original power and are marked with a clubfoot. Henry Foster of Turning Creek is a Remnant of Hephaestus.

Hera - Hera was the wife and queen of Zeus. By the time of the uprising, she had became angry and bitter over Zeus's many affairs and bastard children. She turned a blind eye to the work of the harpies and fled before Olympus fell.

Ioke - Ioke is the personification of onslaught and pursuit. She is part of the Shield of Zeus and her main weapon is the crossbow.

Iris - The original Iris has golden wings, delivered the messages of the gods, and had the gift of prophecy. She shared parentage with the harpies and argued on their behalf often, softening their punishment when Zeus's anger turned against them. The Remnant of Iris, also called The Messenger, is marked with a birthmark of golden wings. The Messenger chronicles the history of the Remnants and the harpies in particular.

Ladon - The Ladon is the serpentine monster child of Typhon and Echidna. Also known as a dragon or a drakon.

Laelaps - A mythical hound, created by Zeus, who never failed to catch its prey

Lernean Hydra - The hydra is another serpentine-like child of Typhon and Echidna. It is a nine headed serpent who occupies bodies of water and spits acidic venom on its victims.

Medea - A powerful and vengeful witch who helped Jason of the Argonauts in many battles and later became his wife, bearing him six children.

Maenads - Maenads are women controlled by Dionysus who turn into raving, mad women. They have been known to tear apart men with their bare hands in their rage.

Manticore - This creature has the head of a woman, the body of a lion, and the tail of a scorpion. It was a meliai, a kind of nymph from the island of Melos.

Medusa - Medusa, in the old myths, was a creature with snakes for hair and eyes who could hypnotize a man. Lily Hughes, the Remnant of Medusa, has the power of persuasion if you look into her eyes.

Mount Olympus - The mountain that was the seat of Zeus and the center of his kingdom during the time of the old myths.

Nemean Lion - The Nemean Lion can only be killed by strangulation. It is one of the monster children of Typhon and Echidna.

Nymph - A nymph is a fairy-like creature with an affinity for nature.

Orthus - Orthus is a two-headed hound and the son of Typhon and Echidna.

Phobos - Phobos is the personification of fear. She is part of the Shield of Zeus.

Satyr - A creature with the lower body of a goat and the upper body of a man. They were creatures of Dionysus and known to harass and sometimes rape women during festivals.

Scylla - Scylla was a sea goddess with a woman's head and torso and the body of a serpent.

Sphinx - The Sphinx had the body of a lion and the head of a woman. It was the offspring of Typhon and Echidna and was known for asking riddles of men and then eating them when they answered incorrectly. The Remnant of the Sphinx is Pearl Nasso.

Styx, River - The River Styx is the body of water that separates the underworld from the living. To swear on the River Styx is to give a binding oath.

Tartarus - Another name for the underworld where souls go to be punished for their bad life choices.

Typhon - Typhon was monstrous being. He had one hundred dragon heads sprouting from his neck, a human torso, and a snake body. He is called the Father of Monsters because he sired the worst of the Greek monsters with his wife, Echidna.

Zeus - The Father of the Gods, Zeus was the tyrannical ruler of Olympus. While heralded as an innovator of culture, he ruled with violence and vengeance and held his kingdom together with blood and war. He was notorious for his hundreds of bastard children. Zeus was unseated in the Fall of Olympus which occurred during the uprising led by the harpies.

ABOUT THE AUTHOR

Michelle Boule has been, at various times, a librarian, a bookstore clerk, an administrative assistant, a wife, a mother, a writer, and a dreamer trying to change the world. She is married to a rocket scientist and has two small boys. She brews her own beer, will read almost anything in book form, loves to cook, bake, go camping, and believes Joss Whedon is a genius. She dislikes steamed zucchini, snow skiing, and running. Unless there are zombies. She would run if there were zombies.

CPSIA information can be obtained
at www.ICGtesting.com
Printed in the USA
BVHW03s0108160718
521691BV00003B/135/P